The King of the Two Sicilies

Andrzej Kusniewicz

The King of the Two Sicilies

Translated by
Celina Wieniewska

Harcourt Brace Jovanovich, New York and London

Library of Congress Cataloging in Publication Data

Kusniewicz, Andrzej.
The king of the two Sicilies.

Translation of Król obojga Sycylii.
1. European War, 1914–1918—Fiction.
PZ4.K9716.Ki   [PG7170.U75]   891.8′537   80–7935
ISBN 0-15-147271-8

Printed in the United States of America
First edition
B C D E

The King of the Two Sicilies

This might be the opening sentence:

"Once upon a time there were two sisters, Elizabeth and Bernadette, who had one brother, Emil."

Or else:

"On July 28, 1914, the river gunboat *Bodrog* of the Imperial and Royal Navy fired the first shot in the direction of Belgrade at — hours. On a small island overgrown with osiers, about one kilometer from Pancevo, two officers were observing through field glasses the not-too-distant Serbian bank of the Danube. They were looking into a fiery purple sun hanging low over the water, a sun that was like a balloon on a line being pulled down by invisible hands. But the two officers were busy with things other than comparisons. For a moment the glare from the water, now almost touched by the brick-colored sun in two places streaked with white mist, was so strong that the officers saw something like molten copper in the oculars of their field glasses. This lasted perhaps half a minute, perhaps a little longer, after which one of the representatives of the Imperial and Royal Army jumped into a boat hidden among the reeds, which at this spot were almost two meters high, and slowly proceeded toward Pancevo. The other officer, a captain, remained for a moment with the field glasses in his hand. From his position, he could see with the naked eye a dark plume of smoke spreading fanlike toward the indigo blue silhouette of Kalemegdan, looming against the now greenish sky."

Or still differently:

"On the corner of Kiralyi Street opposite Lajos Winter's bakery in the town of Fehertemplom (otherwise known as Bela Crkva or Ungarish Weisskirchen), there was a tavern once owned by one Supicich, nicknamed by his customers Nandor-Bacsi." And so on.

Or else:

"After a very hot day when one could at last breathe with

relief the somewhat cooler air blowing from the direction of the old clay pits in the Gypsy Quarter—a breeze coming at almost musically rhythmic intervals—there, just beyond Garden Street, where the Gypsy Quarter begins (because one cannot consider Garden Street as being *in* that quarter) a sudden scream resounded, followed by a prolonged silence. Thick layers of dust lay on the road and on the leaves of burdocks, wild chicory, and wild mallow. A flock of sparrows rose for a moment, then settled on the nearest acacia tree, whose leaves had curled up from the heat. Copper color dominated the street, combined with the grayness of sand. Here and there some fragments of walls, wooden fences, and acacia trunks began to turn purple. The same evening, at about eleven o'clock, someone will inform the local gendarmerie that he has found, in one of the abandoned clay pits, the body of a young gypsy girl. Istvan Vilajcich, the sergeant of the Royal Hungarian Gendarmerie on duty that night, will get up ill-humoredly from the table on which an unfinished bottle of wine is standing. He will slowly buckle on his belt and, having donned his hat adorned with a bunch of green feathers, he will go out into the street."

These facts appear to be logically unconnected and surely not interdependent. Nonetheless, each of them occurred at a strictly defined time, and therefore has been lastingly preserved. Nothing can be changed that happened in the past, nothing can be erased or left out. The past is indivisible. It is possible, perhaps, although there is no proof for it, that the absence of any element might have affected the course of future events in the public or private sphere. This assumption is not so absurd as it seems. What is or is not important is relative.

When on June 28—exactly one month before—at 10:10 a.m. in the city of Sarajevo, close to the police headquarters and only a few steps from the hardware store of Racher and Babich, a youth in a black coat with a black hat tilted low over his eyes threw a bomb under the motorcar carrying His Imperial and Royal Highness Archduke Franz Ferdinand, the heir to the throne, together with his wife and Artillery General Oscar Potiorek—a bomb that slightly wounded the Archduchess Sophia von Hohenberg in the shoulderblade, and injured Lieutenant Colonel von Merizzi of the archduke's entourage more severely—

in the town of Fehertemplom the first squadron of the Twelfth
Regiment of the Imperial and Royal Lancers was returning in
open formation from their morning field exercises. The horses'
hooves churned up the dust, their shoes clanked on the uneven
pavement of Franz Josef Square. A few youths gaped at the
soldiers, whose trousers, jackets, and spurred boots were covered
with the grayish-yellow summer dust. Unless we are mistaken, at
exactly the moment the young man in black was raising his arm
to throw the bomb under the archduke's car, Lieutenant Iodkay,
riding alongside the second troop, sneezed, after which, screwing
up his face, he covered his nose and mouth with a silk handkerchief sprinkled with Eau de Cologne 4711. The day was already
hot; at 10:00 a.m. the thermometer hanging next to the window
display of Csilag's "Under the Star" pharmacy registered over
forty degrees centigrade in the shade. Leopold Soyka, the
chauffeur of the archducal couple, noticing a black object thrown
in an arc, accelerated, instinctively leaning forward over the
wheel. The grenade hit the folded roof of the open car and then
the pavement, where it exploded. The archduke, also instinctively,
put his arm around the Archduchess Hohenberg, who gave a start.

Because of the heat, some officers of the first squadron returning from the morning field exercises—among them the commander, Cavalry Captain Peter Malàterna, and Lieutenants
Gruber, Iodkay, and Franilevich—decided to call at the nearest
tavern, located between the Lancers' barracks and the station:
the Golden Lion Inn, an establishment renowned throughout the
city and belonging to a German, Alois Kellermann.

They dismounted and walked down the middle of the road,
talking loudly. The gypsy children were gathered near the open
market, waiting for the opportunity to steal a melon from the
stalls or peasant carts, or a piece of liver sausage red with
paprika that had been fried on a piece of tinplate propped on
two bricks. Then they took to their heels, hiding in gateways to
let the officers pass on their way toward Kellermann's tavern.

At the same time in Trieste, in the Quarnero Hotel, Emil R.,
still in civilian clothes and entirely unaware that soon he will
have to don the uniform of the Imperial and Royal Sicilian
Lancers, will light his first cigarette of the day and prepare to
do some writing. Two days before, on a sheet of white foolscap
paper taken from a green chamois attaché case, he began to

write an essay upon somewhat undefined subjects: about a new
approach to the understanding of music, also about certain feelings that have been absorbing him for years. He takes up a pen
from a marble urn that is the base of an inkwell representing a
reclining nymph. The marble used by an unknown artist to make
this artifact is light gray, with slightly darker veins thin as a
spider's web. Holding his pen in his right hand, Emil R. will
become pensive, looking at the half-open window, half-covered
with a lacy curtain swaying in the gusts of the sirocco that has
been blowing since the previous evening. A branch of acacia
growing beside the wall, also waving in the breeze, will brush
rhythmically against the corner ledge of the second-floor balcony.
Emil will place his cigarette on a heavy ashtray that sticks to
the cloth covering the hotel table under the window.

And the gypsy girl Marika Huban will at that time still be
asleep in one of the wooden shacks in the Gypsy Quarter of
Fehertemplom. Hot and glowing with sweat, she lies on her
back, covered with a red shawl that she will soon kick off in her
sleep. She is sleeping with her mouth open. On the earth floor
next to her and also on the cool hearth in a corner of the room,
children are playing. On the threshold, in the open door, sits
Czilko, an old gypsy, cleaning his teeth with a broken splinter
of wood and spitting, while a curly-haired black mongrel dog
will start barking and run toward a clump of dust-covered dwarf
acacia bushes, where something has moved. Who is there? Perhaps a crawling baby? At the given moment, however—exactly
10:10 a.m., Central European time—the dog is still lying next to
the gypsy Czilko. Its hair bristling, its ears pointing, its nose
wrinkling.

On the neck of the sleeping Marika one might admire a string
of small beads. After a while, we notice that it is not a string,
but a thin, strong wire. The sleeping girl holds the necklace with
two fingers of her left hand, almost black in this light, while her
right arm is thrown to the side, resting on the earthen floor of
the shack. From time to time she moves the fingers of her right
hand.

And in the various parts and climates of the world, precisely
at the same time—10:10—there will occur many trifling and
important, private and public, secret and known events that, had
they not occurred, would have nullified and canceled the plans,

intentions, and activities of various people acting or intending to act at this precise moment.

Perhaps Cavalry Captain Malaterna and his colleagues would not have opened the door of the Golden Lion Inn; or the gypsy boys would not have hidden in the corners of Franz Josef Square, more particularly behind the fence of Winter & Gethner's timber store on the corner of Munkacsi Street; and Emil R. would not have looked at the window behind which the branch of acacia—or perhaps it was laburnum—made a scraping noise as it brushed against the balcony. Marika Huban might have removed the fingers of her left hand from the necklace made two days before with beads stolen from the stall of a certain Nathalie Kosma, and later laboriously strung on a thin wire found in the rubbish outside Misitich's store in Kiralyi Street. Had all these events—objectively trivial but subjectively very important at that given moment—not taken place, perhaps the Daimler motorcar, registration number A-11-118, with chauffeur Leopold Soyka at the wheel, and the archducal couple with the governor general of Bosnia and Hercegovina, His Excellency Potiorek, on the back seat, and Lieutenant Colonel Count von Merizzi next to the driver, might have passed half a second earlier the spot where the young man in black was standing. Perhaps then the young man would not have had time to lift his arm and strike the firing pin of the bomb against the metal pillar of the street light, before throwing this lethal object straight at the motorcar of the distinguished guests.

And when the burgomaster of the city of Sarajevo, Effendi Fehim Curcich, bows deeply to His Highness, who is crossing the threshold of the reception rooms of the town hall, the situation will change totally; Captain Peter Malaterna with three of his colleagues will sit at the oak table in the tavern redolent of wine, and the owner of the shop, Kellermann, will come up to them, bowing just as the burgomaster had bowed to the archduke at precisely the same moment. Emil R. will at that moment turn his eyes away from the window and reach for his Memphis cigarette still burning in the ashtray, but his hand will hang in the air long enough for the bluish wisps of smoke to move lightly between his fingers. Only the twig beyond the window will still perform the same movement to and fro.

And it is quite probable—we can check it with our watch: it

is now precisely 10:39 and His Imperial and Royal Highness still has one hour to live, or more accurately an hour less a few minutes, on condition that nothing interferes with us, nothing stops the river flowing to its mouth. It is quite probable that there is still time, but will it be made use of? It seems unlikely.

Perhaps exactly at the same moment Marika Huban removes her fingers from the beads, strung on a thin but firm wire, and in her sleep turns her head toward the wall, while only a few kilometers away the third platoon of Sicilian Lancers, under the command of Cavalry Captain Count Alois Kray von Krayova, while returning from morning exercises, will pass the first suburban gardens, and then the buildings of Moravich's farm which, like most of the hamlets, arable fields, pastures, and vineyards, belongs to the family of Count Festetics de Tolna.

On the plain that stretches as far as the eye can see up to the misty yellow horizon shimmering in the heat, on the left side of the road that the Sicilian Lancers will take, a tall cloud of dust will rise, not unlike a storm cloud, and move nearer and spread upward and sideways, so that some of the horsemen screening their eyes from the sun will look that way, checking their horses to see a moment later—but this is still in the future—a herd of big-horned white Magyar oxen, running, racing each other, climbing on each other's backs as they are driven to the watering place, to troughs hollowed out in oak trunks, where water buckets hanging from rods (there are several of them, standing in a row) will move forward, squeaking, manipulated by farmhands clad in blue aprons and linen trousers tied at the ankle.

The lancers (still riding in twos in an extended column across the immense plain of the Banat) will hear the lowing of the cattle gathered at the troughs, knocking each other with their horns, while more oxen, still running, just begin to emerge from a cloud of dust shot through by rust-colored and pale pink rays of a rising sun.

And somebody (this is still the same time of day, that same undivided reality fulfilling itself at that moment) who leans against the window frame of Ludwig Wintermann's shoe store on the corner of Franz Josef Square at Fehertemplom will yawn, adjust his black hat, and walk away.

Somebody else (elsewhere—for instance in Trieste, the port of the monarchy) will walk, heels clattering on the sidewalk, under

the window at which Emil R. is sitting in a pink damask chair.
But Emil R., deep in thought, will not notice. He will reach for
his pen, having forgotten the cigarette, which has gone out. But
the person walking under the window—a young woman in a
light yellow summer dress and a fashionable little hat tied with
a *jaune de Naples* net—will cross the road at an angle, playing
with the handle of a partly folded parasol that looks like a
flower with its calyx turned downward. She will then stop at the
corner of the square now lit by the glare of the Mediterranean
sun, its lawn striped by the shadows of tamarisk trees, and will
look around, as if waiting for someone.

And at that moment Effendi Fehim Curcich will begin his
welcoming speech. Behind him will stand the councilmen of the
city of Sarajevo and representatives of the four local denomina-
tions. In the first row, Moslems in fezes; in the second, Catholic
dignitaries in dress suits, holding their top hats in their hands;
and behind them the Orthodox priests. There is also a representative of the local Jewish community. And as everyone knows,
his Imperial and Royal Highness will rudely interrupt that
speech, and the burgomaster of the city of Sarajevo will lose
his composure and stop. After a while the archduke will signal
with his hand—"You may continue now"—and Effendi Curcich,
overcoming his nervousness and embarrassment, will continue
with the interrupted sentence: ". . . our hearts are filled with
happiness . . . our deep gratitude for the fatherly and gracious
care of Your Highness . . . the newest jewel in the Holy Imperial crown, Bosnia and Hercegovina . . ." Then a large, hairy
fly will emerge from behind a curtain hanging on either side of
the open door and will circle around the distinguished visitor,
who will follow its spiral evolutions while at the same time pre-
serving his poise, and even a benevolent severity suitable for so
elevating an occasion, so that only his eyes will follow the insistent insect, until the fly settles on a cornice of the audience
chamber of Sarajevo's town hall.

But this will occur later. Meanwhile, the fly is still airborne
and the burgomaster, stammering and sweating, is delivering his
address. What is to happen in a moment, will or will not happen.
Now there is a break.

We repeat: all these facts of different objective significance,
yet subjectively important and therefore of equal weight, form

an inseparable whole from which nothing can be omitted, because each component is crucial. However (although this might strike some as strange and even shocking) the demise of His Imperial and Royal Highness on June 28, and the death of the young gypsy girl Marika Huban precisely a month later, on July 28, 1914, will be equally important. Such a trivial occurrence as the leap of a dog from the door of a gypsy shack toward the dust-covered acacia bushes in which something suspect had moved, and the rustle of a laburnum twig that exercised an indefinable influence on the thinking of Emil R.—everything counts, everything at a given moment is extremely important for someone, therefore nothing can be excluded or dismissed.

If one were to tear out even one component, remove one piece from the chessboard, the whole film now in incessant movement would stop still and freeze. We would behold a kind of film in which life has been trapped; persons in motion would stop with one leg in the air, with a piece of chocolate cake impaled on a fork, or carried to an already opened mouth but never ingested. The cream dripping from the fork would hang in the air. The mouth would remain dead, absurdly open forever.

While on the subject of films, it is perhaps worth mentioning that during that week the only movie house in Fehertemplom, the Bio-Moderne, was showing a film in two parts entitled *The Queen of the Nile*; having been shown with great success in more important towns of the monarchy, from Vienna and Graz to Budapest and Arad, it was finishing its run here. In the two movie houses of Trieste those interested could admire the famous star Asta Nielsen in her latest film, a psychological drama entitled *Engelchen*. In front of one of the Trieste movie theaters a motorcar is parked, an Audi 1912, painted cream, a four-cylinder model that, according to the driver clad in a white dust coat with a navy blue collar and a flat hat with a visor and goggles on it, can go a hundred kilometers an hour. He tells this to three workmen who, having interrupted their work repairing waterpipes in the nearby square, have come up to admire it. The chauffeur tells them about the journey he made the day before from Vienna via Semmering, Mürzzuschlag, and Judenburg, and about his employer, the deputy director of the Länderbank in Vienna who, a moment before, had entered a shop nearby. The doors of the Edison Theater are closed at this hour. One of the workmen will walk away from the motorcar, abandoning his mates who are still discussing the good and bad features of the new Audi model, to look more closely at the colorful posters advertising the film.

At the port a group of travelers on the dock are crowded alongside the Austro-Hungarian passenger boat *Prinz Hohenlohe.* Her cruise has been canceled at the last moment. Passengers of various nationalities, variously dressed, intending to travel to the eastern Mediterranean, to Pireaus and the island of Corfu, to Constantinople and Alexandria, inquire about the schedule changes. Somebody—probably a representative of Austro-Lloyd— provides information. Farther along, one can recognize the silhouette of the old, worn, but still highly serviceable liner *Carpathia.* Under a canvas on her deck awning are some seamen. One of them, his white-trousered legs hanging over the water, is singing a nostalgic Croatian song. The air is mild, there is no wind, so the words can be heard even on the dock.

Events that create an inseparable whole either by their convergence in time, the combination of circumstances, or the whims of fate, can belong in the purely physical sense to two spheres. Thus the existence and the fortunes of the R. siblings, in the phase that touches directly upon other facts occurring simultaneously in time and place, might be inscribed within the circles formed by water as it runs out of the bath when the plug had been pulled. The law of gravity—or the earth's force of attraction—forms a lively whirlpool that tries to penetrate the outlet of the pipe, helped by the pressure of air on the surface of the water. The whirlpool will eventually form a funnel, its tip pointing to the drain. In the last stages of that speeding ebb, that emptying of the bathtub, we will hear a slurp, like the last sigh of a dying person, and the funnel will vanish.

The facts parallel in time already mentioned above—facts that are both real and irrevocably fulfilled or in the course of becoming so—have a different aspect. These might be likened, if one proceeds with the water metaphor, to circles not converging concentrically, as in a bathtub after the plug has been pulled, but spreading centrifugally. It is enough to throw a stone into water to verify this commonly known fact. Around the place where the pebble has landed, circles appear that spread wider and wider until they disappear and the surface becomes calm again. These circles, this movement of the water, cannot be stopped either with an outstretched arm or with an oar. Only a strong dam, barring their progress, will stop them, and then the watery pools and circles begin to recede. But these phenomena are too obvious and commonplace to be described further.

Thus we repeat:
"Once upon a time there were two sisters, Elizabeth and Bernadette, who had one brother, Emil."

Should this information be insufficient (and there is always somebody thirsting for details, and even for inessential gossip that strikes him as important), we might add the following:

The above-mentioned persons were fathered by Emmanuel R., at one time a well-known attorney at Graz, later domiciled in Vienna, legal adviser to the Bodenkreditanstalt and to one of the branches of the Länderbank. Each was conceived under different circumstances, a fact not without meaning and therefore worthy of attention.

The eldest, Elizabeth, had been conceived after her parents returned one evening from an operetta, the title of which is immaterial, and after a pleasant supper with friends in the restaurant of the Elephant Hotel at 13 Murplatz in Graz, in July 1890.

The attorney, a tall and vigorous man of middle years, and at the height of his masculine powers, had entered his apartment at 3 Seebacherstrasse in an excellent post-operetta and post-prandial mood singing an aria he remembered, hung his bowler hat made by Habig on the coatstand in the hall, and deposited his cane with a silver top in the shape of a greyhound's head in a basket in the likeness of a vase decorated with Chinese dragons; then, still whistling the aria, he looked at himself in a mirror and, curling his moustache, set off resolutely toward the marital bedroom. Meanwhile, his wife, married three years before and graced with a rather melancholy beauty (particularly underlined by the expression of her eyes and the shape of her eyebrows), had also been standing before a mirror, a full-length one, where she removed a long pin securing her summer hat adorned with a pendant blue-gray feather while singing softly to herself. Having taken off the hat and placed it on a table next to the mirror, she leaned toward the mirror and began to observe

her face with a meticulous and concentrated attention. She did
not like the tired look around her eyes, especially at the lower
lids, now slightly swollen and heavy. Her eyes, however, still
sparkled with liveliness after this pleasant evening. Having
folded back a corner of a light green bedcover, Mrs. R. sighed
and sat on the edge of her marital bed. Just then her spouse
entered the bedroom, unbuttoning his patterned piqué vest. His
suspenders had already been removed.

The middle child—a boy who at baptism in St. Leonard's
Church received the names of Emil, Henry, and Joachim—was
conceived, one might say, under extraordinary circumstances,
because it was on His Majesty the Emperor's birthday, August
18, 1892, a date easy to establish and remember. To be more
precise: it was the night of August 18–19, so the claim to a connection with the Monarch's birthday may be a little far-fetched
and misleading. Mr. and Mrs. R. had been in Vienna for a few
days, staying at the Klomser Hotel. (The same one—the very
same—in which, in 1913, Colonel Alfred Redl will commit
suicide; Redl of evil memory, the chief of staff of the Eighth
Corps at Prague. This fact, occurring much later than the events
here described, should not influence their assessment unduly, or
unnecessarily create a semblance of Destiny.) Mr. and Mrs. R.
had witnessed in the main streets of Vienna the celebrations that,
as every year, were an occasion for popular enjoyment. And there,
in one of the coffee houses in the Prater, the attorney noticed,
while drinking wine with his wife and friends (a couple named
Jacobi), a young cavalry soldier's energetic courtship of a still
younger and attractive waitress, which put Mr. R. in a lyrical
and aggressive mood. On his return to the hotel, not even having
doffed his hat, but having thrown his cane with the silver greyhound's head somewhere or other, he suddenly felt lusty, which
made him perform a rather violent amorous act after—let this
be mentioned, too—a prolonged erotic drought. He performed
the act, and, after a short interval, two more acts, which astonished quite pleasantly, but at first slightly frightened, his spouse,
unaccustomed by now to the kind of love-making bestowed on
her by her husband that August night. It seems—we are not
quite sure about this—that the attorney, having removed his
black frock coat in the hall, kept his bowler hat on, forgotten in
his amorous frenzy, while his wife, after her husband's hasty

removal of her corset, purchased the previous day in the Mariahilferstrasse, as well as an item of her underwear of the best quality, permeated with the scent of verbena much in vogue in certain circles, remained in her festive imperial-anniversary gala clothes: her summer straw hat trimmed with a navy blue ribbon, and laced boots coming halfway up her leg—exquisitely elegant boots made of the finest leather, with fairly high heels. It might be assumed that she was still also wearing her gloves of thin chamois leather, ivory colored, although her handbag lay on the rather shabby rug by the bed.

With all this, and knowing Attorney R., one can assume that, having tightly closed his eyes, instead of his wife he imagined that charming little waitress from the Prater, having himself been transformed into the young lancer, the waitress's admirer who—and this seems likely—was at the same moment performing with similar frenzy a similar act, only without having to rely on his imagination, because the object of his passion was precisely the one he was embracing. Although separated in space, both ladies and both gentlemen were united at the same minute in the same activity, emitting similar, because universally human, cries and groans of delight.

Given these circumstances, Emil became a child of a somewhat split character, because he was begotten by someone thinking of one object while embracing another. The wedded wife was the attorney's partner in the physical and not in the essential, psychophysical sense. The intention was split into two not strictly contiguous elements, hence the undoubted peculiarity and separateness of the offspring Emil, born seven months later, the result of that stormy Imperial and Royal night.

For Emil, born at Graz, was a premature baby. Perhaps the reason for it was that Mrs. R. gave birth to her only son as it were by proxy, because it was that young waitress of unknown name who should have been fertilized by the lawyer. Perhaps the foetus, conceived by accident and reared in Mrs. R.'s womb, felt like an interloper, a foundling, a stranger. One might indulge indefinitely in speculation without anything being gained by it, for the future, at least in part, is always as impenetrable as the fate of Oedipus.

Emil was born two years after the first-born Elizabeth, later nicknamed Lieschen, and a year before the birth of the last of the children, Bernadette, called Detta. About the latter, only the briefest, most concise information.

Her conception occurred in circumstances that were undefined, imprecise, and not easy to remember, because ordinary and colorless. It was perfunctory, arising out of the habit of performing, from time to time, the gradually less attractive marital duties foreseen by the law, by custom, and by religious precepts, considered at the time by the attorney as additional office work, thus obligatory and boring, especially as during that period Mr. R. was interested in a certain Mrs. K., while Mrs. R. was passing through a not quite happy or auspicious period of her life, if one takes into account her chronic kidney trouble and the gingivitis brought on by that winter's cold winds. She regularly visited a dentist at Hartenaugasse on the first floor left, at the same time undergoing renal treatment administered by the local medical wizard, Dr. Max F. That winter had been particularly unpleasant. There were winds from the river Mur, and fogs that originated there penetrated into the canyons of the streets, filling them with freezing air; snowstorms followed thaw, and in the garden of 3 Seebacherstrasse were puddles covered with ice, or whose muddy bottoms shone darkly. On some days only the Schlossberg was visible in the sea of fog. The attorney's bowler hat had been resting in the cupboard since autumn, the fancy cane was replaced by a less fancy umbrella, and for daily wear Mr. R. took a Persian lamb hat, worn with a coat with the same fur lining. All this had its importance, so these seemingly trivial details ought to be mentioned.

To be precise:

When little E. (Elizabeth/Lieschen/Liselotte) was five years old and becoming a thin creature with a foxy face and fair hair that, much to her mother's disappointment, would not grow, her brother Emil had his third birthday, and B. (Bernadette, nicknamed Detta) was two, and had just started to talk. She was a rather fat, serene baby, slightly slow to develop. Luckily, this righted itself as she grew older. Even later she was characterized, one must admit, by a certain docility, by a slightly sleepy, lazy passivity. In time (one must patiently wait a few years), her helplessness caused her to become the object of all kinds of experiments on the part of her elder sister, who from early childhood had a tendency to willfulness, extravagance, and perfidy, but was endowed with considerable fantasy and imagination.

In advance of events we might mention that at the real time, the one that actually occurred (we refer, clearly, to the end of July and beginning of August 1914) Detta had been married for two years to a promising young banker, who thanks to his father-in-law was given a start at the Bodenkreditanstalt and had hopes of advancement. In 1913, Bernadette had presented him with a daughter, named Ethel after her mother.

And this would be almost all.

True, there has been mention of some childish "games." Yes, indeed. It is difficult to establish the date when they had begun. The initiative was undoubtedly Lieschen's on some winter evening in the lounge-cum-waiting room of Attorney R., her father, who a year or two before had moved from 3 Seebacherstrasse in Graz (where the family continued to spend the summer months) to Vienna, where he rented a largish apartment in the Stuben-ring. But it could have happened in the morning, on a Saturday for instance, after the general washing of the three children by the governess, at the time when Mama had already gone to a café to meet her lady friends and when Mr. R. was at court.

It is not the date nor the time of day, however, that is important, but the course—or rather the type or model—of the game. Its initiator was Lieschen, and the object of the experiments the obedient and docile Detta, while Emil was the eager observer, recipient, or medium. The games were immutable in their assumptions and similar in their nature. The details might differ, but not the essence. The variations were decided by Lieschen's fantasy and inventiveness.

At some time Cornelius Blatt, their confessor, will become (indirectly, of course) part of the action. And he will in some measure be the witness to the games.

So on tiptoe we enter the drawing room in the Stubenring and stand in the corner. We may preserve our identity and observe the events from our own point of view, or we can assume Emil R.'s personality. In that case it would be difficult for us to witness anything objectively. For lack of anything better, we might be left with assumptions arising from Emil's notes or his few letters (mostly never posted). Otherwise there is nothing tangible.

Unobserved, on a certain day we enter the drawing room, which is lit by a lamp of dull pink fluted glass in the shape of an open waterlily. The spiral ridges and elliptical scrolls of the pink shade will cast on the walls and ceiling fluted, pink-yellow, slightly smudgy, and fleeting shadows and streaks. At the windows of the drawing room, overlooking the Stubenring, hang heavy curtains held by thick cords ending in rich tassels. It might happen that the heavy curtains will be drawn for the night, and making invisible the fine net ones beyond them, next to the windowpanes. Through a crack in the curtains, the glare of a lantern might glimmer. It will be the lantern of a fiacre driving by with the clatter of hooves on the cobbles. And it is worth mentioning that a thick carpet covers the floor. Of the five armchairs in the room, one will be pushed into the shadows toward a large Biedermeier sofa.

We are in the era of late Art Nouveau, of fading modernism; it might therefore be worthwhile to mention a few books in the glass-fronted mahogany bookcase that in style is nearer Maria Theresa than Biedermeier. If we tiptoe over to it, its glass doors will allow us to see three upper rows of shelves; next to other works, we shall find the latest editions of the dramas of Frank Wedekind; several issues of the magazine *Die Fackel; Die Farben* by Hoffmannsthal; *The White Manor* by Hermann Bang; a year's run of *La Revue des deux mondes*; and the newest novels by Marcel Schwob and Maurice Barrès. Attorney R. and his wife count themselves among the enlightened who follow the latest fashions and the newest trends in culture. Mrs. R. follows them more closely than her husband.

Somewhere in the neighborhood someone is playing the piano. The walls, the carpets, and the furniture deaden the sound, but on listening more closely, one can recognize the music. Chopin? Perhaps. But if anyone would prefer some Brahms, or the piano transcription of any of the operatic arias—like for instance those from *Tosca*—no one will dispute it. And here is Emil. Somebody has declared (perhaps Mrs. Martha Jacobi, the councillor's wife, or perhaps someone else) that he resembles the youthful Schubert. To relate this resemblance to the source, to the tune, we might choose a song by the composer of the *Unfinished Symphony*. Perhaps the serenade "Leise flehen meine Lieder." And this musical tune in the distance will not leave us, it will stubbornly accompany us, along with the insistent scent of "Violettes Impériales," Mrs. R.'s perfume. It forms the background and—as long as it lasts—a component and indispensable accompaniment irrevocably connected with the aura both of the drawing room in the Stubenring and of the youthful games of the R. siblings.

One of the armchairs covered with a brocade in Pompeian pattern has been pushed to the side. The leg of the armchair had got caught in the corner of the carpet, which, turned back, revealed a piece of the parquet floor, somewhat lighter and duller in this place because, being covered, it was less frequently polished.

In that uncovered place little B. is now kneeling. She hangs her head and does not look at her elder sister, who is standing over her, her legs wide apart, looking at her imperiously. Lieschen is knitting her narrow, fair brows, which are almost invisible in the pink light. Her eyes are also very light—grayish yellow. Cat's eyes, the chambermaid maintains, and so does Father Blatt.

"Moo! Come on—like a cow!" Detta attempts to emit, in accordance with her sister's order, a suitable mooing. Emil stands on the side, not important, taken into consideration by neither of the two girls. But this is only pretense. He is standing, almost hidden by the folds of the heavy curtains, which are permeated by the smell of "Violettes Impériales."

"And now, *baaa*—like a sheep! Well?" Lieschen stamps her foot with impatience, because the other child does not manage to do it, although she is desperately trying. In a moment, perhaps, with the point of her shoe—still almost a child's, with a bow or pompom adorning it—Lisa will nudge her sister on her forehead or shoulder. Or perhaps this will occur after we have left the drawing room of Mr. and Mrs. R. in the Stubenring. We shall leave on tiptoe, carrying with us the sultry, faded scent of "Violettes Impériales" and the memory of the tune still returning like a wave, an obsession drifting in from elsewhere, perhaps from another floor of the house, or another apartment. We shall descend the red runner covering the marble stairs. On the landing, at the turn of the staircase, is a plaster figure, a dryad or another nymph, holding a lamp with a glass shade in the shape of a lily or perhaps a gladiolus. And we shall tell ourselves, upon reaching the street: "To be continued." For there will be a proper time for each installment.

After Supicich's death, the tavern in Kiralyi Street was taken over by his widow, the stout Erzika Supicich, always laughing noisily, and popular with her customers. Some of them address her familiarly as Bezsi.

Years before, the site had been occupied by a Turkish bath (or hamman), probably from the time of the Danube expeditions of Prince Eugene of Savoy, or perhaps from an even earlier time, though this is not certain. Now it is the place where the officers of the local garrison meet for a glass of wine.

Most of them are officers of the Imperial and Royal Twelfth Regiment of Lancers, known today as General Bothmer's Cavalry—formerly, the Lancers of the King of the Two Sicilies.

In the late evening of that fatal July 28, 1914, some of the officers were still sitting in a side room of Mother Bezsi Supicich's tavern, where they learned from her that in a nearby clay pit the body of a fifteen-year-old gypsy girl had been found. Mother Supicich heard it from a boy, who in turn heard it from a witness, the one who had found the corpse and, running to the gendarmerie, had told his friend all about it.

Mother Bezsi went up to the table where the officers were drinking, stopped, and crossed her thick arms, bare to the elbow, on her generous bosom. She delivered a few commonplaces about the young gypsy girl's death and her apparently none-too-praiseworthy life, while shaking her head in wonder. She advanced some guesses, commenting on which, the officers began a noisy conversation. As it appeared, some of them had known the dead—or perhaps murdered—girl. The gendarmes had been informed, so by the next morning at the latest, everybody would know what had really happened.

The first to clear his throat was Cavalry Captain Peter Malaterna, who raised his bushy black eyebrows. Then Lieutenant Baron Lajos Viranyi, nicknamed "Handsome Louis" by the regiment, showed similar astonishment. Reserve Lieutenant Kottfuss Freiherr von Kottvitza, who had joined the regiment only the previous day, burst out into loud and light-hearted laughter. After which he adjusted his monocle, twirled his moustache, and took a long sip of wine.

It was 10:15 p.m. And it was about 11:00 when the officers left Mother Supicich's tavern in a noisy group. Baron Kottfuss looked up at the sky, then uniformly black and strewn with stars. The brightest and largest of them, greenish-blue and silvery-emerald, shone just above the horizon toward the Danube. Could it be Venus? The lieutenant could not remember its name, try as he might. Just then his colleagues were talking on subjects which had nothing to do with stars. The news about war with Serbia and the mobilization of several army corps dominated their conversations, which is entirely understandable.

At that time, the river gunboat *Bodrog* had stopped its bombardment of Belgrade. Had it continued to fire salvo after salvo from its deck guns mounted in armored turrets that now shone martially in the Serbian moonlight, they could not have been heard in dark and dusty Kiralyi Street. Everybody knows that the town of Fehertemplom is at least seventy-five kilometers distant from the capital of Serbia.

Gendarmerie Sergeant Istvan Vilajcich gets up heavily from an unfinished glass of wine on the table, and without hurrying starts to fasten his belt. He is slightly sleepy. The heat, and the additional work connected with the just declared mobilization of the Fourth and Seventh corps, have tired him. Having fixed his belt, Vilajcich dons his Hungarian gendarme's hat, adorned with a bunch of green cock feathers. He goes out with a young guide named Yano, the one who first reported the discovery in the old clay pit on the edge of the Gypsy Quarter. The night is a typical July night, close and very dark. En route, the sergeant still hopes that perhaps the young gypsy girl drowned accidentally in the pool left by the recent torrential rains. Maybe she fell in while under the influence of drink. Such things happen often. Recently, for instance, the body of a male gypsy called Metko was found near the town brickworks. The post mortem stated that he was mortally drunk. He stumbled on a stone, fell, and never got up. There was a police report, and that was that. As for gypsy women . . . One must say, all the same, that the officers are not above having their little games from time to time. Not all of them, but some. They are capable of forcing whole liters of wine down the gullet of a girl who begs too insistently for alms, or even a quart of plum brandy. Not in Mother Rozsa's place, because Mother Rozsa keeps an eye on things—only rarely is there a brawl. But in the other taverns, especially in Ujvaros and at the far end of Kiralyi Street and Kerti Street, it's another story. The day before yesterday, for instance, three gypsy girls were over there, in the bushes beyond the market place, completely unconscious with drink. One of them wearing only an officer's belt that nobody has yet claimed. It still hangs on the rack in a corner of the police station, as a "corpus delicti."

Vilajcich also remembers another incident when some joker tied a live cat to the leg of a drunken girl asleep under a hedge. The sergeant felt a secret and long-lasting dislike for all the officers stationed at Fehertemplom. They were to some extent beyond the reach of his authority, and treated him—indeed all the gendarmerie—with contempt; the majority—no use denying it—did not take any notice of him. So he put down to "typical gentlemen-officers' jokes" all such offenses, especially those of a sexual nature. The belt hanging unclaimed on the rack was tangible proof of a crime, while regarding the cat one could only surmise, as there were no witnesses: a gypsy youth might have tied it to the drunken girl out of spite, or an ordinary soldier might have done it out of exuberance. But Vilajcich obstinately assumed that it must have been one of those gents in white gloves who had committed this latest practical joke. Had the garrison not been so large, blissful peace would have reigned in Fehertemplom. People would walk on tiptoe, bowing low to the man in a hat with cock feathers. Sergeant Istvan Vilajcich had previously served as a corporal in the Royal Hungarian Gendarmerie in the small provincial town of Kiskunfelegyhaza south of Kecskemet. There was no military garrison there, so peace, order, and discipline prevailed. It was enough that he should knit his eyebrows—Vilajcich's brows were black, thick, and fierce—or that he should move his moustache—which was turned up, pitch black, and famous even in such a moustachioed formation as the Hungarian gendarmerie—for people to tremble and move out of the way. Everybody: peasants, Jews, gypsies. Even most of the poor lowly townspeople, merchants and artisans. Everybody except the bailiff of Count Andrassy's estates—but he was unimportant. And the count himself, of course, but who set eyes on him even once in a lifetime?

At Fehertemplom, on the other hand, let's see: the Franz Josef Barracks: first battalion, Fourth Royal Honved Infantry

Regiment; the so-called "Iron Works" Barracks (official name,
Archduke Josef Barracks): the supply depot of the Fourth
Cavalry Brigade, together with the stores, smithies, and orderly
rooms of that unit; the Emperor Ferdinand Barracks: the
Twelfth Lancers Regiment (they gave the most trouble), also
the three field batteries of honveds transferred from Arad only
two weeks before (God help us, what a bunch!). Thus cogitating,
inwardly fuming and spitting in the darkness, Sergeant Vilajcich
followed young gypsy Yano, the apprentice of the butcher in
Kiralyi Street (next to the pharmacy), still hoping that the
gypsy girl found by the boy had drowned accidentally and that
the matter would end with a report, but without a tiresome
investigation.

It appears, however, that he would be spared nothing. Yano
(the devil take him) declares on the way that somebody had
probably cut the girl's throat. The sergeant curses heartily.
Pulling back his hat, he scratches his temple, then spits again.

Meanwhile the officers are already far away. Walking, pausing
to light a cigar, talking about this and that, they are now approaching the Emperor Ferdinand Barracks. Most of them live
in the barracks, and the whole roomy left wing is given over to
their quarters. Only two or three have managed to find suitable
billets in the town, like for instance Major Markovich, who is
near retiring age. He lives with his wife on the first floor of the
pharmacist Smugich's house. He has been in the regiment from
time immemorial and intends to remain here at Fehertemplom,
or so he maintains, when he retires from active service. The
regimental vet also lives in an apartment, but he doesn't count
either socially or professionally. Anyway, he comes from these
parts, has his own private patients, and is a dedicated hunter
besides.

Sicilian Lancers—good God! Just think: "On March 4, 1854,"
(we read in the regimental chronicle) "this unit is awarded
(*mil allerhöchsten Befehl!*) its name and recruitment area,
which from now on will be the territory of the Thirteenth Corps,
with headquarters at Zagreb." But with the passage of years the
regiment was moved to different corners of the vast monarchy
and attached to various units. It was stationed in Lombardy as
part of the Fifth, later the Eighth, Corps (what good times
those were! what beautiful garrison towns—Piacenza, Cremona,

Mantua—when Lombardy was still one of the most precious
jewels in the imperial crown of the Hapsburgs! . . . *tempi
passati* . . .), then later at Varazdin, at Banja Luka and Mostar
(during the occupation of Bosnia and Hercegovina), at Arad
(not too bad a garrison!) and finally at Fehertemplom, as part
of the Eighth Cavalry Brigade to which, apart from our local
regiment, the Ninth Regiment of Hussars also belongs.

In the same chronicle, published in an elegant edition by the
Imperial and Royal Institute for Military History, one could
read that the successive honorary colonels of the regiment were,
first, from 1854 on, Ferdinand II, King of the Two Sicilies—
"King Bomba" whose portrait hangs in the officers' mess in a
place of honor, facing the entrance door, to the right of the
buffet: a pink, as if slightly powdered face, with thick gray
whiskers, and majesty seemingly veiled by a light mist of melancholy and kindly joviality. In fact, at a closer look the Neapolitan
monarch reminds one slightly of Jacques Offenbach—a likeness
pointed out to Emil R., the day after he joined the garrison, by
Reserve Second Lieutenant Kocourek, his old friend and colleague from Vienna. It is quite possible, of course, that we are
wrong: perhaps the jovial smile of the first patron of the regiment is due not to kindliness but an innate and perverse cruelty,
mellowed by age; but to be sure about this one should be better
acquainted with details of the life and habits of the ruler of
Naples, Palermo, Syracuse, and Taormina. In his journey to
Italy, in the summer of 1911, Emil R. did not omit Syracuse,
Taormina, or Agrigento. Perhaps when visiting the palace at
Naples he fleetingly remembered King Ferdinand, not having
foreseen that he would ever know him as the first patron of his
regiment, and that under his auspices and blessing from beyond
the grave he would set off to the Great War of the nations.

The second on the list of patrons and honorary commanders
of the regiment is Francis Bourbon II, irrevocably the last King
of the Two Sicilies.

Looking at his likeness in the officers' mess at Fehertemplom—
to the left of King Ferdinand, nearer the window—Emil R. will
think: "The duality in the name of a kingdom which perished
years ago bears in it the seeds and sentence of death. Our monarchy is also double in name: Austro-Hungarian, and so is the
imperial line: Hapsburg-Lorraine, and I myself, too—" Here

he will interrupt his train of thought and approach the buffet, summoned by his friend. Second Lieutenant Zdenek Kocourek is waiting for him with a glass of plum brandy. Several other reserve officers, mobilized a few days before and hailing from various parts of the monarchy, are also calling him, so he must not linger.

At that very moment when Emil R.'s thoughts are ranging far afield, in Naples and perhaps in Reggio di Calabria it is night, and in the roads of Palermo the Royal Italian Navy battleship *Dante Alighieri* lies at anchor. On her bow, near the forward turret from which the sheath-covered barrels of two powerful 305 mm guns project, a few sailors are busy. Their feet are bare on the freshly washed, still wet deck. One of them lights a cigarette while approaching the ship's side. A small light hanging on the forward yard is blinking. The light can be seen from the city, on the docks where the market stalls are now empty. A dog runs here and there, sniffing. The lighthouse sheds an elongated beam of light on the gently undulating water. In the white moonlight the oriental domes of the church of San Giovanni degli Eremiti look like fragments of a stage set for *Scheherezade.*

Later—but one should wait a moment—a sailor will begin to sing, while a paunchy, elderly gentleman in silk trousers and a straw hat, who is leaning against the low wall of the dock, will throw his cigar butt into the sea and it will go out with a small hiss. Apart from this, there is nothing to report. Perhaps only that the lonely greenish star, which some moments ago the officers of the Sicilian Lancers returning from Mother Bezsi's have been looking at, is now not over Belgrade, but perhaps over Tunis and Pentelleria.

1859: the year of Magenta and Solferino. A year of ill omen. Then a longish gap in the history of the regiment, if one does not count the dates connected with maneuvers, personnel changes in the officers' ranks, marches from garrison to garrison. Only in 1896 does a new patron of the regiment appear—a man worthy of the dignity: Cavalry General His Excellency Otto Freiherr von Gagern. His full-size portrait hangs in the officers' mess to the left of the buffet, in full dress uniform, his white-gloved hand on the guard of his saber as he smiles at his predecessors, the Kings of the Two Sicilies.

Perhaps because of the portrait's proximity to the buffet, or perhaps because he stared at it for so many years, the manager of that buffet, Istvan Barabas—the master and pride of the officers' mess and its famous cuisine (especially his Hungarian fish soup, called "Szegedin soup," unmatched throughout the monarchy)—has become so like Baron Hagern, the honorary patron of the regiment, that at times, when Istvan is serving young Dalmatian wine or old plum brandy from the Banat, one has the feeling that the Imperial and Royal officers are graciously served by His Excellency in person (now, alas, His Late Excellency). "Prosit, Excellenz!" The glasses are lifted high.

And here is the latest, the contemporary patron of the regiment: since 1902, Cavalry General His Excellency Wilhelm Freiherr von Bothmer. Everybody here knows him: he has been entertained on several occasions. He participated on horseback in the imperial maneuvers of 1904 north of Temesvar and in the subsequent tactical exercises of the cavalry brigade, galloping along with the third squadron, stirrup to stirrup with Major Emmerich von Magyarpecska, commander of the First Division, over the fertile, clear, open Banat plain in the clouds of dust raised by thousands of horses' hooves, amid the snorting of horses, the clank of stirrups and saber sheaths, the glint of harnesses and spurs, far, far away, following the tracks of Prince Eugene's expeditions to the lowlands of the Danube and the Sava—as far as the spot where the high Serbian bank can be seen, Kalemegdan Hill and the crosses of the Orthodox churches of Belgrade and its royal residence.

This regiment of ours, "The Twelfth Sicilian Lancers," is not to be sneezed at, in spite of the fact that all those rulers have been dead a long time, their dual kingdom of Hercules and Proserpina, too, yet the memory is still fresh and so is the legend. "The Sicilian Lancers" sounds better than "Bothmer's Lancers"—everybody knows that.

From a window of the Emperor Ferdinand Barracks, one can see that Major X is preparing to mount a black horse. He is resting both hands in their immaculate white gloves against the bow of the saddle and is trying to put his foot in the stirrup without looking. Unfortunately the stirrup is swaying, whether jarred by the tip of Major X's boot or by the jerking of the horse's head while it tries to avoid the insistent bumblebees.

There are always swarms of these, not counting the ordinary flies, in the vicinity of the cavalry stables, from which soldiers in white summer shirts and red trousers are now leading out the saddled horses.

Looking out the window at Major X, one can, at worst, "escape into music," just as one can "escape into illness" from the worries of the day. Emil R., therefore, still looking from the window, stops thinking about the major and begins to think about imminent problems: marching orders expected soon—perhaps tomorrow at dawn, perhaps in the evening or at nightfall. Since the First Squadron may entrain on time—though one must consider the complications arising from the simultaneous arrival at the railway ramp of the Thirteenth Regiment of Hussars, whose marching orders have changed at the last moment, God knows why (there's complete chaos in the wake of mobilization, so what's going to happen later on, when whole army corps have to be moved?)—since they may entrain on time, one must escape fast into music from the despair of expectation and the boredom of waiting. What for, in fact? What am I waiting for? Nothing—therefore why not escape into imaginary pictures of war, or rather various wars, a synthesis of warfare from various eras? That's how I've been re-creating it often in different versions: a medley of battles and struggles, all different, chaotically combined into the whole gamut, and chords and attempts at études or symphonies created in an instant from fragments of colors and sounds, real musical *Images d'Epinal* conceived from illustrated magazines, etchings, photographs, and reproductions.

Emperor William II on maneuvers somewhere in Mecklenburg: a cuirassier's helmet with an eagle, upturned whiskers, a map lying on a folding stool, and next to him the staff. The French general staff—probably also somewhere on maneuvers: red kepis trimmed with braid, loose pantaloons with broad stripes, their upturned heads observing a captive balloon at Epernay or perhaps Saint-Quentin. A squadron of battleships sailing from Wilhelmshaven, and now the Japanese jump into this image, penetrating the fortifications of Port Arthur. Now the Boers. General Botha at Pietermaritzburg or perhaps Bloemfontein. It is 1901, it seems. *Wiener Illustrierte Zeitung, Leipziger Illustrierte Zeitung*, and so on. A complete show of costumes, colorful but somewhat demonic. A carnival and funeral rites. "Violettes Impériales" and the stifling smell of disinfectant. Carbolic acid. For a few days the local station has been reeking of it, because the sanitary authorities ordered disinfectants sprayed inside the coaches prepared for the troops in the event of mobilization—carbolic acid and lysol—for fear of a dysentery epidemic. Dysentery is linked with war. Sometimes it breaks out during the summer maneuvers. Last year, apparently in the area of Nagybecskerek. And in our native or mother regiment to boot!

One image after another, each arising from the previous one: General Nogi out of Lord Kitchener, Marshal Niel out of the leader of the Zulus, and so on, like the famous Russian toys, those wooden dolls painted in garish colors, brought back from journeys to Moscow or St. Petersburg by one of the uncles. Each one contains a smaller one, a progressively smaller and smaller effigy of a ruddy-cheeked Muscovite woman with scarlet blushes on her cheeks, a woman in a bell-like skirt with her hands folded modestly in her lap.

In this medley of images there is room for the lonely escape of the Russian light cruiser *Zemtchug* from the hell of Tsushima to the distant Philippines. It was an especially garish and persuasive genre picture, seen once in an illustrated magazine and now firmly lodged in a memory fed by imagination.

The sea the color of mignonette, high shaggy waves with scarlet crests, like flowers or cocks' combs, a blue-golden, transparent depth and, on the bottom, coral reefs and lurking fishes. Ah, the southern seas of our childhood dreams, of distant sailing adventures! How green they were! So were the fortunes of the sister ship, the light cruiser *Izumrud*, which in the flight from Tsushima to the north (through yellow Chinese seas where the dominant colors were sulphur, and whose waters were evil, seething and burning like molten metal) foundered in a hurricane at night on submerged rocks in the roads of Vladivostok. Here black waters dominate, streaked with illusory flashes. Is it the moon shining behind the clouds? Or a searchlight from a sinking ship sending calls for help? A blackness cut with flashes the color of pewter, like thrusts of a sharp knife. Deep blackness— ah, to be able to paint it as an illustration to a nocturne! A musical blackness and silver squiggles like music signs—certainly

B minor—like embroidery on someone performing a funeral rite. The ritual would have been Chinese or Mongolian, at any rate mystical in its secret cruelties, about which one had read some time ago, perhaps in the *Garden of Torture* by Mirabeau. And there is the moon rising over the battlefield of Solferino. The night of June 24–25, 1859, that famous night! But this is a separate, especially important page of history. Grandfather—mother's father, it was—died in action that night, and so many stories, so many memories of the earliest years were centered around that date and that name: Solferino! And that's not all: a lonely rider, into whom I myself was transformed while the picture expanded in my imagination even then—how many years ago was it?—when I tried to compose something, musically or not, in pictures and faint sounds, *Sons et Tableaux*. Nothing resulted from it, but the aura has persisted. A musical etching? Or perhaps a fabric of sounds?

And next to it a well-known painting by Vereshchagin, *The Battlefield of Plevna*: a priest in a chasuble, long-haired, with a silver beard, swinging a golden censer emitting smoke, and fields covered with rows of neatly arranged bodies of soldiers, row after row, as far as the eye can see, faces covered with hats without visors, other faces bare, unprotected, blanched.

That same Vereshchagin painting—there must be some logic in that seemingly chaotic scheme, that morbid review—sinking in the troubled yellow sea, an evil Chinese sea, as in a hellish pot of boiling water. The surging bright lemon-yellow waves of the Far East, and in them the battleship *Petropavlovsk* lying on its side, sinking with Admiral Makarov on board. A flag with the blue cross of St. Andrew the Apostle, jutting out proudly from the water. And following that image, probably remembered from a contemporary illustration, Orthodox choirs and the smoke of incense, and priests singing an Orthodox Requiem—what does it sound like?

And something else, a clear recollection of a book read in bed not so long ago at Gmunden, and finished on a train going from Klagenfurt to Graz—the net result of a very strong impression: wounded soldiers of the American Civil War crawling through a marshland full of serpents and small reptiles, muddy forest thickets resounding with the croaking of frogs. Strips of torn, bloody uniforms, bandages trailing over stones, along forest paths, on and on, amid groans and curses. This image can wake me up at night. Half-human figures crawling or half-rising on elbows and knees amid swarms of gnats in a steaming, damp, black night in Virginia or Carolina. A year ago in one of the Vienna movie theaters I saw an authentic report from the war in Tripoli and I still remember every detail clearly. The figures of male nurses—or were they burial details?—dragging off by their shoulders or legs the corpses of their comrades or perhaps the mortally wounded? The passionless workers of death dragging the bodies over sand, on which long, dark traces of blood remained. Or were they shadowy furrows left by the bodies?

For some time I've been unable to get rid of premonitions. They're quite vague, but nonetheless tormenting. They arrange themselves into unclear musical sequences, fugues ending in a question mark of sound, something like a warning, something threatening, obscure too, but evoking the image of a well or a deep chasm. Reasoning in a simplistic manner, I might have concluded that these are, for instance, premonitions of an impending war that indeed has been threatening for at least two years. The thought of war, however, and my part in it has been and still is something that I don't concentrate upon; such subjects have never preoccupied me. Politics and its ramifications and complications, all assumptions and forecasts connected with it, have always bored me. The premonitions plaguing me belong to a completely different sphere of phenomena. They are private and exclusively mine. I've lived with them for years and would feel impoverished if they left me. Just like at Merano some eighteen months ago, when I became aware that my mild fever had passed and there was no more threat of consumption, and I felt a sudden deprivation. As if somebody had switched on a light in a dark room where I'd been dozing in a warm blanket, or had drawn the curtains to admit a sunny day. All the delusions and fears born in darkness had left and I remained alone, deprived and cheated. And somewhat ridiculous.

Now, on the margin as it were of that antidote of recalled visions and premonitions, there is still *it*, for I know that I must never fool myself. A vicarious situation returns: the striped sea tigers of the China Sea (cheap *Images d'Epinal*, pleasant to look at: Tsushima and so on, a kind of decoration: tea wrappings, but transformed and grown into the grandeur of a largo) wind-

ing their movements musically (even now, standing by the barracks window, watching soldiers take out their horses to be
watered, I might express it by musical sequences, chords, and
scales) and at the same time voicelessly. (A logical absurdity?
Perhaps, but watch out, it only seems so: musical silence exists
or can exist, when colors are substituted for sounds.) And so a
symphony of yellow seas, saturated by a bright sulphuric color,
a jungle of watery tigerlike lianas, twisted and animated spirals,
winding themselves in fluid chords. A sea aura, but born from an
image of great growths of greenery on river banks spattered by
incessantly falling droplets of water, a sight known to me from
the mountains of Styria viewed a few years ago. And following
this image come memories of smells: partly medicinal, bitter and
salty, iodine and mountain gentian, and at the same time a real
or imagined smell of the ocean, and a shark that belongs to the
previous image. A huge, oblong shark swimming up from the
deep, seen at once from below and from the side: a monster
opening its mouth cut in the shape of a sickle or a rising moon.
Around the head of the beast swim swarms of small, agile pilot
fish, leading the blind hunter to its prey. Small fish seen in an
aquarium, resembling hummingbirds and swallows, red and
black, waving their veil-like tails and fins; also white water
butterflies and sea moths, gray, with huge heads and bulging eyes,
seen through glass panes and enlarged to the size of monsters. A
wreath of white sharks' teeth approaching me unawares after
one jerk of its shiny body, profiting from my contemplation of
the water fauna, and I now know: the white uniforms of those
historic years of Solferino and Magenta, specters dragging themselves along through mist or fog, the battlefields on the Lombard
plain, ghosts chanting in chorus in the Elysian fields. Or perhaps
these are Doré's illustrations for the *Divine Comedy,* a melopoeia
in the boundless lowlands of purgatory or heaven, since choirs
of angels accompany the wanderings of the white shapes. Bach?
No, this isn't any of the works I know. Violins and violas, and
the obtrusive smell of "Violettes Impériales" that saturated my
days and nights at the Stubenring, perhaps also the interior of a
Vienna opera box. And thus the dull but shining pearl-violet
opal of Mrs. Martha Jacobi's gown, not quite leaning against the
back of a chair upholstered in purple velvet with gold braid—
you've been dead a long time, Martha; when looking through my

papers before leaving the hotel at Trieste, I found the announcement of your death on a card with a broad, black border.

And the stifling smell of violets (in the background, perhaps at the very center of events), the purple of Mrs. Jacobi's dress, rustling at every movement of her knees or shoulders, and a leap of thought: I caught myself in the act, as if I had experienced that leap from here to back there, physically and in reality! When had E. worn a purple dress? Ah yes, on Mama's name day, in the year . . . ? I had been looking at her surreptitiously and she felt my look although she was standing with her face turned from me—yes, I really noticed then the purple of her dress, bordering on red. Let's turn back, turn back fast, because it still hurts, in spite of everything, even now, now perhaps more than ever, when I know, when I expect and foresee, and feel as if I knew for certain that never again . . . The flat mouth of the shark, making a leap in one strong, slippery move of its tense body, somewhere from the side, from inside the Opera, to the opening of the proscenium box, like a slippery bit of wood, from its mouth down to its slightly bent tail, and the fin cutting through the air like a knife, leaving a barely visible furrow, like a long corridor immediately filled with music and the sound of violins, then a viola. And this is already another year, another day, another date, and there's a balustrade hanging over a void filled with a light resembling the depths of the sea. Light is shed on something that doesn't exist, that has a color defying description in the known spectrum of the rainbow. I couldn't call it by any name, but it might be expressed by sound. The smell of moondust perhaps, of dust gathered in the velvet armchairs and hangings, in the folds and bends of gilded Art Nouveau ornaments, the caryatides supporting the front of the box, an unreal light, but one that existed in reality, and I could swear was moved by the waves of the floating music, seizing any pretext to assume forms either already existing or newly invented, but shapes capable of being described or even painted, now crowding insistently in swarms of metaphors. Music must be received in total abstraction from any analogies—yes, yes, yes!— after a total exclusion of similes with things nonmusical. But then again, what about the broad stone flanks of a castle (the Villa d'Este at Ferrara?), balconies and cloistered arcades receding to infinity in cascades of sound? And now a slow proces-

sion down wide Gothic stairs, as silvery as the walls of the Villa
d'Este (this is without any doubt the memory of Ferrara seen
with E. two years ago in the spring, when the air was exactly
like that silvery note of the upper scale in C major). And once
again moonlight suggesting metaphors, but in its literalness deriving from the worst paintings, from kitsch and songs about
moonlight on water. Hence a violent attempt to free oneself from
these obtrusive images. Music should be ingested in total abstraction from any analogies! And I repeat once again (I said it when
I sat in the box behind Mama and Mrs. Jacobi), there is a pure,
unadulterated musical world: Bach; the smell of dry timber;
curd cheese in an earthenware bowl; creaking, steep stairs; a
bust crowned with a wreath of small rosebuds (the so-called
"ramblers"—see Mauthner's catalogue or the issues of *Garten-
laube* read by Mother and collected in stacks on the shelves);
the reflection of stars in a pond surrounded by black walls, or
else a slippery stone floor on which someone is walking noiselessly, slightly dragging his feet in slippers of red leather. And
balconies. Rows of balconies overhanging empty spaces, existing
independently from background and surroundings, a symphony
of balconies, balconies as symbols, and an endless procession of
arcades. Incense? But this would be too insistent a reminder that
Johann Sebastian had been an organist. Hence a nervous search
for a way of retreat, an escape from the maze of symbols, this
new visual trap. Escape. I remember it as if yesterday, yet it was
several years ago. At least nine years since that theater box and
that Bach, heard with tension and concentration, humility and
pain. Attempts to reduce the strength of impressions, the wish to
purify them. A flat receding wave, a tinkling husk, returning
over and over again in the same pitch and color, as if in expectation of something or someone, I don't know. The view from the
Sacred Mountain of Music—from Sinai—at last, at last! And a
total release from any imaginings, from any nonmusical feelings
apart from this one: height, going up and falling down. Fluctua-
tion in a state of weightlessness. A road from somewhere to
wherever. The goal is unimportant, going is what matters.
Where? Why?

Beyond the window: dust and heat. A mounting heat, white
and blinding. The clatter of horses' hooves comes from the direction of the stables. The lancers are leading their mounts by their

bridles toward the gate. The left half of the open gate is in shadow, the right half in glaring sunshine. And the wispy acacia tree is burnt by the blazing sun.

Tired by the glare, I shut my eyes, I wipe the sweat from my forehead, I recede into the past, but return quickly: a wind tugs at a violet-colored veil. I know it: Karlsbad. Sprudelbrunnen. Mrs. Martha Jacobi's profile, or rather its fading outline when she turns her head away from me and, lifting the veil from her lips, begins to sip the medicinal water through a thin tube of greenish glass. Mrs. Jacobi's protruding lips in the action of sucking. And superimposed on this image the shape of Lieschen's mouth, licking with the tip of her pink tongue a wafer covered with a layer of ice cream. Graz, Hilmteich. Then a delayed awakening from meditation and a deep bow while doffing my hat: "Madame Martha, if I'm not mistaken?" and an immediate reflection—"Ah, excuse me, didn't you die four years ago?"— and a withdrawal, backing away on tiptoe, deeply ashamed, bowing, almost dancing. A ballet scene?

Fashions in 1912 (a gloss on the above): this season hats will be much smaller than last year. Toques will be fashionable. Materials: velvet and felt. Feathers rather than flowers, the veil tied at the back of the hat in a loose knot, not too large, or else a small ribbon bow. Aigrettes, but used without exaggeration. Also fashionable will be medium long, pointed single feathers, or better still whole wings, the colors blending with the dress, coat, or two-piece outfit. The feather to be stuck into the hat askew, from the front toward the back. Long, bushy feathers—in fashion in 1911—are out. Colors still recommended: violet in all shades and tones, from vanilla pink to deep purple, almost as deep as navy blue. Also plum color and, as always, the most elegant black velvet. Last season, the fashionable new shades "Tango" and "Electric Blue" were introduced for the first time.

A milliner's salon in the Graben in Vienna, large windows, mirrors, glass panes, and behind them Madame Flora. A row of women's heads with fashionable hair styles stuck on small neat stands of polished ash or blackened oak. The eyes of the dummies, without any pupils, always make a strange impression on me. I stop and look at them. One of the milliner's manne-quins has a nose and cheeks very much like El.'s, but only in profile. Or perhaps it seems so only at first glance. Probably. I

approach the shop window to look at it from the side, from left
and right, to make quite sure. Then I walk away quickly, because one of Madame Flora's assistants or shopgirls is looking at
me. A shortcut toward the Burg. The Kohlmarkt. Regulars at the
Graben-Café, who sit there for hours on end: retired Royal
Councillor Justus Kämmerrer, Councillor Max Jacobi (of
course!), and Colonel Desiderius Spack, also now retired. None
of them is still alive. They drink coffee with whipped cream or
Pilzen beer. Newspapers attached to bamboo sticks, dreamy
voices that summon the waiter: "Waiter, the check, please!" A
senile smile on the thin lips of the waiter, who probably can remember several generations of regulars, from the time of Sadowa
to the recent years. His familiarity is held in check by excellent
manners, years of training, an unbridgeable distance.

All of them dead now, one could count: one, two, four years—
all of them, together with the old head waiter, Franz. But they
still sit stubbornly, continuously, around the dead hearth—the
table in the corner to the left from the entrance. The place
hallowed by years of unwritten privilege and exclusiveness. A
marble top and curved legs made of cast iron, pure Art Nouveau,
but early, from the time of the first World's Fair, perhaps, or
from when the café was redecorated, I believe around 1900.

The rainy weather has settled in now, real autumn weather,
with mist that blurs the spire of St. Stephen's. Windows are
misted over. They should be wiped clean with a napkin or better
still with an angel's wing, for we now linger in the café haunters'
paradise.

And a waltz tune, picked up somewhere or other. From near
the Sprudelbrunnen at Karlsbad, from the shell-like kiosk in the
promenade, where the Eighty-eighth Infantry Regiment band
had been playing?

Our regiment of Sicilian Lancers has no tradition of military
glory or exploits, so one must be content with what there is. It
did not exist at the time of the Napoleonic wars, when the First
Lancer Regiment—at the time bearing the name of Merweld—
or the Second, Schwarzenberg's, covered themselves with eternal
glory on the battlefields of Donau-Eschingen, Aspern, and
Leipzig. Not to mention the cuirassier and dragoon regiments
in existence for many, many years. Some of them go back to the
great Empress Maria Theresa, others to Prince Eugene of Savoy

or even Wallenstein. Well, what can one do? Our regiment missed the battles of Custoza, but it took part in the campaign of 1859 and fought gallantly at Solferino. Yet it's difficult to compare it with, for instance, the First Regiment of Hussars (named after the Monarch himself), which under the heroic Colonel Edlersheim made several gallant charges. Trampled under the hooves of the Imperial Hussars, with saber cuts straight from the shoulder, the companies of Zouaves and Turkomans ran off screaming with terror. The mounted African rifles of Baron de Richepanse fled before the hussars. The Bersaglieri lost their hats adorned with cock feathers in the cornfields and vineyards. Their blood filled the furrows of Lombardy. Nothing will erase from our memory those days of glory of the heroic regiment of Imperial Hussars. Nothing will remove their name from the pages of history.

Looking through the regimental history of the Twelfth Lancers, one can also read that, by the wish of the high command, the regiment of the King of the Two Sicilies fought in the Second Corps of Field Marshall Prince Edward von Liechtenstein, and partly in the Ninth Corps of Cavalry General Count Schaafgotche.

"The Sicilian Lancers received their baptism of fire on May 3, 1859, and merit the highest praise," we read word for word on the third page of the chronicle bound in dark blue morocco.

These are the important dates of the Italian campaign: May 5, Valenza; May 20, Montebello. In that battle the regiment was engaged for the first time with the independent cavalry brigade of Prince Alexander of Hesse. The division of Major Baron von Appel gained distinction there, and the baron personally led the third squadron in the attack. Fourteen lancers were killed and twenty wounded, among the latter one officer.

"The archduke, heir to the throne, was killed on Sunday, June 28. Today is Tuesday, July 28. Dusk is falling. Yesterday at that time I was still on the train, somewhere between Laibach and Zagreb. I watched daybreak, I think, near Brod. A wide expanse of the river. Bustling crowds on the platforms. Recruits and reserve soldiers in regional dress dragging wooden luggage boxes. A crowd of peasant women. Later, willows could be seen through the windows, their leaves brushing lightly against the wet panes, and from beyond the river there emerged the blinding ball of the sun, golden lemon in color. Against the sun, the willow leaves seemed completely black. The Honved Major riding in the compartment with me, with whom I have not exchanged one word, unscrewed the metal top of a flat bottle and drank a gulp of something that smelled like plum brandy. He glanced at me while screwing the top back on, and after some thought made a gesture toward me, as if offering me a drink. I refused by shaking my head. He spoke only Hungarian. He got off, I think, at Vinkovci."

Written in the cavalry barracks, in a room on the first floor. Terrific heat and thick dust behind the window.

"Fehert-m, July 30, 1914.

"Dear Mama,

"I arrived here safe and sound amid incredible heat, dust, and commotion, noises of all kinds and no information whatsoever concerning our future movements. At the station, Magyar Brod, I learned that as of today we are at war with Serbia. There are all sorts of rumors here at F. That it will all end in threats, or at most in a punitive expedition, and the enemy will give in, or else a major row will develop. This latter opinion seems to prevail with the local Jews, who seem the best informed. In any case our so-called 'fighting spirit' is not to be faulted, a fact of which I am informing you, dearest Mama, though with some embarrassment. Your son, in spite of the long journey and certain discomforts connected with it, is holding up bravely, as behooves a second lieutenant of the reserve. You probably know me well enough to imagine what I think about all this. On the platform at Brod I managed to wash at a basin used by a crowd of other people as well, because there was no water in our coach. Only here in the barracks have I been able to take a bath and shave. Luckily, the coffee in the officers' casino isn't bad. On the train a moustachioed Magyar offered me some brandy, of which he himself partook copiously straight from the bottle. If I had drunk like that, I'd have dropped dead before I arrived. Councillor L., whom I saw at Trieste before my departure, stubbornly maintained—trying forcibly to persuade me, although I did not say a word to contradict him—that everything will blow over, that there'll only be a lot of talk and some threats, and that at most we'll occupy Belgrade in order to make our point and show our strength. Afterward—still according to Councillor L., who says he's very well informed—the Great Powers will intervene, with peace conferences and so on—and in the end the Serbs will get scared, because Russia won't support them. Perhaps he is right. And even if he isn't, the war can't last more than a few weeks in view of modern technical equipment. Just think: in 1859 war lasted only two months, and the one in 1866 not much longer. So the present war, should it be declared—with modern artillery, machine guns, and so on, even airships and airplanes that might also be brought into action—can't possibly last any longer, and might not last as long. Who in the world could stand such a horror? I'm writing about this because, from your letter that I received at Trieste just before coming here, I see that, under the influence of panicky rumors in Vienna, you are anxious about me. I beg you, Mama, don't be afraid! Your Emil will return safe and sound sooner than you expect—sunburned, hardened, and manlier from the fatigue of the campaign, and with the added glory of a hero. I can imagine a wreath of laurel on my brow—oh yes, quite clearly! I'll enter the hall, hang my heavy field saber on the hatstand, and embrace you heartily, saying: 'Well, it's all over!' You can't imagine how heavy a field saber is! I'd never have guessed. When I got it here, I tried to draw it from its gray sheath. It would not come out at first, and when I tried to cut the air with it, my arm collapsed and I almost beheaded good old Zdenek! Luckily, he jumped aside in time. Zdenek—you must remember him from Vienna, a thin blond boy, a poet, I read you his poems about a year ago, they were published in one of the issues of *Moderni Revue* in Prague, his surname is Kocourek, he used to visit us in the Stubenring last year. He's now sharing a billet with me, he insisted on it, so we live together and you know how I dislike sharing a room with a stranger.

"I embrace you and kiss your hand. Yours ever, E.

"Ps. As soon as I arrived at Trieste from Grado, the warm underwear was handed to me by good old Schani, who was waiting at the station. I have it in my suitcase, although I'm sure it won't be needed. Winter is still far away, and anything—provided it even begins—will end well before winter. Otherwise it would be an absurd thing, contrary to nature, the forecasts of politicians, sound strategy, and other valid considerations. But I brought those wool shirts, though I was tempted to leave them with Schani, so you won't worry or be disappointed, my darling Mama."

This letter was mailed in the post office in Fehertemplom and reached Mrs. R. only on August 5, when extras were announcing war with Russia, general mobilization in many countries, and the Monarch's address to the nation.

Montebello, May 20, 1859. There is a beautiful watercolor, painted in 1899 by a talented amateur painter, Reserve Lieutenant Rezeda, on the fortieth anniversary of the battle, when the regiment was visited by Baron von Gagern, its patron at the time, as well as several military and civilian dignitaries.

This watercolor now hangs in a narrow gold frame in the officers' mess, on the wall between two wide windows, facing the buffet. With the passage of years the frame had faded, there are traces of flies or perhaps spiders on it, and the colors have faded. Even so, the painting is quite impressive: to the eternal glory of Montebello. It is a beautiful thing to witness posterity honoring its gallant and heroic forefathers. On the days of maneuvers, as well as on May 20, the anniversary of the battle, the painting is decorated with branches of acacia, oak leaves, or a wheat sheaf. When the regiment was stationed at Varazdin, oak leaves predominated. Here at Fehertemplom it is usually decorated with wheat of the Banat, still green and frail in the spring. Facing the watercolor with their backs to the buffet, the officers lift their glasses and say in German, Hungarian, and Serbian: "To your health! Long live the nation! Long live the Emperor!"

The watercolor represents Major Appel, rising in his stirrups and turning toward the Sicilian Lancers who follow him at full gallop; he is shouting something, probably urging them on. Or perhaps he is shouting praise of the Emperor and the Fatherland. Or something simple like "Charge!" The expressions on the Lancers' faces testify that they don't need such encouragement. They follow their gallant commander in a compact group. Judging by their open mouths, the Lancers are shouting, too. They utter fierce soldierly battle cries. The white teeth under the uniformly black moustaches have been rendered excellently and in great detail by the artist. The horses are depicted with great skill in various attitudes. Reserve Lieutenant Julius Rezeda must have been fond of horses, as he could paint them well. We also possess another watercolor of the same artist painted from nature: the commander of the regiment at the time, Colonel Berzeviczy von Kakas-Lomnitz, on a magnificent chestnut horse that hangs its thoroughbred Anglo-Arab head. The colonel looks to one side, but is seen by the onlooker full face. He is wearing a lancer's hat, from which a long horsetail, knotted at the top, hangs down over his left ear. In the background are fragments of the barracks buildings at Varazdin. The commander's horse had been depicted even better and with greater accuracy, it seems, than the colonel in the saddle, although he is suitably manly, serious and of martial mien, but at the same time gentle, as a commander should be.

Reserve Second Lieutenant Emil R. and his comrade of equal rank, Zdenek Kocourek, pass from painting to painting: from the two Sicilian kings to the panorama of the charge at Montebello, admiring on the way Generals Gagern and Bothmer, and Colonel Maurice von Berzeviczy on his splendid mount. Some of the Lancers' horses at Montebello are lifting their forelegs, others lowering them to make the dust of battle whirl behind them as their hind legs rise. All the mounts without exception have their manes and tails flying. Some of the horses are chestnut and bay, one is even a roan, but the majority are coal-black. The Twelfth Regiment has preferred black horses for years. They are magnificent specimens from the Hungarian plains.

In those years the Lancers still wore green uniforms, and their headgear, the so-called Tartar caps that are now no more than a historical memory, had a different shape from the tall modern shakos: four-cornered like the present Lancers' hats, but soft, without a visor, and trimmed with lamb's fur. Instead of the horse's tail hanging on the left, they boasted an erect eagle's or heron's feather. The color of the Tartar caps of those years was also different. The Twelfth Regiment once wore cherry-colored headgear, while at present the crown of the hats is navy blue.

Montebello! Cavalry Captain Baron William von Hammerstein, while attacking the railway embankment held by French skirmishers (in wide red trousers and white gaiters), was hit by a bullet, fell off his horse, and died. Night falls after the battle. Castel Venzago. A cloudy Lombardian night, close and uncannily black. Mists rise from over the canals that cut the plain. The withdrawal must be covered. The horses are neighing in the darkness.

And then Solferino. Those who distinguished themselves in the battle and who figure for all time in the golden pages of the history of the Sicilian Lancers: Rittmeister Baron Karl von Skrbensky (a hero! a hero!), Baron Johann von Appel (the one who distinguished himself at Montebello and is depicted in the watercolor)—both have received the Maria-Theresa Order (what a prize!), while Rittmeister Ludwig Müller, Major Friedrich Barres, and Edler von Perez got an Iron Crown. Reserve Cavalry Captain Bela von Schönberg also distinguished himself.

The regiment's losses on that day: over one hundred lancers killed, and twice as many wounded and missing.

On this note one might close the great memorial book bound in dark blue morocco, the present color of the regiment. However, it might be worth casting an eye on the other pages of the album, heavy and solemnly smooth, with gilded edges. When you turn them in awe, they rustle with the peculiar rustle of history. Written on them are the names of those who on various occasions and at various dates honored the officers' mess with their presence. We read here: Congratulations on the gallant battle-readiness shown during the imperial maneuvers in 1862—Archduke Albrecht (of Custoza!), and following him two others from the House of Hapsburg who visited the garrison and the officers' mess in later years. On the following pages—at a suitable distance from Their Highnesses—the signature of the Minister of War, General Baron von Schöneich. On the next page, a few words written in a bold hand: "God Bless You, Sicilian Lancers!" and the signature of Archduke Franz Ferdinand and the date and the place of the maneuvers: July 7, 1902, Uj-Bela. And later, under the same dateline, the signature: "K. und K. Artillery General Heinrich von Pitreich, Imperial Minister of War." Turning a few empty pages, we find a couple of short but beautifully rhymed compositions, the fruit of the patriotic military muse, and also some rhymed trifles, written for somebody's name day, several cartoons—some witty and to the point—of various officers from all periods. Not to forget amateur snapshots of maneuvers, jubilees, anniversaries and other similar occasions.

And a flower, completely dried and flat like tissue paper, but so carefully stuck in that it looks fresh—a large field poppy.

Having examined the regimental archives, the two young second lieutenants of the reserve walk to the window overlooking the courtyard of the barracks. At the buffet one of the stableboys is polishing the wineglasses and arranging them in rows on the shelf. From the window one can see the lieutenant of the first squadron, Clement Okliczny, walk unhurriedly across the grounds of the riding school, pass the wooden jumping bars, lean over, wipe perspiration from his brow and, holding his forage cap in his left hand, brush his dusty trousers with a glove. He is wearing dress trousers: dark gray, nearly black, with a strap for shoes, and a thin red piping along the seams. The lieutenant disappears beyond a wall to the left. He is going, it seems, to the tavern of Kato Zoltan, known otherwise as Katerinchen. Her husband, Lajos-ur Zoltan, was drowned a year before in the well beyond the local cemetery, almost in the open fields, on the night of August 3–4. Lord keep his soul, even though he was not a pious man! At Mother Katerinchen's one can drink cold wine not only inside the tavern, but also straight from the barrel while sitting under a chestnut tree, next to the cellar. One can also go down several steps and there, perched on one of the vats, draw wine from it with a tin half-quart measure. Katerinchen serves an excellent bacon cut into strips and covered with red paprika and raw green peppers. There are people who like raw bacon; others prefer it lightly burnt over an open fire. In the evening a gypsy band occasionally plays here. To go to Kato Zoltan's, walk left from the barracks past the horse market and then down Munkacsy Street, which is like a long country lane.

In the courtyard Major Franckl's orderly is polishing six pairs of his chief's high boots, and six pairs of low ones with inset elastic on the sides, until they shine. With those low boots one wears dress trousers and light spurs without the dented wheel at the end. Instead of the wheel, there is a rather blunt end. The orderly, polishing yet another pair of boots, sings. Although it is still early morning, the air is hot and close. There is no breeze.

Major Franckl's orderly now begins to beat his officer's clothes on a bright green stand. Having beaten two lancer jackets, a coat, and two pairs of trousers, he goes on to some warm gray blankets. The dust raised by the orderly hangs in the air and does not disperse. Only slowly, after a few minutes, does it settle on the dry grass. A grayish, sandy dust, the color of camels' or perhaps lions' fur, almost a desert color, has settled over Fehertemplom and the vast plain all around it, reaching almost to the Danube and the Nera and the distant hills in the east, called Shepherds' Mountains, from where, if the air is clear, one can see Bazias on the Danube and also—but this might be too distant—the Orthodox monastery at Kostolac on the Serbian side. And the forests in that region. On the farms of Count Festetics de Tolna the wheat harvest is over, the gathering of tobacco and corn is nearing its end, threshing machines and reapers are roaring. You can count them on the infinite plain, recognizing them by the clouds of dust above them.

About 8:00 a.m. on June 24, 1859, the Emperor set out on horseback from his headquarters at Valeggio toward Cavriana, in a white general's uniform of the period and a hat adorned with a bunch of green cock feathers. At 9:00 a.m. he stopped at the village of Volta, the headquarters of the First Army. General Wimpffen was not there; he had ridden at daybreak to Guidizzolo. Since early morning there had been chaotic firing in the brush and vineyards: skirmishes of the vanguard, it was thought. The local stony hills looked white and pink in the Lombard sunshine. Bells were ringing at Medole or perhaps at Castel Goffredo.

On the flat plain near Medole the Third and Ninth Corps have been fighting for an hour against the French Fourth Corps of General Niel, advancing from the west. From a small coppice near Campo di Medole one could see with the naked eye the long streaks of dust raised by thousands of French troops marching in columns and then reordering themselves, after random firing, into loose formations in the valley. One could observe the First Division of General de Luzy, Marquis de Pélissac, forming hurriedly into squares. Their red trousers, tall patent-leather kepis, even the flashes of single bayonets could be seen. To the left, beyond some clumps of bushes, was the Third Division of General de Failly.

Close behind it, the mounted rifle brigade of Baron de Richepanse was emerging at a gallop from behind the ranks of infantry.

The Emperor was now looking through the field glass handed him by his chief of staff, General Hess. Mounted, he was observing the field of battle, while General Hess stood next to him, his horse held by an orderly in a navy blue hussar's cape with yellow braiding thrown over his left shoulder and held by a cord.

In the magnification of the field glass, in a circle bounded with brass and seemingly within reach of his arm, the Emperor could see the dense underbrush, the silvery gray vineyards with each little leaf separately outlined by the sunlight, the furrows of dried reddish soil, and every stone in the walls dividing the small fields. And, farther off, the white uniforms of the infantry that had so often distinguished itself at Aspern and Esslingen, Custoza and Mortara, and that only a few days ago was blooded at Magenta and Melegnano. The backs of the soldiers' white jackets, crossed by the black belts of their powder pouches (with two-headed eagles on the flaps) and the gray trousers of foot soldiers in single file going out to face death. Regimental standards. The Emperor recognizes them: these are the soldiers of General Schwarzenberg's Third Corps, probably Baron Schönberg's division, which had covered itself with glory a few days before. He adjusts the field glasses, trying to see the color of the facings and collars. He recognizes the infantrymen of the Archduke Stephen Twenty-seventh Regiment, deployed in a long column. Above their heads, shrapnel is bursting in the dust-filled air. French grenades tear out clods of earth and stones. There are black, dun-colored, and almost pure white cloudlets of smoke in the air. The Emperor lowers the field glasses and, leaning from the saddle, asks General Hess, still standing next to him, a question. At that moment a courier on a foaming gray horse rides up, dismounts, salutes, and presents a message. General Stadion begs to inform that the French army is now attacking the village of Solferino with superior forces, and that with difficulty he has repulsed the Sardinian attacks on San Marino on the extreme right. The courier stands stiffly to attention. His white jacket is in tatters, its right sleeve stained with blood.

Major Franckl's orderly collects his chief's blankets, folds them neatly, and carries them toward the door on the right. The two reserve officers, freshly arrived by train from the region of Budapest, stand at the mess buffet, drinking coffee and brandy.

Or maybe it is cognac. They talk in Hungarian. One of them, a cavalry captain, yawns. Then both light cigars. A large buzzing fly circles, then settles on the collar of King Francis II of Naples and Syracuse. It sits there a moment; when the reserve major, his elbows on the counter, reaches the third time for a glass, resting his cigar on the edge of the table, the fly begins to walk on the portrait in oils, avoids the royal chin and the King's lips turned up in a slightly contemptuous and skeptical smile, and finally stops on the nose of Taormina's ruler. You could swear that the King has twitched his lips and his nose, and that his right eyebrow has slightly risen. Later, after the fly has left the august face to settle near the gilded frame of the portrait, the King's face freezes in his half-smile. It now seems to look mockingly at the two officers, who are still smoking their cigars at the buffet counter.

Beyond the hill at Cavriana the Emperor can now see with his naked eye the French columns deploying to storm the fortress.

To the left, facing Guidizzolo, defended by General Veigl's Eleventh Corps and by Prince Schwarzenberg's Third, are the massed battalions of the French Guards, and almost the whole of Mac-Mahon's corps. The cries of soldiers advancing in ranks to attack, the words of command, the thud of drums, and rifle volleys can all be heard from the copse. Through clouds of smoke and dust one can observe the tall fur caps of the French Guards, the braided coats, red vests, and white gaiters of General Mellinet's Zouaves. They press relentlessly toward Casa Morino and Campo di Medole. They pass the Austrians in white uniforms, their coats rolled up and slung across their backs, loading their rifles with a regular movement of the shoulders. Somewhere on the left, in the dust and smoke rising high over the greenery of the vineyards, the divisions of Count Clam-Gallas's First Corps fight the French infantry penetrating the narrow streets of Solferino. A light breeze shifts the dark, dense smoke toward the overgrown ravines. A few houses catch fire in the narrow streets. Somebody runs out from a gateway, stops, stumbles, falls. On the Emperor's hill one can hear a bell ringing the alarm from a tall campanile. On the slope of the hill, brightly lit by the sun, a riderless horse gallops away blindly and disappears into the brush.

Major Franckl's orderly emerges from the gateway and stops. Another lancer in a white, slightly soiled summer jacket goes up to him. For a moment both talk heatedly, then the lancer walks away, while the major's orderly remains there motionless for a while, gaping, not far from the now empty bright green frame for beating clothes.

News from Generals Benedek and Stadion: Benedek has held Martino, but cannot support the center in the battle for Solferino, because almost the whole Sardinian army is now attacking him. The Bersaglieri have penetrated from the direction of San Rocca, pushing boldly toward Pozzolengo: only the efforts and exceptional bravery of Roden's brigade made possible the repulse of the Italian attack. General Benedek reports that it was the Eleventh Infantry Regiment of the Saxon heir to the throne that has proven itself so honorably, at the cost of serious losses.

General Count Stadion's report is no more optimistic: the situation in the center, at Solferino, is critical.

The heat increases. Dust fills their throats. The sky is cloudless, the sun stands high over the horizon, almost at its zenith, somewhere over the houses of Valeggio. A few pigeons circle here and there, soaring high over the tiled roofs. Above the deep ravine of the River Mincio, a lonely white cloud hangs immobile.

There is now a clear view of the chessboard, the white fields have assumed an ivory shade, and the chessmen of bone seem very fatigued, worn smooth by fingers and somewhat soiled. The right knight looks rather seedy, so does the knight on the left. The players, alas, deliberating over their next move, have the rather unpleasant and tiresome habit of holding a chessman a long time in the air and even twirling it, or massaging it with the tips of their fingers. Perhaps such procedure has some effect on the result of the game; the views on this vary. Nonetheless, the knight now held over the black field, which from that perspective looks like a deep well, is visibly impatient and uneasy, trying to free himself. Deep in mournful thought, the player does not see this. His adversary has time to read the headlines in the morning paper. It is the *Wiener Tageblatt*, attached to a bamboo stick with a wooden handle. The foam in an unfinished glass of beer has settled, and hangs on the outside of the glass like the jellified but not-too-clean mouth of a deep-sea monster.

Attorney Emmanuel R. and his faithful partner, Mr. Max

Jacobi, a now-retired councillor at the Finance Ministry, are playing their sixth game of chess today. Two have been won by the attorney, three by Councillor Jacobi. Now the game is for serious stakes—there might be a draw, or perhaps a triumph for the councillor. Lately, Attorney R. has been winning. Has luck abandoned him today? Before he moves his knight, he has to collect his thoughts. The knight looks down fearfully, but the square black abyss has disappeared, has moved to one side, and there is a white, bony desert below. He does not see the bishop that is threatening him, hiding cleverly behind a row of dwarf-like, potbellied pawns. Some of these, obviously jeering, point to the knight, still held in the air. One, particularly thick-skinned and bearded into the bargain, has stuck out his tongue. The bishop discreetly closes his eyes like a young lover's and at the same time reaches under his cape for his sword.

In his youth Attorney R. was said to have resembled His Imperial Majesty in his earlier years, the years of Magenta and Solferino. At present no one seriously mentions this supposed likeness. Mr. R.'s face has become broader, his side whiskers, having grown, have lost their youthful grace, and his double chin sinks into his stiff collar. There are some people, however, whom kindness prompts to mention the former likeness. The attorney then smiles enigmatically, as if embarrassed.

The knight waits on the white field, looking around. It now is Councillor Jacobi's move. The councillor rests both elbows on the marble table top, and his fingers delve into his bushy side whiskers, skillfully blackened and intricately trimmed, silky to the touch, and stroke them thoughtfully. From time to time—time, measured by the moves made by his adversary and himself, lasts from five to ten minutes and is punctuated by puffing on a cigar and gulping beer—the councillor takes in his fingers thin strands of hair from his side whiskers and plays with them. He winds the hair around his fingers, pulls it lightly, smooths it. He is waiting for the attorney's move. The knight, struck by the bishop's sword, lies dead on the cold marble of the table, at the foot of a towering beer glass from which a thick tongue of dried yellowish foam is trickling. The play with the whiskers seems to be a partly vicarious gesture, but one can be sure that it is not motivated by any thought of Mrs. Jacobi's hair. Mrs. Jacobi, who recently celebrated her fortieth birthday, has preserved the figure and the stance of a young girl, a fact that Edward VII, King of England and Emperor of India, was apparently gracious enough to observe, when he met her some two years before on the promenade in Marienbad. All the same, for a long time she has ceased to play a role that would stimulate the councillor's erotic imagination. His titivating his side whiskers, his stroking his hair strands and winding them around his index finger, are therefore entirely neutral and sexless manifestations, one might almost say chess-orientated and strategic. They might be included among similar magic manipulations used in chess.

The councillor, his right hand attending to the hair on his right cheek, at the same time massages the castle with his left. Both gestures are coordinated, almost identical. The fingers of the councillor's right and left hands perform simultaneously those preparatory gestures. The attorney is observing his partner with half-closed eyes. The castle can make either a move called a "rochade," to which the attorney has a ready response, or else can move to square x or y. Then we shall move the queen from square — to square —. And then . . .

Immediately after 4:00 p.m. black, dense clouds lined with evil sulphurous streaks suddenly blew in from the direction of Lake Garda, from over the fortress of Peschiera in the Alps, and advancing swiftly, blocked the sun. The valley of the Mincio was obscured. Almost complete darkness descended, the sky was lit by lightning, and rain fell in sheets. In these appalling weather conditions the imperial army began its retreat to beyond the Mincio. Only General Wimpffen, the commander of the First Army, disregarding the order to retreat toward Monzambano, Valeggio, and Peschiera, fought alone and hopelessly in the torrential rain. Forty thousand dead covered the field of Solferino on June 24, 1859.

One can read about it in the regimental history which, illustrated by battle plans, pays particular attention to the consecutive positions of the Twelfth Regiment of the Lancers of the King of the Two Sicilies. Turning the pages of the book with his friend Zdenek Kocourek, Reserve Second Lieutenant Emil R. sighs deeply. Then, from a small breast pocket, he produces his gold cigarette case and thrusts it toward his friend. Both light Memphis cigarettes, while continuing to stand by the table in the officers' mess on which the volume rests, bound in dark blue morocco with an embossed golden two-headed eagle and the inscription: "Memorial Book of the Twelfth Lancers." The mess steward, Istvan Barabasz, who resembles General von Gagern, appears behind the table and arranges rows of wine glasses on it. He lifts some of them against the light, not trusting the mess orderly, and looks at them critically, half-closing his left eye under a gray, bushy eyebrow. Istvan's moustache, combed rakishly upward, with ends sharp as needles reaching to his ears, is completely, authentically, and convincingly pitch black, being, together with his resemblance to the patron of the regiment, a second rightful reason for his pride. When the two young reserve second lieutenants, who Istvan has not previously met, walk away at last from the buffet, the mess steward sinks into a reverie. All the while the mess waiter covers the tables with white cloths and lays them for the next meal. Istvan Barabasz observes him critically. He will not allow the slightest inaccuracy. He is stern, but as just as God the Father.

The noon meal today will consist of consommé, an entrée, and saddle of mutton. For dessert, pears in vanilla sauce, then black coffee and plum brandy or cognac.

Both young second lieutenants have found themselves in the Lancers quite unexpectedly, a fact that someone uninformed might consider a whim of fate. Having their choice of unit as volunteers for one year's service, they selected this particular cavalry regiment, stationed far from Vienna or Prague—one that they knew nothing about, composed for the most part of Hungarians and Croats, although they could have served in any other regiment, like the Seventh Lancers at Stockerau, close to Vienna, or the Fifth Dragoons at Graz. Zdenek Kocourek might have felt much better in the Prague Liechtenstein regiment of dragoons, or in the Eighth, which was organized during the Thirty Years' War. Yet they both came here to Fehertemplom, almost on the Serbian border, looking for memories, pursuing a romantic idea of the past that in effect has long ceased to exist. It was Emil R. who had decided and Zdenek, as usual, followed his friend's whim. Emil was looking for a legend, the legend of the regiment in which his grandfather had served years ago, the hero and victim of Solferino. Solferino meant defeat, death, a black night filled with the premonition of catastrophe, with groans of wounded men, with caravans of white ghosts dragging themselves across the battlefield. Solferino was the sum of those images: a requiem. That fact had its importance. It meant the end—both extermination and consolation. The sound of the name Solferino was like a stem of a musical flower, a lily, or perhaps a dark purple funereal orchid that emits a humid, marshy smell, and whose petals are fleshy, yet delicate like human skin.

Elizabeth, Emil R.'s sister, on a certain summer's day many years ago was given for her birthday by her godmother, Mrs. Martha Jacobi, the councillor's wife, an almost grown-up dress reaching down to her ankles. Emil has remembered that dress, and also its color, fashionable at the time: "solferino." It was a dark violet that looked saturated with blood. And the name of the color gave birth to a musical phrase: three or four notes of ill omen.

Emil's mother, touched by the present for her elder daughter, thanked her friend, while young Liesbeth, without much enthusiasm, agreed to try on the "grown-up" dress. Mrs. Martha Jacobi assured her that violet, a color perhaps a little too dark and too old for the recipient, had recently become very fashionable in Paris and was named "solferino." In the window displays of Worth and Lanvin one could see a whole range of clothes in that color, together with accessories—for instance, bows—considered *le dernier cri*. In view of her goddaughter's youth, Mrs. Jacobi had selected an exceptionally light shade of "solferino," akin to *rouge Bourgogne*, almost pink with tones of lilac—quite lovely, isn't it?

Liesbeth, having dressed in Mrs. Jacobi's bedroom (the whole R. family had been invited to supper) and now clad in the solferino gown, will enter the small corner drawing room and graciously allow both ladies—her mother and Mrs. Jacobi—to turn her round and round, while Emil, who at the time was fourteen and still in school uniform, very slender and anemic, stands in the half-opened door to the balcony, because the evening was mild, almost warm, and the thin curtains were not moved by breeze. Liesbeth's new dress marked her entry into womanhood—a kind of accolade like the one by which squires with clear faces surrounded by blond locks cut straight over the eyes and forming a fringe, were made knights. Liesbeth's face, seen in the light of a lamp with a broad shade, seems dark and boyish at that solemn moment. Only her cat's eyes are shining, and she casts from side to side quick, cunning, mocking glances.

Just then Emil will think: "This is a symbolic verdict on both of us: myself and her." And he will add (or perhaps this addition comes from a much later period, that of Gmunden or Graz): "*Nous sommes maudits, tous les deux.*"

The train of thought of the young man in the school uniform of the Jesuit monastery at Kalksburg—his thoughts as he was standing in the half-open balcony door of the Jacobis' apartment in the Alterstrasse—would not be easy to explain rationally. There were, however, other trains of events, the consequence of matters arisen a long time back. In the box at the Burgtheater, on the evening following that party at the Jacobis, he consciously realized his separateness and otherness resulting from the need to conceal the mortal sin in which he had been living; sitting behind his mother and sister, he whispered to himself almost aloud: "Now I'm sure, I'm sure!" In the darkness of the box, not looking at the stage, he remembered the glaring eyes of his Jesuit confessor, Father Cornelius Blatt. And his trembling lips, now blanched with horror: "My son! . . ." And his hand with dry white fingers feverishly grasping the confessional, and at last the index finger raised in a gesture of condemnation or perhaps supplication of the Almighty for the gift of grace for the penitent.

Emil will realize, too, that he is reconciled to being damned during his lifetime. He will understand the insidious joy that this condition provides during the presentation of *Oedipus Rex* while he sits in a darkened box full of the stifling scent of "Violettes Impériales," filled with solferino-colored light, a sin-polluted atmosphere transferred in a seemingly innocent way to his sister. This consciousness of sin will cause a short, painful euphoria, and young Emil will accept the curse and damnation.

All this happened the day after his sister tried on the grown-up and outlandish dress, "solferino" in color, in the small boudoir of the Jacobis' first-floor apartment in the Alderstrasse, just as retired Court Councillor Jacobi was passing the boudoir, walking toward his study to look through the files sent by the Bodenkreditanstalt, uninterested in the trying-on scene where the decolleté of the dress that fitted to perfection was being discussed. It was immediately after the military parade observed by the siblings from the dining-room window of their own apartment in the Stubenring.

Having moved the edge of the heavy curtain, from the first-floor window Emil saw the military band of the famous Deutschmeisters marching with a bandleader at their head. That magnificent man—tall, portly but not obese: a real man in the full vigor of life—wore a tightly fitting dark blue dress uniform with an azure collar and cuffs, and a sash across his breast, and held a baton wreathed in a garland; he had shining black, pomaded sideburns, and his cheeks seemed lacquered or covered with still wet tar, while his moustache was equally black and curled up in an irresistibly manly and almost lecherous way. This masculine figure, his slight paunch aggressively protruding, now advancing smoothly, almost dancing at the head of the band, has so strongly affected the anemic young man that for a long time he will be unable to forget him. Particularly so because Lieschen, standing on tiptoe behind her brother's back and shaking with laughter, makes some remarks about the bandleader's girth as well as his sideburns and moustache. She pinches Emil all over. She cannot control her malicious glee.

Behind the band that marched in fours, behind the shining glossy scream of trumpets, French horns, and trombones, behind a pony carrying an enormous drum painted in black and yellow stripes, and a row of flutists, came the Imperial and Royal Lancers on horseback, also in full gala with white gloves, and white cloth caparisons on their horses' backs, whose necks and withers have been brushed until they shone. The lancers' trousers made a red splash, horsetails dangled from the sides of their eagle-fronted hats, the sabers clattered, and there was a flash of stirrups and of spurs on boots that shone like mirrors. The horses were stepping with the grace and lightness of ballerinas, shaking their manes and lifting their necks and heads, the bridles held short in the lancers' hands gloved in cotton and the officers' in glossed kid. The young first lieutenant riding at the head of the column would later become the hero of a night's wandering over the battlefield of Solferino. Bent over the horse's neck, he will gallop to the rhythm not of the band directed by the proud bandleader of Deutschmeister regiment but, curiously, to the strains of "Solveig's Song" from a Grieg suite heard on another occasion. Solveig will complain in the artificial moonlight of the stage, in a gray blue mist, while Anitra, seen from a proscenium box in the second tier of the Vienna Opera, will rock in time with the music—the same music that, in another reality and another dimension, will intrude into Solveig's plaint, disturbing with a grotesque dissonance the lonely wanderings of the rider on the battlefield of Solferino. Whereas the impure and lustful masculinity of the bandleader will mix with the bass of the King of the Mountain, a bass droning throbbingly in a lower register, his singing echoing high among the frescoes of the ceiling and in the gildings and Art Nouveau ornaments of the opera box, becoming one of the many double or even manifold variants of the symbol, of Solferino, a symbol at that early moment still being formed with strands of colors, music, and a simultaneous feeling of discovery: I am irrevocably damned, and being thus sentenced, I am happy.

In it there are impressions from earlier years and subsequent nervous reactions, now difficult to recollect and even more difficult to explain with precision. When a June night is enveloping Lombardy after tempest and rain, a lonely rider will appear on the bare, stony hill of San Cassiano. Simultaneously the moon will rise among the vineyards. The sky will be cloudless, dark blue, almost black, and filled with stars. Far away to the north, the Alps will shine in the light of the rising moon. Night-scented coolness will descend from over Lake Garda.

The horse's gallop, and later its trot, will resound across the empty plain cut by a net of ditches, irrigation canals, and low stone walls amid vineyards, between rows of high poplars and cypresses in the direction of a silent, deserted village or hamlet that with its campanile looks now like a graveyard. The bare hills are silent.

Behind the trotting rider, a platoon of lancers is scattered in the vineyards. Later the rider will remain alone in the emptiness and funereal quiet. The others, following him, will lose themselves in the darkness and call to one another for a while; later still, there will be total silence.

The image is white and black like an etching. Everything within the orbit of the rising moon is chalky white. The sky is black, as is everything hidden on earth outside the compass of moonlight. Thus the rider, his horse, and his lancer's shako hanging from one arm are black, as is his face, shaded by a hat from which a heron's feather juts. Only the tip of his chin and, with the horse's rhythm, the sheath of the saber shine like silver in the dead moonlight. There is complete silence in which the only sound is the thud of the horse's hooves, galloping on the black and white stones. The black shadow of the rider and his horse slip through the misty, silvery space.

The lonely rider is now faced by the rising moon that resembles a balloon. The black Romanesque outline of the campanile at San Cassiano will glide across the moon's face. The moon will appear in the open bell chamber at the top of the campanile, then on the empty balcony; the white stones, the white sheath of the lancer's saber and a part of the wall surrounding the vineyard and the cemetery will darken. The moon will soon slide to the right side of the angular, blunt tower, peep out from behind it, and for a moment light up the bell. But this will take no more than a fraction of a second, after which the bell will immediately blacken and disappear, and the tower, now again uniformly black, will merge with the blackness of the sky in which the stars are fading. Only the distant peaks of the Alps on the horizon will rise uniformly white and icy cold.

From the direction of Solferino the voices of the wounded, who are covered with blood and dust and crawl in groups, some on their knees and elbows or even on their stomachs, will be heard. Some will fall on their faces amid the stones. Their cries will come in waves like a distant, elusive echo, a faraway song, or perhaps like the low sighs of grass moved by a gentle night breeze.

The tall darts of the cypresses pierce the sky with their own separate darkness, deeper even than that of the sky. They loom from the left and right, but soon disappear. But perhaps they have never grown in this region.

And again the trot changing into a gallop. The clatter of hooves on the stones that will be blanched by the moon, as it passes the campanile and rises over the roof of the church. The campanile will grow smaller, merge with the darkness, disappear. Perhaps it has never been there? For a moment a lone, small bell, hanging in space, dangling in darkness, will remain, one half of a bronze fruit. And then this will disappear, too.

("The moon rising over the battlefield of Solferino.")

Moonlight enters the window that reaches almost to the floor, it throws the pattern of the curtain net on the folded edge of the carpet. Miss Elizabeth R. is having her daily dance and deportment lesson with Monsieur Dufis. Somewhere to the side, removed to the chair by the wall, a small lamp with a green shade is lit. Its light falls only on a small section of the floor. The crystal chandelier under the ceiling is not turned on.

"*Mettez-vous dans l'ambiance, mademoiselle!* Quickly now, *mademoiselle*, one position after another. Pay attention and look at me.

"*Arabesque—fouetté—pas de bourrée—pas jeté—plié. Très bien, mademoiselle! Vous êtes délicieuse, mademoiselle!*"

("Nighttime in those regions. The moon over the battlefield of Solferino.")

"And now, *mademoiselle*, I ask you, I beg you for a moment's attention. We shall do a beautiful *battement*, yes, like this— excellent, wonderful! And an *effacé*, yes, just like this, wonderful, excellent, fabulous! And now an *entrechat*, and another *entrechat*, and now a tiny, charming *glissade*—lower, lower, along the floor with the feet—*bien, bien!* Careful, careful! A *pirouette* to finish it—and a *plié*. Lower, lower please, Mademoiselle Elizabeth—*rond de jambe, merci, mademoiselle, grand merci.* You might one day become a celebrity, *mademoiselle*, a prima ballerina of the Imperial Opera, yes, yes, my word of honor, what a pity, of course, I know, I know, of course I know, *mademoiselle* is exercising only to attain perfection, to have graceful movements like a deer, a gazelle, flowing movements, for the general culture of the body, yes, yes, I know, but it's a pity, a pity all the same."

("Nighttime in those regions is somewhat strange in character. There is a continuously receding and yet lasting clatter of horses' hooves on cobblestones, on roads and empty byways of the Lombard night that seems never to end.

"The moon is motionless, so is the lonely, motionless Romanesque campanile of San Cassiano that lurks in darkness—or perhaps it isn't San Cassiano? It exists in the darkness of the night in imagination rather than in its shape and reality. And the *campo santo* with its cypresses that rise up to the star-filled sky, and the white uniforms of soldiers wandering like ghosts in the darkened vineyards, entangled in the wires stretched low over the earth and connecting the criss-crossed black vines.

Specters that appear to accompany the lonely rider with their
groans, cries, and funereal whispers; that disappear and reappear as white shadows on a neighboring bare hillock, only to
disappear once again. And the horse now at a walking pace, its
head hanging low over the ground as if to sniff the spilled
blood. Right foot, left foot, right foot, left foot, night, night,
night . . .")

"Grieg? All right, if the young man desires it. I shall play
Grieg. Your taste is a bit cheerless, young man. Hmm . . .
Maybe it's better to listen to Grieg by moonlight. I just realized
it. Where have you disappeared to, young man? Aha, you're
standing by the window. *Eh bien*, let's begin together. Mademoiselle will be good enough to change now, she must be hot and
might catch a cold. Mademoiselle's mother asked me to see that
she didn't, God forbid."

Once upon a time there were two sisters, Elizabeth and
Bernadette, who had one brother, Emil. This must be repeated, if
one is to get back to the beginning, Alpha, and to dig down to
the source.

Perhaps after many years the name Emil suggested to the one
who had received it at baptism in the church of St. Leonard's at
Graz, a comparison with the hero of Jean-Jacques Rousseau's
novel and that hero's fortunes. Perhaps this thought even exercised an influence on the development of events, although this is
by no means certain.

Once a long time ago, but not so long ago as to be forgotten,
there was a fashion for masquerades in certain circles. Even
Emil's mother, the beautiful Mrs. Ethel R., eternally young and
flighty in the opinion of her husband, liked to dress up her
children at any opportunity such as children's parties, festivals,
and balls. One must go back to two years—1899 and 1900—that
on the face of it form a break, the advent of a new era, a dawn,
and a watershed, but only in appearance: nothing has changed
nor will change; the nineteenth century will continue in its full
though slightly wilting glory until Sunday, June 28, 1914, when,
stricken by a sudden paralysis, a brain hemorrhage or apoplexy,
it will crumple on the pavement of the Kaiser Franz Josef
Strasse at Sarajevo, at the very end of the world, at the foot of
the Balkan volcano of which the world press has been writing

continuously, making gloomy predictions about its ominous smoke.

So we revert to the beautiful years 1899–1900, to the authentic *fin de siècle* marked by the decadence, pride, and joyous despair of some. From pockets of jackets nipped at the waist, men produced small handkerchiefs, batiste squares perfumed with the scent of the era—"Trèfle Incarnat," "Cuir de Russie," or "Quelques Fleurs" by Houbigant of Paris, or "Black Poppy" by Atkinson of London—and lifted these to their noses. A "sad fatigue" and melancholy were in fashion. Indeed, behind the scenes something was withering but, as frequently in nature, flowering at the same time.

One read the poems of Alfred Mombert and the French symbolists. Jiri Karasek, the enthusiast of modernity in its latest edition, far ahead of metropolitan Vienna and following Berlin step by step, was just twenty-six, and his *Moderni Revue* was six years old. In the Danubian capital Kraus was publishing *Die Fackel*. Vigeland's sculptures, in the original and in reproductions, were scandalizing or gladdening people's hearts. The products of De Dion-Bouton and Gobron-Brillie were triumphing in the Paris motor show of 1899, and in London the famous Napier presented a model of Kennard's invention, a nine-horsepower vehicle of incredible construction and small fuel consumption for amateur drivers. "The Regional Section of the Friends of the Feline Race" at Vichy, in the hall of the Saint Petersburg Hotel, loaned for that purpose by the directors, presented a show of pedigree cats, in particular cats brought from Anatolia and Persia. The town of Fehertemplom in the district of Temes (destined to play a certain part in matters of interest to us) was inhabited, according to the last census, by 10,107 people with a German majority of about 65 percent, while other population groups could be divided as follows: Israelites, ca. 6 percent; Protestant and Roman Catholic Hungarians, 21 percent; Croats, Serbians, and gypsies—the remainder—8 percent. As for the Austro-Hungarian armed forces that will become one of the main strands of the story, we can note as follows toward the end of the *Belle Epoque*: the minister of war was His Excellency General Kriegshammer, the head of the Fourth Army Corps was General von Pitter. The governess, Miss Traut, taught the R. siblings that they had to recite together a little poem before they went to bed: "Eins, zwei—Polizei; drei, vier—Offizier; fünf, sechs—eine Hex; sieben, acht—gute Nacht; neun, zehn—schlafen gehen." In the Stubenring the street lamps shone and the trees in Schwarzenberg Park threw shadows on flower borders and lawns. Then the chestnuts and lindens lost their leaves and the first snow fell during the night of November 29–30. Mrs. R.'s maid, Greta, looking through the window, was the first to see it. She stepped out on the balcony and swept the white layer of snow from under the door. In the apartment everybody was still asleep except the master of the house, Attorney R., who was just beginning to shave in the bathroom. He had to be early at court, where that day he was appearing at 9:00 a.m. in the case of *N. Rappaport vs. Bodenkreditanstalt.* Mr. R. was appearing for the defendant, the bank.

Lieschen was usually dressed up as a page. The first time we remember her in that costume was for a family birthday and the *tableaux vivants* usually arranged on such an occasion. Unfortunately, Lieschen would not keep still in spite of solemn promises that she would be as motionless as a statue; in spite of the admonitions of Miss Traut, she spoiled a little the effect of the performance. When the curtain (made from linen sheets by one of the older cousins and hung on a wire) was drawn, when the audience was finally seated, Lieschen spun around and stuck her tongue out at her younger sister, who was sitting on a cushion in a corner of the room, dressed in the costume of a princess. Detta, as far as we know, burst into tears, but quietly, not having moved an inch from the place allotted to her, for which she was praised.

A little later we might have seen Emil dressed up as a fairy from the Grimm fables, and Lieschen as the witch. This time again the unruly little girl could not remain still to the end; while the curtain was falling, she thrust a long pin into the arm of the fairy and fairy Emil for the first time in his life experienced a peculiar sensation: feeling pain in his arm, he steeled himself and instead of screaming or bursting into tears, he smiled at his sister as if to thank her or show that he considered it an excellent joke, so much so that he almost disappointed Lieschen, who had, it seems, expected and secretly hoped for a scandal, loud sobbing, and a scene. But Emil, like Saint Sebastian, in spirit tendered not only his arm but his whole body to the darts of his sister, desiring them, anticipating them, and realizing with some apprehension that he was made happy by having been chosen as a living target.

At the next celebration—the birthday of Mrs. Cecily Babo, a friend of Mr. and Mrs. R. closely connected with the bishop, and for many years devoted to good works—little Emil played the part of Saint Cecilia in a group of children-angels. He was chosen apparently because of his face, which at that time was surrounded by blond locks cut in page style, and looked most spiritual, prompting talk within the family that perhaps Emil would end up as a priest, even a Jesuit, to which he himself was not averse.

On the small stage, arranged on that occasion in the spacious salon of Mrs. Babo in Elizabethstrasse, Emil took part in a *tableau vivant,* holding in his hand a harp cut from cardboard and covered with gold foil that had been saved from chocolate wrapping for weeks; on his head he wore a small halo, also made of gilded cardboard. He was most embarrassed and protested to the last, but so politely, gently, and quietly that it was not too difficult to persuade him that "it must be done." He was embarrassed because during rehearsals, of which there were several, the girls, standing in corners dressed as angels, laughed at him meanly, perhaps because they were jealous that none of them had been chosen for the part. Lieschen, the eldest, was clad in a kind of violet smock, with wings pinned to her shoulders that flapped each time she moved, and she was never still; Detta, fat and somewhat apathetic, stood immobile in white stockings and a long white dress among the other angels, just as she had been told to do by Miss Traut, who was in charge.

Emil, we remember, was crying in a corner, turned toward the wall; he calmed down only at the première and stuck it out honorably.

Canon Pflaum applauded him and even called him over and stroked his blond hair, upsetting the halo. He gave him as compensation a picture of Saint Cecilia. In it the saint was shown as a grown girl who seemed to walk blindfolded, holding a harp. Father Pflaum said: "This is your patron saint, my child. And what is your name, little girl?" (As became evident later, he thought Emil was a girl.) "Come nearer, little one. What lovely blue eyes you have, like forget-me-nots." And so on, in the same style.

The other children-angels were laughing in their corners. In the maid's room, the improvised changing room, Emil was later kicked and painfully pinched. Little Irma Ludolff, the daughter of an artillery colonel and older than Emil, twisted his nose until it hurt. He will never forget her. Wasn't she one of the fallen angels on the walls of the Sistine Chapel? Years later, Emil will discover her likeness there. Standing in a crowd of tourists and looking up, he will see her there quite distinctly. She has been falling for centuries in the crowd of the other damned, but a little apart. Her arms look like spreading wings, her fingers are held wide apart, and her eyes, blinking and narrow, seem to smile equivocally.

In 1909 she will marry Major von Rottenhahn, a garrison commander in one of the small Slovak towns near Eperies in the area of the Imperial and Royal Sixth Corps of Koszyce. Emil will lose sight of her.

The next day Lieschen said; "Cecilia won't get any cookies today, only an almond from her brother the Little Devil, as a reward for being obedient." This alluded to her brother's performance as Saint Cecilia and to her own, on a previous occasion, as a little devil.

And Lieschen, digging the almond out from a piece of cake, will add: "Does Cecilia know what it is? Cecilia has to guess what it is." Raising her eyebrows, she will squeeze between two inkstained fingers a half-bitten, white, slippery almond, its brown skin peeled with a fingernail. "Well?" Emil will instinctively bite his lips. Suddenly he will be afraid. The almond assumed the identity of a Host. The scene occurred less than six months after his first communion. The pupils of his sister's eyes shine between her fair, sparse eyelashes and the half-closed, always reddish eyelids. Recently Lieschen had an attack of conjunctivitis. In her eyes her brother will read encouragement and expectation, and perhaps also a threat: "Try to oppose me, just try!" With a feeling of mortal sin he accepts in anguish the diabolical Host from his sister's inkstained fingers. She then wipes her fingers on the edge of the table cloth.

On another occasion, in the park in the summer, Emil will be a Greek shepherd; this will be Lieschen's idea. This will occur at Baden near Vienna, in a grove of tall, shady linden trees, on a clipped lawn. Lieschen will transform herself into a forest spirit from a story that they had read together. She is Silenus, or perhaps a nymph just being transformed into a satyr with goat's feet. Or perhaps this is a later impression that Emil entered in a notebook bound in green leather—a book he will never show to anyone during his lifetime.

Never having read a single page of that diary or rather notebook—because, apart from drafts of letters never sent and a diary kept from day to day but not in chronological order, it contained also some drafts of compositions for piano and violin—it won't be easy for us to unravel the numerous crisscrossings and narrowing knots of feelings and their secondary reflections. During the scene among the linden trees at Baden, Lieschen had her shoulders twined with ivy. But perhaps not. Isn't it maybe a product of her brother's imagination?

The coils of ivy grow from her arms, rise over the nape of her neck like a bundle of lianas entwined cunningly in her hair, and fall in festoons on her cheeks. Is it then that Lieschen cuts the tip of her finger—the index finger of her left hand—and sucks it violently, knitting her brows and stamping her foot before Miss Traut can find a rag to bandage it? The piece of linen becomes saturated with blood, and Emil must then fight the wish to put his sister's bandaged finger in his mouth to sample—as he imagines it—the sweetish taste of her blood. Yet perhaps all this happened much later in a dream when, feverish after a bout of pneumonia in the spring of 1909, and threatened by tuberculosis, he spent a long time at Merano.

From this perspective we could see the sea, ruffled by a slight sirocco blowing in from the tip of a desert island. What island would that be? One of the unnamed reefs jutting in isolation from the sea near the island of Krk? Possibly. In that area there are whole archipelagos of similar, nameless small islands.

We might read in Emil's green book:

"Abbazia, September—, 1913. On the deck of a small warship whose name I've forgotten. Courtesy of Frigate Captain Max N., a friend of L.'s fiancé. He has allowed us, at L.'s request—seemingly, against regulations—to make this small excursion on a torpedo boat. Abbazia—Krk—Pula and back. We returned

shortly. *Une petite excursion pour s'amuser.* Standing almost at
L.'s feet—having found a place at the stern, on a metal cylinder
with a thick metal cable wound around it, she looking at the sea
behind us—I confided my Great Worry to her. It was somewhat
embarrassing and not easy to admit openly. I added that it was
all her fault. She listened without a trace of surprise, as if she
had expected it for a long time, not interrupting while I was
making my intimate and desperate confession. Then I fell silent,
stopping in mid-sentence. She remained sitting in the stern of
the speeding ship, looking at the sea. Then she said, "Poor
Emil . . ." I thought perhaps my words had passed unheard because of the roar of the foaming waves, and that she hadn't understood everything I said. On the return trip, the sun began to
set behind the rocks of the tiny islands."

So we too walk on tiptoe to the cable housing in the stern of
the boat. Abbazia falls away to the left and soon will be ob-
structed by the rocky outcrops of the peninsula around which
we are turning. Dark thickets of trees, a narrow strip of stony
beach, hotels surrounded by greenery—all this is hidden behind
the exposed point.

Listing slightly to port, the torpedo boat *S.M.S. Scharfschütze*
describes a large arc, heading for the open sea straight into the
sun, whose disk hangs low behind the cliffs of the coast of Istria.
The Gulf of Quarnero is calm, and only beyond the peninsula
just passed does the strong breath of the warm sirocco hit us
frontally. One can see a fairly distinct line that divides the belt
of sirocco from the sphere of calm, and how the sea acquires a
different color, ruffled into tiny sapphire scales over which bright
yellow glimmers appear. Behind us, from this distance a bluish
green, cool, severe expanse seems to have remained almost
immobile.

S.M.S. Scharfschütze seems to speed straight into the disk of
the sun. The watery horizon is folded into gentle hills and
valleys, almost musical in its rhythmic rocking, rising and falling. Emil R. is thinking about it. He follows his sister to the
stern. Behind her a foamy furrow is formed. Two fishing barks
appear and brush lightly against the ship. Then a stronger wave
tosses their bows up, so that they rise and dip simultaneously.
Their masts with folded sails perform the same kind of salute in
the same rhythm. On the mast of one of the boats a lantern is

already lit, in spite of the early hour. Somebody calls out something in Croatian to the racing torpedo boat, cupping his hands to his mouth.

The smoke, rising from the low funnels, describes a slightly broader arc than the wake behind the poop. Its black plait falls on the waves, dances on them, disperses to the sides, settles for a second on the water, then disappears. On the first wave beyond the promontory, the bow of the ship will rise on a sizable wall of water driven by the sirocco, then cut the emerald green water like a sharp knife, falling at the same time. The white splashes fall on the steel deck with a thud, flowing with a hiss of receding foam from the rivet-studded metal plates. The next wave follows at once, then the next, the third, the tenth.

A few watery tongues edged with a piping of transparent foam penetrate to where the young couple is standing, where the red-white-red pennant is flapping in the gusts of the sirocco.

A year before, in the spring of 1912, not far from here at Volosca, Miss Elizabeth R. was riding the Reisachs' black mare at a gallop, clad in black riding clothes, while Emil, standing off to one side, was trembling lest she fall. Although Elizabeth reined him in with all her strength, the horse raced up and dug its hooves into the ground but a few inches from where Emil was standing. Then Baron Reisach senior, also in riding gear, walked up to them. His son, a young boy still in school uniform, was playing tennis on the adjoining court. Tamarisk leaves trembled in the light breeze coming from the gulf. A glaring sun shone in the direction of Abbazia, but here, under a row of tall trees, there was shade. Lieschen's face, bending over the horse's neck and patting it, was memorable.

Now from the deck of the ship one could still see that same clump of trees and even the fence of the tennis court, on which at the time young Reisach was running with his racket. A few white rocks, jutting out of the water, seemed from this distance like a skulking animal.

Looking at the profile of his sister standing on the ship, hardly visible when the wind ruffled her veil, moved it to the side, or else lifted it for a moment before a subsequent gust pasted it over her features like a gray spider's web, Emil perhaps thought: "Look at her, look while she is here, profit from this opportunity and don't waste a moment to preserve her image forever and ever."

Tightening his fingers on the cold, wet rail, he looked at her knitted brows, the oval of her cheek, at her lips visible now through the tulle of her veil, almost black in the fading light, probably moist and salty from the spray, palpable and physically material as never before, not even when he had looked at her standing close by in conversation during confidences never withheld—lips known in every detail for years.

"Oh God," he thinks suddenly, "grant me only this one thing: to die looking at her; I don't wish for anything else, I don't ask for anything more!" All of a sudden he is overcome by a premonition of death so powerful that he has to clutch the steel rail.

"If I jumped into the sea now while she's looking toward Lovrana, she would probably not even notice. Perhaps only later, alerted by some sailor. They would certainly take me out, but a moment too late. What would she think, leaning over my slippery corpse, lying face up like a dead fish? That she had anticipated it, foreseen it? That one would have to explain this unfortunate accident to strangers? Her brother suffered from vertigo, the excursion wasn't well planned, and she . . . Something of the kind."

And afterward, without any connection with those thoughts, another memory of several earlier years comes to him: the cat at Kreuzbach that Lieschen had tried so hard to teach acrobatic tricks, inventing methods of instruction that always failed because the animal was either not very gifted or simply lazy. Together with Detta she had made him a formal suit out of Mama's old red dress and forced it on him. The cat at first was astonished, then seemed to mind, and after a moment escaped to the villa's attic spitting fiercely; they had to climb a ladder to entice him back. Emil had to hold the ladder while Lieschen, having climbed up, put her head into the small opening of the attic window, attempting different voices, from a thin caressing miaouwing to a threatening growl, even declaiming snatches of a speech and then a poem composed on the spot, to persuade the fugitive to return. In her "ode" the cat was referred to as "Mr. Cat," and that's how Lieschen at last succeeded in persuading him. Following this memory that had filled him with tenderness, Emil remembered how the previous year Baron Erich von Reisach, helping Elizabeth to jump off her horse and holding its reins, had declared that Lieschen might in time become an accomplished rider, whereupon Emil, standing close by, took the elderly gentleman's compliment as inexplicably unsavory and highly inappropriate. He turned his head away, not wanting to look at his sister while she was dusting her riding boots and breeches with a short whip and saying something to the baron about the horse, which she had just ridden along the coast as far as Voloska. Emil did not want to look at the sunburnt face of his sister when she moved a strand of blond hair from her eyes, nor listen to the boastful pride in her voice.

At the time he had been reading Strindberg's *Inferno* at night and still clearly remembers the impression that the book made on him. Lieschen took the book away from him and, it seems, read it in one sitting, but Emil cannot remember now whether they discussed it afterward.

This was one year ago and now . . .

"I kept following her eyes fixed on the sea behind us, on the foamy furrow broadening like the tail of a mysterious comet, and on the spray leaping up from the side and splashing on the deck, then disappearing in a thin trickle into the seams on the deck of the torpedo boat. Isolated rivulets reached my feet; others receded with a dry note, like desert sand swept by the wind. Close behind us another ship, black and low, was sailing full speed ahead, her skulking and rapacious silhouette like a salamander rowing with short forelegs. With her prow the ship cut the waves left by our boat, rising slightly above them, then falling, then, dripping with water, rising again to climb over the next green water wall. She tore whole constellations of watery lace, of bursting bubbles of spume, shoving these to the side. Blowing from behind the cape, the wind pushed far into the sea the black smoke belching from the two low, slanting funnels. I saw it all, not looking at anything except L. standing on the prow, yet I must have noticed all these trivial details since I remember them so well. O the misery and the perfidy of memory!

"A sailor was working nearby around a winch with a steel cable wound on it, a strong barefooted fellow in white summer trousers wet up to the knees that in the wind sounded like a flapping sail; he said something to us and laughed. In the opening of his shirt, on his broad, hairy chest I noticed the tattoo of a shark and around it an inscription—in Croatian, I think. Leaning over the winch, he continued to talk to us, but the roar of the sea prevented me from understanding a word. On his muscular arm I noticed another tattoo in blue.

"L.'s eyes were still turned toward the sea, after following for a moment the movements of the sailor manipulating the cable. She must have noticed the shark tattoo on the breast of that muscular fellow. She pursed her lips and turned her face to the sea, observing the ship that followed us closely, while I saw nothing but her profile, now visible through the veil that clung to her face. The nape of her neck . . . Her somewhat raised shoulders when she leaned forward, propping herself on her palms with fingers spread. A few gulls flew by, circling above us and screeching, then L. raised an arm as if to chase them away or perhaps catch one in flight."

Dated at Trieste the same year, probably a few days after that trip on the second-class torpedo boat of the coastal defense squadron stationed at Lussinpiccolo:

"When we passed the naval base of Pula, I saw several ships in the roads. Second Lieutenant F. of the torpedo boat came up to us and began explaining to L.—I wasn't in the least interested, but she listened closely, or pretended to listen only through courtesy—that three coastal defense battleships are at anchor in the roads: *The Monarch*, the *Offenpest*, and behind these, already in the port basin, our newest first-class battleship, and pride of the navy, the giant *Viribus Unitis*, launched quite recently. And lying at an angle to them and nearer our boat, so that we could see the sailors in white summer uniforms standing near the ship's side, there was a training frigate painted in horizontal white and red stripes. Our informant told us that he had served on her two years before; he seemed proud of this fact and deeply moved.

"Later, the docks and stores of the port of Pula lay off somewhat to the left. Through the forest of masts, cables, and cranes, I could still see the barely visible outline of the Roman arena and the tower of some church. Our ship set its course—this is apparently the correct naval expression—for the port of Trieste, and Pula disappeared behind the point of the peninsula. Some time later we passed the small Miramar palace. I thought: the tragic and lonely spirit of Empress Elizabeth of Austria, L.'s namesake, must hover there in the shadow of the two black cypresses and look at us both. Perhaps she is blessing us, while with a long transparent hand she screens her eyes from the sun that is now standing low over the waves, so low that single waves are pierced by the rays and begin to shimmer with purple, shot through unexpectedly with green and gold, before becoming rust and violet, then dark blue, almost black, to revert in a moment to the color of bottle glass."

And after half an empty page, a few lines erased so thoroughly as to be illegible, a continuation without a date:

". . . when the boat returned to its berth, disappearing behind the cliff, L. said, while standing on the stones of the quay and averting her eyes from the sun: 'Well, that's it.' Then, straightening up and shaking off the drops of water that had fallen on her skirt while we were disembarking, she added without looking at me: 'Now throw your watch into the sea. Look, I'm doing the same with mine.' She began to unpin her gold Omega watch from the belt of her skirt and, together with its chain and a cluster of charms, threw it far away into the waves between the rocks. 'Now your wallet. Look, I'm throwing my handbag, too. There! Now let's go! We must see what that little island, our uninhabited kingdom, looks like.'

"She began to climb up the rocks and I followed her, negotiating the steep empty slope, overgrown with tufts of tall, sharp sea grasses and thorny bushes. Dusk was falling. A light breeze blew from the sea and made the grasses rustle. Then there was complete calm, and again the growing rustle of the leaves. She said, not turning round, not looking to see if I could keep pace with her: 'We have no watches, so time has ceased to exist. There will be no minutes, no hours, no day or night. Nothing, do you understand? There will be no seasons either. This is what I want, that nothing should remain. No background, no scenery. Nothing. Only the two of us. You and I.'

"I was silent. The sun disappeared behind a jutting cliff, everything was dark blue and empty. Somewhere down below, the sea was roaring. The waves broke regularly against the coast. Above us neither the stars nor moon could be seen. A solitary gull flew from the direction of the Bay of Quarnero, or perhaps it was a hawk. The bird hung above us almost immobile in the air, its wings spread, emitting now and then a sharp, angry screech.

"And then . . .

"She gathered in her hands a tuft of tall, spiky grasses. She brushed one of these against her bare skin, where if a sleeve is lifted, delicate blue veins are visible. It was so dark that I sensed it rather than saw it. I could only see her profile when she lay leaning over me. The hissing gusts of sirocco penetrated even to where we lay between the rocks. I gave her my arm without a word. She rolled up the sleeve and bent over me silent and serious. 'Look,' she whispered, 'My blood and yours have mixed and are now flowing in one common stream. I hope you aren't afraid!' "

At 9:05 p.m., after a considerable delay caused by congestion on the rail line from Arad to Temesvar, Marvita, Vercecs, and Fehertemplom, and on the one from Nagy Beckerek to Zriny, Orlovat, Pancevo, Vercecs, and Fehertemplom, a troop train carrying the second section of the Thirteenth Regiment of the Imperial and Royal Hussars, bearing the proud and ancient name *Iazyger und Kumanier*, arrived in the station.

Even before the long train halted with a screech and a thud at the empty, ill-lit platform at Fehertemplom, the soldiers began to jump from the coaches and run toward the station pump. They were hot and thirsty because in the heat of the day, especially after the frequent stops at small stations or even in open country, the water in their bottles and buckets was overheated, muddy, and furthermore smelled of disinfectant. The temperature at midday apparently reached more than 40 C. in the shade.

It was now completely dark on the platform. From behind the wooden ramp for unloading horses, a soldier appeared with a rifle slung over his shoulder. He stood there looking at the hussars who crowded around the pump, splashing themselves with water and shouting. The soldiers spoke Hungarian, while stamping their feet, laughing, and swearing. Red forage caps, red trousers, and dark blue dolmans with yellow piping jostled around the pump, from whose short, thick pipe spurted a torrent of water. Distant oil lamps in the station made the surface of the water opalescent, like icicles catching the sun in a winter dawn. Then the impression vanished, because the backs, shoulders, and heads of the hussars intervened. Puddles formed under their feet. A late-comer jumped down from a coach and ran with buckets in his hands, stumbling on the stones, slipping in the water spilled near the pump. Horses began to neigh in their cars. Somebody swore.

After a while, officers began to alight from the three first- and second-class coaches. The locomotive breathed like a tired animal. Far ahead of the train, some bushes could be seen in its headlight, while farther off still, against the black background of the sky, shone the red eye of a signal.

The officers stretched themselves, brushed the dust off their uniforms, asked the name of the station, and lit cigarettes. Some looked at the pitch black sky, strewn with thousands of stars. The Milky Way, clearly visible, turned in a wide arc, disappearing behind clumps of acacias and the roofs of the stores.

One of the officers, his spurs clanking, walked along the cattle cars toward the stationmaster's office. The latter, mobilized two days previously, ran out of his office in a field uniform with creases and traces of fresh pressing after a long period in the army stores, and stood at attention in front of a stout hussar major who was loudly asking for something in Hungarian.

A few officers of the Sicilian Lancers already in Fehertemplom appeared, attracted by the noise. They had been drinking beer in the station buffet. Among them was the regimental surgeon, Dr. Oplustil, a former hussar of the famous regiment that had just arrived at Fehertemplom—a regiment that he had left less than two years before. He stopped on the platform in front of the buffet, asking a corporal the name of his unit that would leave the same night on its way towards Mitrovica. From Arad, not too distant, the journey had taken fourteen hours.

It is quite possible that one of the surgeon's former colleagues will recognize him in spite of the darkness on the platform. And that, upon seeing him, he will quote the words of a song popular in the Imperial and Royal Army: "Hail Brezina! Is that really you?" and embrace Dr. Antonin Oplustil, whom he has not seen for several months.

And behind him the fat padre, Father Geza Karinat, will follow in a field uniform half ecclesiastical, half military. He will giggle, adjusting a wide field belt to which he has had no time to grow accustomed. And Father Geza Karinat—having had a drink or two en route—on seeing the godless Oplustil, against whom he has waged a none-too-serious battle, will utter words expressing at the same time a joy that he cannot hide, and a regimental pride completely understandable at a historical moment when the god Mars has become his patron. He will exclaim in his broken German, in accents acquired at Temesvar: "Look, old man, I'm an authentic Iazyg, aren't I?" and walking toward Surgeon Oplustil he will stumble, perhaps, and embrace a lamppost. It is quite possible that the whole officers' party won't limit themselves to drinking a few glasses of the excellent Banat brandy that they took care to bring on the journey, but will go in fiacres (driven mostly by the local Jews) straight to Mother Rozsa's place. Besides officers of the Thirteenth Hussars, those going will include a few Sicilian Lancers such as Lieutenant Alois Svjeticianin, Second Lieutenants Istvan Bihar de Barabas and Lazar von Magyarpecska, not counting the commander, Major Emmanuel Vidos de Kolta.

Talking loudly, laughing, and clapping each other on the back, they will pack into a fiacre three, four, and even five at a time and go rattling over the cobblestones of Munkacsi Street. After a while their singing, cheers, and laughter will be heard from Mother Rozsa's.

In the wee hours of the next morning, Father Karinat will dance the czardas on the top of a small table beside the leader of the gypsy band, the black-haired, dark-skinned Jozsa. In the spring Jozsa had led the gypsy musicians of the whole area— eleven fiddlers, and what fiddlers they were!—in the funeral procession of Master Jotka, who had died the previous May, following behind the cart pulled by a pair of long-horned white oxen with wreaths on their heads, behind the coffin on which the orphaned violin of the deceased had been placed. By the side of the coffin walked his weeping women with black kerchiefs on their heads, wailing and scratching their cheeks until blood showed. This procession had been led along field paths among ripening corn by the dead man's successor, young Gyorgy Jozsa.

But before Father Karinat, having first turned up the flaps of his military cassock, climbs the table to dance the czardas— which he will execute in a masterly way on a space not larger than a square yard, and cluttered in addition with glasses full of wine and brandy that he will not upset—before we admire his performance, the gentlemen officers will conduct noisy conversations in three languages at once, mixing single words and whole sentences of Hungarian, Croatian, and German. They will embrace and slap one another's back in drunken tenderness, shouting and remembering how two or three years ago in one of the garrisons—on the edge of the Hortobagy Plain and more remote places—something funny had happened once.

Names will be bandied about, names evoking by their very sound sighs of love and nostalgia—names like Hajdu-Tarabos and Hajdu-Böszormeny and Kisvarda and Nyirbator and Püspökladany and Nyfregyhaza and others still, Haydouk and Chico, wild and daring like the sounds of soft gypsy violins, at the sound of which the gentlemen officers used to raise their tumblers and having emptied them, threw them on the floor, or broke them against the walls of taverns. And how once—it seemed like only yesterday or the day before—First Lieutenant Janos von Janota left the party at dawn on all fours, growling and barking like a dog, and reached the barracks in this fashion. And during the wine harvest at Count Karolyi's—we have his nephew in the regiment!—twenty-four girls from the count's estates, selected from among the most beautiful, with arms akimbo, working in pairs, crushed with their feet the grapes in twelve casks of a hundred liters each, until the juice squirted up to their waists, and the gypsy band played throughout the night amid the smoke of calves and lambs roasting on spits—eight heifers and twelve sheep roasting on long spits!—and in the morning the dancing began. And once in winter Major Csingay organized a hunt on a great plain: two squadrons in full gallop spread in a wide arc with sabers in their hands drove the quarry, and the collected hares and foxes were graciously shot by the officers and Count Karolyi in person, together with his civilian guests invited to the shoot from Vienna, Budapest, and even Paris.

"And what about Madame Ilonka Irkay? Do you remember Madame Irkay, the uncrowned queen and patron of the *Iazyger und Kumanier*? How could we forget her! We tossed her in a blanket, eight officers on each side holding it, because it was a double one already commandeered for the approaching war from the stores at Szeged. What a time! When at the end Ilonka Irkay was dropped into a cask of the last year's wine—

the cask was at least one and a half meters high and held at least two hundred liters, do you understand?—we had to turn her upside down to pour out the wine under her corset!" At that recent memory, the officers jump up from the table in Mother Rozsa's place, stand erect, and unsheath their field sabers—more like swords if compared with the ones they carried until the day before yesterday: light peacetime things with a golden guard and tassel. The raised sabers, crossed now over the cluttered table, are heavy and warlike, meant for thrusts straight from the shoulder after rising in the saddle for a better stroke, teeth clenched under the curled black moustache, with a Magyar curse or a shout of "Long live!" So now at Mother Rozsa's the sabers are raised in unison toward the ceiling, and at just this moment Father Karinat, in spite of his girth and the liters of wine he has already drunk, jumps nimbly on the table and calls on Primos Jozsa to play something for him, a poignant song but not entirely nostalgic, a song with some merry passages as only the gypsies know how to play, a gypsy song about how wild, beautiful, and untamed is the immense plain of Hortobagy.

Then the day will break—an August day, for it is August 1, 1914—and from the nearby railway station the piercing alarm whistles will be heard in the cold early morning air, causing an involuntary shiver. Into the sky, becoming green in the east white whirls of steam rise from the locomotive. Its short, squat boiler, shining from morning dew and heavy grease, seems at this hour almost dark blue like the armature of a beetle. The hussars and a few Sicilian Lancers who accompany them will rush out from Mother Rozsa's, stumbling and laughing, and emitting cries that will arouse the still sleepy streets of Fehertemplom. They will race one another, raising their sabers toward the sky, where the stars are pale now. Through the little alleys and winding byways of the small town they will rush toward the station, along Kiralyi and Baranya Streets, through Franz Josef Square, already full of carts with melons and watermelons, and thronged by gypsy folk and peasants from the Banat, and along Railway Street with its market stalls, leading past the mills and corn silos down to the station. They will leap on the moving train, onto the steps of the coaches, while the train is gathering speed and the engineer gives several blasts on the whistle as he passes the switches and the tall signal with its green eye shining against the gray green sky. Along the horizon, over the reeds and tufts of osier, a pinkish yellow streak is spreading, into which the black locomotive will sail, cut through it, and almost vanish. Its sharp contours will flatten, the smokestack and the boiler, the wheels and buffers, the hump of the tender, all will be edged with a lemon yellow border. And then the sun will burst out from behind the silhouette of the engine, which will sink in the sudden glare, changing for a moment into a burning bush, then into a fire-blackened star. The officers of the Imperial and Royal Thirteenth Regiment of Hussars are still trying to jump on the steps of the coaches, clinging to handles still cold with dew, waving their hats to the comrades who have remained in the station and are reeling from too much wine and brandy, even attempting to dance a czardas on the emptying platform in honor of the departing men. And the train has now gone a long way. In the clouds of dust, amid the cries of soldiers leaning out the windows, it clatters past clumps of thorny dwarf acacias, harvested areas, and immense fields of stubble toward the horizon lit by the glare of a far distant dawn; it rattles now over a small bridge and past the hut of a crossing keeper, then passes Novo Selo and nears Nagy Becskerek and Backa Topola.

At this morning hour Assistant Commissioner Ferenc Bogatovich sits down at the table in the gendarmerie and, lighting his first cigar of the day, begins to ponder who killed the young gypsy girl Marika Huban the day before yesterday.

Only the day before yesterday Marika was walking, swaying her hips gypsy style and smoking cigarettes offered her by casual admirers or obtained by begging in the street—perhaps from one of the officers just lighting an odorous Memphis cigarette or even a Virginia cigar. "Mister, give us a cigarette!" she would say with a wink of her eyes under her black eyebrows and sniffing half childishly, half deliberately and roguishly, for it must be mentioned that Marika was very pretty. The majority of fifteen-year-old gypsy girls in Fehertemplom and its suburbs were pretty, but Marika was the most attractive of all. Or did she become beautiful only after her death? So she walked, swaying her hips, puffing at a cigarette, nor did she neglect the butts to be collected from the taverns and in the market, stooping gracefully to pick them up with two dark fingers, cleaning the dust off them and hiding them in her torn blouse, displaying to the curious her dark girlish bosom covered with streaks of sweat or dirt. But even gypsy dirt is full of romantic attraction.

Marika Huban also stole cigarettes from the market stalls. We say that she smoked, begged, and stole in an undeservedly past tense, as undeserved as her death in the old clay pit the day before yesterday. We state these facts while taking care to assess mutually the time that we are speaking about and its relativity, for we must consider as certain and irreversible two matters: first, the death of Marika Huban, a person of little objective and public importance, but very important, essential, and unique for herself and her murderer, her existence in its relative poverty and final fulfillment being broken in spite of the promise and expectations of summer nights and the nightly song of birds in dark groves; and second, the death, already a month distant and therefore somewhat forgotten, of the heir to the throne of Austria-Hungary at the corner of the Kaiser Franz Josef Strasse at Sarajevo at 10:47 or 10:48 a.m. on June 28, therefore slightly over a month before the death of his subject, whose precise hour of death is unknown.

Neither of these facts is to be questioned, because they have been officially confirmed and supported by statements of persons legally entitled to do so by the imperial and royal authorities.

A Jesuit priest, Father Anthony Puntigam, who had been summoned to the dying archduke, by a strange coincidence bore a name identical with one of the districts of the city of Graz on the river Mur. In that suburb there is a famous brewery of the same name: Puntigamer-Bräu. The beer brewed there was always drunk by Emil R.'s family, as well as by many officers of the Sicilian Lancers in the garrison at Fehertemplom. Apart from a few Hungarians, clearly unfamiliar with the wider world, half-provincial or completely so—men who had never ventured beyond the familiar acres under the jurisdiction of the Seventh Corps at Temesvar or the Thirteenth at Zagreb—few people had the opportunity to become acquainted with the prodigious taste of the beer from the Puntigam brewery.

The label of that beer shows a Styrian lion on a green Styrian background. The same lion, only in a slightly different pose, is known to everybody who has ever walked through the winding shadowy paths to the top of the Schlossberg at Graz, or who, not to tire himself in view of age, excessive weight, or the elegance of his manners and dress, went to the top by a funicular, in order to gaze with the naked eye, or through binoculars hired for five talers from a helpful city employee, at the magnificent panorama of the city encircled by the river Mur. One also sees the spacious suburbs swathed in the mist of distance: to the north, Andritz; to the south, Puntigam; to the southeast, Sankt Peter. Also, surrounding the Schlossberg, the green Rings from the Keplerstrasse to Annenstrasse. And likewise the tall chimneys of the Puntigam brewery with a plume of smoke over them.

The vista is wide and worthy of the most exquisite taste of the most demanding aesthetes. On a clear summer's day, to the northeast we might see the dark emerald hill overlooking the residential villa quarter of Kreuzbach, well-known to us and remembered with the sentiment surrounding our earliest memories, its green cupola of leaves surmounted by the white towers of the church at Maria-Trost. We won't be able to see the second place of early pilgrimages: the distant monastery of Maria-Trost. We can only see—especially through the binoculars obligingly handed to us by a man wearing some kind of livery—a shining narrow ribbon of the suburban railway line, or the narrow-gauge streetcar running from under our feet—right down there—along the Zinsendorfergasse and proceeding in curves to disappear from view behind the roofs of Kreuzbach and the clumps of trees in the direction of Maria-Trost.

Directing our eyes, or a telescope mounted on a brass tripod, slightly to the right, we can admire the shady park around a pond on which swans and gray green ducks are swimming and where, on narrow gravel paths, mothers or nurses with children walk in the shade of chestnut trees or sit on benches: this is Hilmteich—our native Hilmteich!

And beyond it—let's raise the telescope, but not change its direction—we shall see, magnified, the quarter of Sankt Leonhard with its baroque church worthy of a visit, cool even during the greatest heat, with its stained glass and gilded altars, and we might, tiptoeing on the stone floor, approach one of the confessionals at which, years before, we confessed in whispers our half-childish sins or their disturbing, only lightly imagined foretaste. And a little farther down we shall see the recently erected buildings of the provincial hospital.

Those for whom these parts are not unknown would easily find
the Sankt Leonhard cemetery. They will walk on, having replaced their hats after they doffed them at the cemetery gate,
and reach the Seebacherstrasse, in which, at No. 3, the R. family
has been living for many years. They will climb the stairs, stop,
and through the staircase window will see the crown of the great
chestnut tree and hear its rustling, the melody which put us to
sleep, and the nocturnal song of a bird in its leaves. Or perhaps
no memories at all will meet us there. Is young Emil R. still
leaning from the open window? Certainly not. So many years
have passed from the moment when he stood there and looked
at something below, waiting for something which was about to
happen, to fulfill itself, or perhaps fearing that event. It is too
late now for any fear. So, with a sigh, we shall direct the telescope to the south. We shall see two factories very clearly in that
light: Puntigamer-Bräu and Puch-Werke.

A cousin of Mr. and Mrs. R. had recently bought a magnificent
automobile produced by Puch-Werke. When one presses the
strong-smelling rubber bulb of the horn, on the right side of the
proud vehicle's dashboard, it emits a melodic sound that makes
the heavy cart horses pulling a dray of Puntigam beer over the
uneven cobblestones prick up their ears and even shy to one
side. The bewhiskered driver will draw the reins and the cart
will continue on its way with a rattle of wheels, and the barrels
of beer, laid in two rows and additionally hung on hooks on both
sides of the dray, will give out a heavy slurping sound, almost
like distant thunder. The day will be sunny and summery, and
children led out by their mother, who on this occasion will
wrap up a dense veil over her light sports hat, break away and
run toward the car. Uncle Prohaska, the owner of the automobile,
while cleaning the glass of the headlights with a chamois cloth
will hum, *"Lisboa mea—mi passion"* or perhaps *"Gretchen,
Gretchen, you are my dream . . ."* but then, having noticed the
children, he will stop singing. Attorney R. will come out last
from the house, closing the door behind him and then the gate
of the small garden with its large chestnut tree. 3 Seebacherstrasse. And he will come up last to the door of the white Puch.
He intends to take the seat next to the driver, to keep an eye on
him and to restrain, if need be, his unrestrained enthusiasm.
Attorney R. proceeds with dignity from the little gate to the

automobile, clad in a white duster and a hat resembling those worn recently by cyclists—who, according to Mr. R., "are a plague of our times, an invention of both modernity and stupidity," and then he adds with disgust, "Road bugs!" On his hat there are goggles that he will use during the drive to protect himself from dust and wind. What speed! Cousin Prohaska, a wealthy industrialist from Wiener Neustadt, maintains that his Puch can achieve a speed of over eighty kilometers an hour, naturally when the road is empty and there are no obstacles to impose caution and extreme attention. Mr. R. won't believe it. Eighty kilometers! Out of regard for his wife and children who are just taking their seats in the rear, the promised test of maximum speed won't take place that day. That would be much too risky.

Little Emil, dressed also in a white duster with a small cape, and wearing a cap with a button on top, sits on the folding seat. Both his sisters are in the rear seat next to his mother. Lieschen as usual has a red nose and suffers from a cold. Detta sits quietly, motionless in a blue jacket, licking her lips nervously, her eyes bulging with excitement. Lieschen, on the other hand, unable to sit still, wriggles and asks questions about the car's engine. Mrs. R. is adjusting her hair behind the veil. On her lap lies a bag with provisions. They are to drive to Sankt Peter, at the foot of the mountains. Mr. R. looks at the sky: what marvelous weather—not a cloud! Even the two little ones that he saw before have disappeared, melted like sugar in tea.

Beyond the river Mur one can admire the hills that surround the industrial, smoke-swathed district of Wetzeldorf. Nearer, almost below us, are the Annenstrasse and the station of the Southern Railway which begins at the Südbahnhof in Vienna and ends in two branches: one at Trieste and the other at Pontebba and Pontafel on the Italian frontier.

At this very moment an express train rolls into the station, the Blitzzug from Vienna to Trieste. The porters come running, their red caps clearly visible, and in front of the station you can see one-horse and two-horse fiacres pull up and take their places in an orderly manner, one close behind the other. One can see the dust circling in the air—perhaps not dust at all, but swarms of flies.

Someone with a large family waves his arms and doffs a hat ringed with a green cord and decorated with a woodcock's feather. He wipes perspiration from his brow and looks around helplessly, but then a porter comes running up to him. Reassured, we turn the telescope somewhat to the left. Somebody has got into a two-horse carriage at the station—seemingly, an officer with a young lady in a mauve hat with feathers. The fiacre turns into the Annenstrasse and disappears from our sight.

The express train starts from platform 2. The engine, very modern, is from the Imperial and Royal Railway Works, with a low smokestack and a boiler elongated like a cigar, and expels toward the sky short, noisy puffs of dense smoke. The wheels painted with red lacquer turn faster and faster. Someone leaning from a first-class compartment waves a hand, then a handkerchief. The last coaches disappear, hidden by the station buildings; the sun glints on their windows, the light leaps from roof to roof, until nothing worthy of attention remains to be seen. The stationmaster walks away, the porters scatter, the platforms empty, so that we direct the field glasses to a closer sight, the park at the foot of the Schlossberg.

The lens of the telescope encompasses the Town Hall, which closely resembles the Rathaus in Vienna, then Bismarckplatz and Jacominiplatz, and the Annenstrasse full of shops and window-shoppers who turn back and reassemble for some reason in another spot. We turn the glasses on the green trees and lawns, the shadowy little paths under the chestnut, plane, and linden trees.

Close under the Schlossberg two officers in the uniform of the dragoons ride their horses at walking pace. They disappear between the trees, but their light blue jackets with yellow facings soon reappear on a narrow path. The right rear leg of the black horse walking in front is tied with a bandage. Now both officers are clearly visible against the background of a small clearing with a bed of white flowers in the middle that shines in the sunlight. There are benches in the clearing and children are playing in the sand. The right hands of both officers rise in unison toward their hats. They are saluting someone walking in the avenue whom we cannot see. The officers' faces are turned to that person and their heads are lowered in a gracious gesture. One of the horses is tossing its head; the officer draws his reins with a white-gloved hand whose cuff goes up to the elbow. Then both disappear from our view altogether.

Now a boy following a rolling ball appears in the telescope. A red squirrel runs up the smooth trunk of a tall beech tree. It crouches on a branch and watches the ball. A boy in a sailor's suit now approaches. We are making a visual journey that is superfluous and in fact futile: it is unconnected with anything useful, serves no purpose, achieves nothing. It is suspended in a vacuum and without any reason. It might happen to anybody, it might never have happened in its unique and concrete form, with the accumulation of these apparently trifling details. Yet it is in some way important, and perhaps even indispensable, because it proves something: its unrepeatable uniqueness. For the doffing of a hat by the irritated traveler on the platform; the handkerchief crushed in his fingers with which he wiped the leather lining of his hat in conjunction with the farewell; the simultaneous gesture of raising an arm by someone energetically waving a handkerchief from the first-class compartment window in the second coach of the Vienna-Trieste express at a precise hour and minute; the departure of this express train; and the horses ridden at walking pace by two officers of the Imperial and Royal Fifth Dragoons along a path under the Schlossberg—all show that the moment we have experienced passively, looking at these unimportant acts, will never again be repeated with an identical composition of the elements. Which is why this moment is relevant, as is the gesture of Father Puntigam, administering the last rites to the dying heir to the Hapsburg throne, or the first draft of cold Puntigam beer swallowed by someone sitting under the canvas roof of the beer tavern in the Annenstrasse, or the barking of the white mongrel dog chasing a child's ball on the lawn below the Schlossberg, on the top of which we are standing.

Still another element connects these others that seem unimportant to us: leaning over the balustrade, propped on her two hands, so poised on tiptoe that we fear that she will rise from the ground, there exists in this landscape—and had existed at that time and in the previous set of circumstances—the real and authentic Lieschen.

But has she really been present there, or have we included her from a strong desire to call her forth from nowhere? For there is no one leaning against the balustrade. Its pillars cast shadows on the sand and on the flagstones of the promenade, slightly below the Styrian lion resting glumly on its forepaws. The shadow of the lion is cast on distant trees growing on the slope of the hill. Has Lieschen really existed in the landscape we have seen through the telescope? She seems to move in the background, materialized in details: a dress trimmed with flounces at the sleeves and at the hem of a skirt now slightly raised as she leans against the balustrade, which is too high for a girl of her age. The very image of her hanging on the barrier under the shade of branches that are pale yellow and green in this light, seems to have been painted by an Impressionist, while in reality the balustrade was gray and rough, full of scratches and crevices, and when the sun covers any of it with a yellow glaze, the stony joints between the rocks become almost black. Lieschen's dress, especially the flounces at her puffed sleeves and the folds of her skirt, which is wide at the bottom like a crino-line, also undergoes elusive metamorphoses of color worthy of Manet or Renoir. But there is no artist at hand who can fix this moment and preserve it.

What is Lieschen looking at, what is she observing with such intense curiosity down below, at the foot of the hill? Who or what on those narrow paths winding to left and right in the shadow of the tall tree—is it a squirrel on a branch? The shadows cast by the sun? The seats on which children sit with their governesses, who chat together while crocheting? Is it the dog with a blue ribbon—that dog white like a ball of wool? It has just run into those bushes that, from this distance, look flat as patches of dark blue and golden pigment on a painter's palette.

The young gypsy girl walks swaying her hips; her long skirt is dirty and torn at the bottom, and skims the dust of the uneven pavements of the Gypsy Quarter. Although faded, the frock is still colorful, with flowers on a paler background, dark blue on yellow, green on orange. The girl's arms are tanned, and on one she is wearing a cheap bracelet, an ordinary ring of light metal. Her dark fingers hold a cigarette, because she smokes as she walks. The stub is so short that it burns the tips of her fingers. Her fingernails are dirty, but the fingers are long and shapely. Finally she throws the cigarette away and continues to walk, humming softly. She leaves the pavement not far from Mother Supicich's tavern and turns into the path leading to the meadows beyond the brickworks. The kerchief that she has just removed from her head disappears from sight. The gypsy girl shakes her hair loose and it falls on her shoulders, black and thick, probably a bit greasy and dusty. She waves her kerchief, throws it in the air, and folds it between her fingers as she goes along the path, still humming.

It is 11:30 a.m., June 28. The body of Princess Sophia Hohenberg lies in the bedroom of General Oscar Potiorek, the Governor General of Bosnia and Hercegovina. The archduke's body lies in the next room. Father Puntigam is by the dead man. He leans down, whispering prayers. Beneath the unbuttoned collar with the gold braid of a general, a gold chain with many medallions hangs on the archduke's breast. Both sleeves of the jacket are turned up. On the left arm a colored tattoo representing a Chinese dragon is visible. Father Puntigam closes his eyes. Perhaps he can still hear the last words of the just expired heir apparent who when asked by Count Franz Harrach, "Is your highness in pain?" replied, "It's nothing!" Through the open windows one can hear bells tolling. They are tolling in turn, one after the other, in all the Catholic and Orthodox churches of Sarajevo.

Gypsy Marika Huban descends from the path toward the first clay pit, its rim overgrown with dense bushes. At the very bottom of the sizable pit, between the bullrushes which grow there, shines a small pool; through the water, its yellow clay bottom is visible. A school of tiny fish, smaller than matchsticks, flees under the rushes when Marika Huban, having discarded her dress, enters the water, which hardly reaches to her knees. On her left shoulder a tattoo can be seen. If anyone were to peep from the thick bushes at the bathing girl, he might discover that the tattoo represents a small animal, probably a lizard. Perhaps there is an inscription around it. But right now no one is looking. As we know, it is half past eleven and the heat is intense even in the shade and at the bottom of the clay pit, where the water has become muddied as the girl's feet stir and flatten the wax-colored slime while she, wary and watchful, bends down. But no one is there to admire the young gypsy.

The girl found at the bottom of the clay pit in the Gypsy Quarter was apparently named Marika Huban. This information is imparted by Ferenc, the bald and pockmarked waiter, to the officers enjoying the cool young wine of last year's vintage on the vine-covered veranda of Mother Bezsi's tavern. Reserve Surgeon Karamarkovich, who joined the regiment three days before, raises his eyebrows. He puts down his glass to light a cigar. He recalls that the day before yesterday a gypsy girl with the cheeky, coquettish eyes of a magpie had begged from him a similar freshly lit, long, well-dried Virginia cigar with a straw in it, and that, after hesitating, he gave it to her, and she at once began to smoke it, inhaling like a man and exhaling through her nose while bending back from her waist, her right foot thrust forward. She smoked looking straight into the eyes of the donor, then walked off swaying her hips, stepping like a dancer, shapely, with a sunflower pinned in her hair, from which her kerchief had slipped down to the nape of her neck. He watched her for a moment as she walked down Kerti Street, sweeping the dust with her skirt.

Sitting on Mother Bezsi's veranda, in addition to Dr. Karamarkovich, is a second regimental surgeon: Dr. Oplustil—the same Dr. Oplustil who will soon go to the station to greet his former colleagues of the Thirteenth Regiment of Hussars.

Dr. Oplustil has endured three full years of suffering and ill-treatment among the *Iazyger und Kumanier*. The exclusively racial Magyars had selected Dr. Oplustil as the butt of constant, never-ending slights, jokes, and leg-pulling. They seemed indefatigable and, not knowing Hungarian, Oplustil guessed rather than understood the tenor of their verbal jokes, which were bearable because he was patient and did not fully understand them. His colleagues, however, took any opportunity to go beyond the purely verbal jests, provoking the thunderous laughter of the whole company at every meal in the regimental mess. Stationed at the time in the Puszta province, compared with which the streets of Fehertemplom looked at least like the Vienna Prater or Graben, the regiment was exposed to long periods of utter boredom. "Ah, the Graben!" they all sighed.

From that hell—from that small garrison, hot in the summer and isolated by ice and snowdrifts in the winter—Dr. Oplustil extricated himself, thanks to the support of somebody high up in the Imperial and Royal War Ministry. He was posted to a regiment in the same division, the Tenth, made up of the three hussar regiments, and the Twelfth Regiment of Sicilian Lancers stationed at Fehertemplom. Thus the good doctor ended up with us—among us and Mother Rozsa and Mother Bezsi—drinking wine, smoking cigars, and enjoying the harmless local gossip.

His previous regiment—the famous Thirteenth, bearing the ancient and historical name of the *Iazyger und Kumanier* and dating from the era of Prince Eugene of Savoy or even earlier—consisted, according to Dr. Oplustil, exclusively of strapping fellows who were a bit on the wild side, and the chaplain was the same. An abomination! What is there to add? It was a compact and very merry company. The boredom of life in a tiny garrison was probably the main cause and stimulus for jokes of which the poor doctor was the butt. Their inventiveness had no limit. The men of the Thirteenth were inconsolable at not having succeeded in thwarting Oplustil's flight. To what lengths can the boredom of life in such a garrison lead? One wintry night, for instance, in a snowstorm, the doctor was forced to escape from the mess stark naked, after his drunken colleagues, led by the major, had stripped him of his clothes. He escaped to the barracks (luckily not far distant) on all fours through driving snow, with only a cockade ribbon to hide his private parts. To mention such incidents is embarrassing.

The doctor now relates that the town physician, one Imre Ludas, an excellent fellow, has reported to him the result of the autopsy on the body of the gypsy girl found in the clay pit. The victim did not have her throat cut, as it seemed at first because of the pool of blood around her. It is true that she had a red mark on her neck, and that the hemorrhage occurred because of the severing of a vein in her neck. No knife was used; she was strangled by the strong wire on which her beads were threaded.

Oplustil reaches for his wineglass. He wipes perspiration from his forehead. Ah, this heat! The report of the regimental surgeon is of interest mainly to young Dr. Karamarkovich. The others are listening only out of courtesy. But Mother Bezsi Supicich herself, wearing a dark blue apron over her multi-colored print dress, now approaches the party, rests her hands on the table, and listens. "She wasn't much good," she says, then adds, "Like all of them." Then she begins to wipe up the wine on the oak table. Dr. Oplustil is now addressing mainly his pro-fessional colleague, Reserve Surgeon Karamarkovich. Of the others, only Reserve First Lieutenant Kottfuss Freiherr von Kott-vizza listens with interest. He is bored at Fehertemplom. Two days before, having to interrupt a pleasant stay at Bad Ischl among a merry, high-class Viennese crowd, he was forced to join his regiment via Budapest. What luck that he met some old acquaintances here—among them Emil R. and Kocourek from Vienna!

"So this gypsy girl was strangled with the wire on which her beads were threaded. Somebody probably approached the girl from the back, yanked the necklace, and when she fell on her back, dragged her a few steps to the bottom of the clay pit, after the two of them had walked down there together for some pur-pose. Gendarme Vilajcich whom I also met at the police station, found footprints in the grass. There's so much dust on those weeds that when anyone moves his foot a cloud rises—one can easily find the traces: the grass in those places is darker because whoever walked by cleared the dust off. There are also footprints of the boy who first reported it, but those two other sets are separate from his. Besides, the youngster had walked down a different side from the dead girl and her killer. And most inter-esting of all, this wasn't a sexual crime, as I admit I suspected at first. And even if sex was involved, it certainly wasn't rape. Perhaps somebody frightened off the killer. The autopsy seems to prove it. I went to the morgue and the town physician showed me what he has found. A red mark on the neck, a few bruises on the fingers—instinctively, the girl put them under the neck-lace to protect herself. I also had a peep at her excised womb placed in a metal bowl. I tell you, this isn't a job for such hot weather, gentlemen! The number of flies! Not a funny sight."

Karamarkovich concurred. Lieutenant Kottfuss shivered. A few years before, he had had to assist officially at a post mortem, when during his one-year stint with the dragoons in eastern

Galicia one of his soldiers had drowned in a well during maneuvers. At that time, too, the heat had been intense. Lieutenant
Kottfuss became thoughtful.

This baron, a native of the region of Vienna, is an old friend
of Emil R.'s. He was an assistant in the governor's office at Graz,
has a law degree, apparently was once a candidate for the ecclesiastical seminary in Rome. From a well-to-do Viennese family.
Willy Kottfuss's uncle is still legal adviser to the Graz diocese.
Young Kottfuss is snobbish about his contacts in the church
hierarchy and in the capital's artistic circles. In the spring of
1910 he bought a motor car and traveled the length of the
peninsula from the Apennines down to Reggio di Calabria. In
Rome he got an audience with the Pope and an apostolic blessing for his whole family, as well as a portrait of the Holy Father
with an autograph of Pius X—recognition of the Kottfuss family's contribution in matters connected with the Faith, including
many gifts of money and foundations. Willy Kottfuss also under-
took two journeys to Spain, where he had lessons with the
famous Seville toreador, Fernando Puneza y Alcaro. In Morocco
he was the guest of the Pasha of Marrakesh and apparently
intended to marry one of his nieces. If only half of these stories
repeated in the Graben Café and at Sacher's restaurant are true,
one has to admit that Willy Kottfuss is an original and colorful
individual.

In Vienna he had tastefully furnished bachelor's quarters in
the Herrengasse. In it, apart from all kinds of souvenirs from
Africa and Spain, was a photograph of the Pasha of Marrakesh
with a dedication in Arabic, and a portrait of Pius X with a
handwritten blessing. Next to these, a few apparently authentic
sketches by Boucher and two anonymous color lithographs derived from the works of the Marquis de Sade. Also, a considerable collection of beautiful Oriental weapons.

In 1912 Willy had done his service with the Ninth Regiment
of Bukovina Dragoons in a small garrison in eastern Galicia,
where he acquired a lot of memories and anecdotes. They were
later repeated by the habitués of Sacher's and of a quiet little
restaurant in the hotel Meissl und Schadn at 2 Neuer Markt, with
a first-floor table for regulars near the window, to the left of the
entrance. He claims that during the spring floods and autumn
rains the dragoon officers had to walk on stilts through the

market square of the small Jewish village in Galicia, literally
in order not to drown in the mud, and not to ruin their boots
and their trousers when going from the barracks to a comradely
drinking session in the only "tavern" in the village. That's how
Kottfuss refers to that wretched little dump, a miserable hole,
which the officers used after having evicted the natives. At the
word "tavern," Willy Kottfuss emits a melancholy sigh: "Ah, an
inn, or if you prefer, *une auberge, albergo*. Like those little
eating places in the south of France or in Sicily!" He smiles and
lights a cigar.

Old Ferenc, the waiter, is serving a dish of salt bacon cut into
small strips and dusted with paprika, reminding one of the thick,
slippery snails without their shells that you can see on country
paths after the rain. The bacon has melted from the heat,
making little puddles on the plate as if somebody had crushed
the would-be snails with his foot or with a wheelbarrow. Baron
Kottfuss averts his eyes with disgust and suddenly feels sick.
The others laugh, clinking their glasses filled with golden
brandy.

Willy Kottfuss lights a cigar, then tells about an eccentric
Galician magnate who lives in his palace as if on an island,
surrounded by a filthy Jewish village. In his palace full of an-
tiques and liveried servants, one ate from silver plates and drank
from cut crystal glasses a prime French vintage burgundy such
as you don't find even at Sacher's in Vienna, no, not even at
receptions given by the Liechtensteins or the Schwarzenbergs.
The count invited the dragoon officers to dinner once a month.
What a cuisine! The count boasted a chef who had served in the
Burg in Vienna—can you believe it, gentlemen? Snipe and quail,
partridges in Malaga wine and thrush on buttered toast, pheasant
à la Windischgraetz and à la Esterhazy. And to think that as a
matter of principle this eccentric never paid the local merchants
for candles, salt, or oil, and that his servants' wages weren't paid
for months on end, although the forests on the estate spread
over an area, I'd say, of over half a million acres! And what
forests!—Here Willy Kottfuss becomes thoughtful and draws
nervously on his cigar. He is, as everybody knows, an enthusi-
astic hunter. Once he hunted gazelle in Uganda. He went to
Africa in the company of Count Salm-Salm.

"The hunting there, in Galicia, at the eccentric count's place!

Age-old oaks, untouched for generations! Some trees, I swear, were so large that three people together couldn't reach around their trunks! And so many wild boars that the forest literally stank of them. And the deer—you couldn't even count them! Listen! One time a lieutenant—I forget his name—was on the edge of an oak grove and missed a wild boar. The beast charged him, the lieutenant climbed a tree, clung to a branch, and started screaming. His feet were dangling not far off the ground, the boar charged, and he had tusks—I swear, *that* long! I know, because all of a sudden the beast turned toward me so I killed him with a shot straight in the heart and later I measured those tusks. And man, was that beast heavy! He names a figure. Not everybody knows the weight of game, but they all laugh, especially Major Rukavina, who apparently is also a passionate hunter. He taps Willy on his back, and winks from under his thick black eyebrows: "Knock it off, Willy!"

So Kottfuss changes the subject. He now speaks again about the little village inhabited mostly by Jews in black caftans, where there reigned a famous *tsadik* or wonder-rabbi who used to sit on a throne with carved and gilded wooden arms upholstered in red velvet in an absolutely empty hall. His footstool was also covered in velvet with a beautiful golden braid. It is possible that this story referred to another time and place, perhaps to the official visit of the Austro-Hungarian ambassador at the court of Sultan Abdul-Hamid or perhaps the Shah of Persia, of which photographs were published in periodicals, so that the story about the silver beard of the alleged patriarchal wonder-rabbi was stitched together, doubtfully—perhaps derived from Constantinople, and not referring at all to a small village in the midst of forests and marshes, called Monasterzyska or perhaps Brody, where once upon a time the Ninth Regiment of Archduke Albrecht's Dragoons had been stationed and a new second lieutenant from Vienna, Wilhelm Kottfuss Freiherr von Kottvizza, served his obligatory one-year service. Or perhaps it referred to the period when the regiment was stationed in Bukovina, for instance at Czernovitz—or perhaps at Sadagora or even Kimpolung. There it was that on behalf of his colonel and at his instructions, Willy gave thanks for the prayers spoken by the wonder-rabbi in the synagogue on the name day of His Imperial Majesty, in the summer of 1912. Entering the great hall of the rabbi's manor, he noticed the retinue of servants of the rabbi, most odd people, posted along the walls. Kottfuss maintained that they wore white stockings and black silk caftans and fur hats made of foxtails. Having entered, Willy stopped in front of the patriarch's throne and saluted according to the rules. At precisely that moment he realized that Jews bare their heads only before the Almighty, so he quickly donned the dragoon's helmet that until then, according to regulations, he had held in the crook of his left arm; later, again standing to attention, he made a short speech that he had previously memorized, while the wonder-rabbi listened from his throne, in silence and completely motionless. Had it not been for the blinking of his red eyelids without lashes and the slight clicking of his tongue, Kottfuss might have thought him dead for years and propped up between the arms of his chair like a mummy or a wax effigy.

Some of those present now leave Mother Bezsi's tavern. Kottfuss turns to the left. Out of sheer curiosity he intends to look at the clay pit. Partly from curiosity, partly from boredom. For little is really happening right now. Nothing except the war (but the war seems really suspended, like a project, a foreboding or perhaps a promise). Nothing except worries about supply services, the railways, and the gendarmerie, which has to exercise increased vigilance. The day before yesterday (Mother Bezsi spoke about it, and she knows everything first and most accurately) near the Danube (and Fehertemplom is only ten kilometers distant from it as the crow flies; at Bazias on the Danube is the end of the railway line from Temesvar via Fehertemplom, the realm stops there, everything stops there, the river is very wide, and on its other bank is the kingdom of Serbia), the gendarmes caught three suspects, undoubtedly Serbians, and this morning they were hanged near the barn of one Niemeyer, the local magnate, a German from the Banat. A girl was arrested and was to have been executed, but because of the suspicion that she was a student from Serbia, disguised in a peasant woman's clothing, she was sent under guard to Zagreb, where experts will no doubt find out who she is and what she was up to in our country.

Somebody in Mother Bezsi's tavern (probably a civilian unknown to any of those present, even to Mother Bezsi—so many strangers around now, you have to be careful!) says that perhaps the young gypsy girl found in the clay pit was mixed up in some spying directed by the Black Hand straight from Belgrade or Nis. The Black Hand is everywhere! So now we have this to cope with, too. Willy Kottfuss wants to look at the clay pit, about which all kinds of suspicions have arisen, and almost a legend.

So they are now walking, all three of them (because Emil R. has been persuaded to come, too—without enthusiasm, in view of the increasing heat). They are walking along Gypsy Street, white with dust, in the direction of the town brickworks, past one-story houses with gardens full of wilting sunflowers, and then across cornfields. In places the fields are covered with yellowish white stubble, completely burnt, emitting a sharp smell, the cadaverous smell of drought, the foulness of intense heat that small black flies buzzing and jumping in the air seem to enjoy. They walk in silence because in such an intense heat one loses the desire to chatter and becomes indifferent to everything— the outbreak of war with Serbia, the prospect of imminent departure for the front. Every word, every thought is unimportant and tiring.

So they are walking along the expanse of china-white heat, among the stench of rubbish heaps and dust, regretting the unnecessary decision to look at the dried-out clay pit where perhaps not even a trace remains of the recent event. Why should they care about the death of a girl they didn't know, killed by some person unknown and for an unknown reason?

But none of them decides to turn back, they are too lazy to do so. Wilhelm Kottfuss, parting the dust-covered twigs of bushes, leads the way through the thorny groves of dwarf acacias covered with spotted black pods and yellowing leaves twisted by the heat. Following him is Zdenek Kocourek, wiping sweat from his face. Emil R. is at the rear.

"I wonder," says Kocourek, "if tomorrow, the day after, or in a few days' time, when the war has obliterated all other impressions, this aimless walk through these bushes, without any clear motive except vague thoughts about what happened here a couple of days ago—a probable crime—won't remain in our memories as the most permanent trace. Why? I don't know. But such things happen in that silly thing called the human memory."

Walking with his head hung down, Emil R. is thinking: "The hotel in which Svidrigayloff in *Crime and Punishment* spent his last night, was called the Adrianopol. Strange how this name affects me. Absurdly. Why does it matter that it was called 'Adrianopol'? And yet . . . That's probably why I've called this whole period of my life right now 'Adrianopol.' When I tried to write a poem on the train here from Trieste: 'A circle of empty lips / the wonder of empty eyelids / the skin peeled off your face when you were asleep / the empty lampshade . . . a lamp in the corridor of the Adrianopol Hotel.' I tore up the paper I wrote it down on, so I can't remember the rest. If there was anything more, that is. I didn't have to serve in the war. With my state of health, any doctor would have given me a certificate, but I didn't want to do it, in spite of Mama's pleas and the advice of my friends. No, I made this choice in order to immerse myself in it all, to leave all else behind. This is how I explain it to myself. The Adrianopol Hotel, with only one exit. When an animal feels its time is up, it hides, leaves its hole, burrows in thickets, and wants to be alone, for it knows that nothing and no one can help it. If one considers the war a thicket of such absurd and completely indifferent events that occupy one's time and thoughts, well, I chose it deliberately. 'Adrianopol'—but in a more modern version."

"You're probably right about memory, Zdenek," says Kott-fuss, stopping and looking around (dried cornstalks obstruct the view). "On maneuvers in Galicia years ago I walked with Lieutenant Hussak through a cornfield just like this and stumbled on the carcass of a dog. It lay in the path, and as the heat was almost as bad as now, it had decomposed and it stank. We raised swarms of flies, those green and blue ones. I took out my handkerchief and plugged my nose, we walked on, and—you won't believe me—that apparently trivial image has stuck in my memory as the foremost impression from the maneuvers. Why? Perhaps you could explain it, Zdenek. For you must admit that this fascination with details can't be fortuitous."

"If I didn't know you so well, Willy, I might have to accuse you of decadent tastes. There is a whole movement in art that is fascinated by death, if you see what I mean. It began, I believe, with Baudelaire. Dissolution—don't you see—and the macabre. But you don't read poems, do you? Perhaps all of us are prone to mystification. To self-mystification. And we succumb to crazy moods. I, for instance . . ."

Emil R. is not listening to their conversation. He is thinking.

". . . I mentioned my various moods to Zdenek a few times when I tried to define my feelings honestly. He can probably guess certain matters, although he had no opportunity to verify anything with his own eyes, so in his own way he ascribes my moods to various creative crises that in fact had accompanied the problem I have named 'Adrianopol.' He agreed, finally, that war may be considered a kind of catharsis. And that the toil and physical effort may help me recover my equilibrium. He himself, as I see it, does not expect anything like this. I sense in him a state of growing apathy, a resignation or acceptance of fate that I had never observed in him before. 'I'll probably die in this adventure,' he said, 'but one way or another, we all will meet the same destiny.' 'Why?' I asked. 'Why do you passively accept such a possibility?' 'I refuse to kill anybody in this war,' he said, 'and you must admit that anyone adopting such an attitude from the outset shouldn't have any illusions.' I didn't contradict him. 'But to you,' he added after a while, 'such a manly adventure can only be of benefit.' He doesn't really understand my situation."

Willy Kottfuss is continuing his conversation:

"Perhaps you're partly right, Zdenek, when you insist that I consider war just another sport. It might seem so. But don't exaggerate, my friend, don't exaggerate. If need be, one might agree that in war there are certain elements of the chase, even conditions that are objectively fairer: the game is an equal adversary. When I was in Africa . . ." And he begins to tell how in Kenya or Uganda he met a lion or some other predator. In any case, in this one instance he had felt a certain satisfaction from the awareness that his adversary might forestall him: should he react one second too late, the lion might attack first and tear him to pieces.

"But he didn't tear you to pieces?" asked Zdenek, laughing.

"No, because I had an excellent weapon, a Schönauer, nine point six. As far as shooting rifles are concerned . . ." He continues with enthusiasm, praising the superiority of the Schönauer over a Winchester used by his best friend, Toni Salm-Salm. "Haven't you any premonitions regarding the war?" asks Kocourek, interrupting Kottfuss's monologue. The other man hesitates for a moment, then shakes his head: "None, absolutely none. Anyway, I never have premonitions," he says and laughs.

They walk on, closely followed by a bunch of stark naked gypsy children, black as pickaninnies, very graceful on the whole, especially one little girl, probably ten years old, slim and agile. Her eyes have a strange expression, combining fear and a half-adult encouragement.

"Let's give them something to get rid of them," says Kottfuss, and he proceeds to throw a handful of coins on the path. The children pick up the coins amid commotion and confusion. The little girl turns around and runs laughing toward Kerti Street, clasping her booty in her fist, while the remaining children, pushing each other with their elbows and shouting, extend their hands for more. One of the officers throws them a few cigarettes. When the officers resume their walk, the whole cluster of children follows, while shouting and chasing one another. But they keep their distance and watch the officers' movements keenly, then disappear around the wooden storage hut of the brickworks.

Only one little gypsy boy, dark-skinned, curly-haired, and naked, continues to walk behind the three officers. He will accompany them at a distance of several steps, more out of curiosity than in expectation of another gift of money. He will stop and crouch whenever the officers turn around, then disappear in the corn and reappear at some turn of the path.

Passing in a wide arc the first of the two clay pits, the path becomes a series of ruts produced, after the spring thaws, by the wheels of carts used for the transport of bricks. These two parallel furrows, in which blades of grass burnt by the sun grow in small tufts, disintegrate into yellowish rubble and dust as one walks over them. From beyond the turn, one can clearly see the pink chimney crowning the low buildings of the brick-yard. The whole compound, with its sheds made of narrow strips of wood and a sizable yard, is empty. Only a large white cat can be seen walking along a thin board fixed to the walls of a storage shed. The path narrows again, and wheel ruts turn off toward the storage sheds. It is stifling in the dense bushes. The three officers are still walking on, trying to drive away swarms of tiny but insistent flies. Dried ears of corn, half-eaten by starlings, rustle as they are pushed aside by the officers' shoulders, then disintegrate, scattering dust. The gypsy boy continues to follow cautiously, his thumb in his mouth. He looks around in astonishment and fear.

"It must be around here somewhere," says Baron Kottfuss, who parts the acacia twigs to look down. Indeed, one can now see a sharp declivity, covered with grass and weeds, its topsoil giving way under the feet of the officers. At the very bottom there is darkness.

The sunflowers loom black against the sun behind the brick-yard, in the open fields stretching toward the Danube. The heat is still rising. Baron Kottfuss takes off his red forage cap and fans himself. Then he lights a cigarette. His match falls in a straight line to the very bottom of the clay pit.

Meanwhile military train number — rolls into the station of Fehertemplom. It comes from Temesvar. The station crew, mobilized two days before, know that, owing to a derailment between Versecs and Moravica, all trains that day have been sent by a roundabout route — not via Versecs and Novo Selo toward Pancevo, but via Fehertemplom. Hence all the commotion.

Some of the trains got stalled on the way. On telegraphed instructions from headquarters, others, after reaching the Fifth Army on the Danube and Sava, will be directed immediately to the north via Senta, Szeged, Szolnok, and Hatvan, or via Kecs-kemet and Budapest, toward the Carpathians. This gives rise to talk about war with Russia.

This train, having come here by accident, directed by orders and counterorders, stops at the station of Fehertemplom. The buffers of a very long series of boxcars hit one against the other with a metallic sound. The locomotive, with a smokestack that looks like a dirty gypsy kettle, whistles plaintively. A squadron of Honved artillery has arrived from distant Nagyvarad with a seven-hour delay. On certain flatcars stand guns and caissons covered with tarpaulins. On a few others there are field kitchens surrounded by busy cooks tired by the heat and covered with dust. They are shouting and swearing in Magyar and Romanian. A stout officer in a brand-new field uniform with a tangle of straps across his breast and also a map case, a pair of binoculars, and something else that sways and glistens in the sun, shouts, standing on legs in yellow leather leggings.

The whistle of the locomotive and the metallic sound of the buffers—like chords, or an extended musical scale announcing or perhaps predicting something—can be heard as far away as the cornfields behind the brickworks at the Gypsy Quarter. The sheds built of thin patches and strips of wood are transparent to the light and mostly empty. Only here and there lie heaps of bricks. Nobody is working in the yard, over which hangs a reddish light like the reflection of a sunset.

Just then, as if to accompany the whistle of the locomotive from the nearby station, Reserve Second Lieutenant Zdenek Kocourek—in civilian life a journalist and poet—begins to recite from memory the order and sequence of field, garrison, and parade marches prescribed for various festivities and religious and court occasions: one of the subjects required at examinations for the officers' academy.

"One: religious march. Two: march by squadrons and columns. Three: march by regimental columns. Four: assault march. Five: funeral march."

("In black clothing or parade uniform, holding the shako according to regulations in the left hand, the left arm bent, one proceeds with a slow, brisk step in time to the march," thinks Emil R.)

"Funeral decorations trimmed with the ritual silver braid. The coffin on a pedestal covered with a cloth, or perhaps on a gun carriage or a stretcher, lined with black velvet. A procession into the labyrinth of mirrored passages, or perhaps to the back of a stage or a masonic lodge. I seem to hear the sound of hammering and at the same time, in the background, Beethoven's Funeral March. The dry corncobs emit just such a mournful rustle, like a musical phrase repeated over and over again, only on a smaller, almost ridiculous scale, because imitative and derivative. I have been haunted for some time by the picture of a catafalque, covered with a black shroud. Since that evening when L. and I sailed toward a rocky, uninhabited island to spend the night there. L. and I, and next to us in the boat two sailors rowing. I stood at the bow while L. sat turned away from me, trailing her hand in the water. And just then our little island appeared against the evening sky like a black catafalque. The two or three solitary trees, probably cypresses battered by the winds and half dried, even seemed like the snuffed tapers in Böcklin's picture Isle of the Dead. It was L. who had insisted that we disembark on that rocky islet, not me. Lieutenant F.,

hiding his surprise and maybe even disapproval of that slightly
wild idea of L.'s, agreed good-naturedly, provided the boat with
the two sailors, and suggested we take warm blankets. He worried because evenings on the sea tend to be chilly at this time
of the year, especially when the bora is blowing. He promised
that in the morning, after night exercises near the island of Krk,
he would send a boat for us, and then put us ashore at Lovrana
on his return to the base at Lussinpiccolo. I remember the low
black silhouette of the torpedo boat against the setting sun, and
Lieutenant F. standing by the gangplank and waving to us. Also
the large bright green star shining just above the island to which
we were sailing. I looked at it all the time, avoiding the eyes of
the sailors, for fear they might guess something. Yet this thought
was quite absurd. What could have they known about the two
of us?"

Carrying what has the appearance of a coffin, the officers
begin to whistle the famous Funeral March written many years
ago, and now played on the occasion of funerals of persons of
a certain rank. It is played by one hundred and two regimental
bands of the one hundred and two imperial and royal infantry
regiments, as well as twenty-six bands of the imperial and royal
rifle battalions, sixteen hussar bands, fifteen dragoon bands, and
eleven lancer bands, not counting the bands of the four regiments of Imperial Tyrolean Rifles, of the Imperial and Royal
Landwehr, and units of field artillery, howitzers, and fortress
artillery. The Funeral March for the generals dead of old age;
for the faded heroes of 1859 and 1866, participants in the defeats
at Magenta, Solferino, and Sadowa and the victories at Novara
and Custoza, as well as the Bosnian expedition; for the colonels
and lieutenant colonels, majors, captains, and cavalry commanders who died in the capital, as well as in provincial garrisons
from various illnesses, also in duels—with the exception however
of suicides, whose funerals are never accompanied by regimental
bands. The Funeral March is a slow procession on the pavements
of the cities of the monarchy on the banks of the Litava, along
the elegant Opernring and on the dust-covered cobbles of some
winding street leading to a cemetery gate in some small provincial hamlet where the Imperial and Royal Army is represented. Therefore also at Fehertemplom, famous for its large
and lively frontier garrison, many wine presses, sunflower oil

factories, grain mills, and great, immeasurable boredom reaching
far, far beyond the horizon during all four seasons of the year.
Ungarisch Weisskirchen = Fehertemplom = Bela Crkva. And in
distant Brod as well or perhaps at Monasterzyska, when that
famous march was played at the funeral of a certain officer of
the archduke's Bukovina Dragoons who had drowned in the
local river on the day of St. Stephen the Martyr, when the ice
broke under him and his horse. According to Willy Kottfuss, it
was a matter of a wager; the officer, apparently named Kalina,
was bald, sported long black-tinted whiskers, and couldn't pro-
nounce the letter r. So much remains of him. *Requiescat in pace.*

At about the same time the *S.M.S. Bodrog,* the gunboat of
the Danube river fleet, fires another salvo toward the capital of
Serbia. Its thunder resounds over the water and its echo can be
heard in the houses of Pancevo, Belgrade, and Zemun, after
which it returns to the river. The echo will rebound from the
hills of Kalemegdan. The roof of some Byzantine church on the
other bank will glisten so brightly for a moment that a young
officer of the imperial and royal artillery regiment will quickly
have to shut his eyes glued to the field glass, for fear of being
blinded by the glare. And somebody is running on the Belgrade
waterfront, waving his arm and probably shouting. But the
breeze from the water obliterates his voice as well as the small
gray puff of the salvo. Then the sailors reload the gun pointed
at the Royal palace. But King Peter has already departed
for Nis.

The three officers are still standing on the edge of the second
clay pit. The deep ravine, its sides overgrown with dwarf acacias,
climbing wild hops, and bindweed, is gray with dust. The mucky
slope gives way as they descend. The officers stoop in unison and,
screening their eyes from the sun, look down. At the very bottom
of the clay pit, like a flower in a buttonhole, grows a lone sunflower, somewhat battered and looking like an angry bird. From
under the feet of the officers a small sparrow rises with loud
chirping that sounds irritated, and flies away, undulating in the
air over the cornfields.

And then the sergeant of the Royal Gendarmerie, Istvan
Vilajcich, hidden in the bushes, will rise to his feet. He is a
dark, portly man in a tight-fitting uniform, sporting a moustache
that might be the pride of the whole Hungarian gendarmerie.

Apart from whiskers that reach to his earlobes, the sergeant also has sideburns, as black as tar, that look as if glued to his cheeks. Gendarme Vilajcich obediently salutes the officers standing above the pit. He can't keep his eyes open, so tired is he from heat and brandy. He did not sleep well the previous night because of the mobilization decree and the order for increased vigilance.

"Is this the spot?" asks Kottfuss.

"Yes, sir! At your service!" Vilajcich straightens up, not moving his hand from the rim of his gendarme's hat with the cock feathers. On his breast shine two medals: the jubilee medal issued in 1908 on the sixtieth anniversary of His Gracious Majesty's accession to the throne, and another one for long service. A ray of sun glistens on both medals, hurting the officers' eyes. A third source of glare is the buckle of Sergeant Vilajcich's belt. When at last he stops saluting, all three foci of glare are extinguished at once. Lieutenant Kocourek blinks.

"Here's the spot. At your service!" Vilajcich repeats and points with his hand. "Over there. At the very bottom, next to that wild rose bush."

On his thick, moist lips, hardly visible under the black mustache, a smile appears. It blossoms on them almost like the rose that down below, at the bottom of the clay pit, has not yet entirely wilted. It is a somewhat enigmatic smile, perhaps ambiguous because tactless under the circumstances, but the officers will not notice.

"Somebody really did a job on her," adds Vilajcich, who unexpectedly licks his lips. Probably his lips are dry from the heat that is steadily increasing. The sun stands at its zenith exactly over the clay pit, as well as over the deck of the *Bodrog*. At this very moment from the far Serbian bank, from the right side, from some bushes probably beyond the mouth of the Sava, some machine-gun blasts resound. Without reaching the deck of the *Bodrog*, the bullets skim the water or plunge into it. The sailors in the armored deck turret point their gun in that direction. The young officer still looks through his field glasses. Another, bending over, writes something in a notebook propped on his knee.

Vilajcich clears his throat as if embarrassed, and the smile disappears from his heat-swollen face. The gypsy boy who had been following the officers, hiding in the bushes and suddenly emerging at the bends of the path, now appears on the other side of the clay pit. He peeps out from among the long stems of a weed, then crouches down, scared, and again shows his black, curly head. For a moment it looks as if he wants to run down the slope, but Sergeant Vilajcich notices him and calls out something in Hungarian that to the officers, who do not know that language, sounds like thunder or the roar of a lion, ending with something like *terem-te-te!* The sergeant stoops to pick up a rock and throw it at the boy, but he has already disappeared in the bushes, which continue to sway for a while, scattering dust, then finally close up even tighter their gray-stained, silver green wall of leaves. A bird rises with a whirr and flies away.

Even so, Vilajcich cannot deny himself the pleasure of throwing the rock. After he has finally found it in the grass, he throws it straight ahead, where a moment ago the gypsy boy's head could be seen. The rock describes a wide arc over the clay pit and falls to the bottom, on the same spot where the day before yesterday the body of Marika Huban had been found. All three officers are now looking at the spot.

"He's escaped, the little rascal!" says Vilajcich, dusting his palms. Then, screening his eyes, he looks down. His stone has raised some yellow dust that hangs in the air a few seconds, then disappears like a pierced balloon or a soap bubble. The sergeant straightens up, adjusts his belt, and says:

"She wore some beads. That's why . . ." The officers guess that the sergeant is referring to the boy, who might have wanted to recover the beads scattered in the grass.

At that moment the sailors on the *Bodrog* fire an accurate salvo into Belgrade, over which a streak of black smoke shot with red rises into the pale blue sky. At the same time Lieutenant Baron von Kottfuss reaches into the pocket of his blue uniform jacket to produce his cigarette case, but suddenly stops, astonished, raising his light eyebrows, while in the pocket his fingers freeze.

"What's this?" he asks himself, or perhaps only thinks it. His fingers have encountered a coral bead. "How did I get it?" he wonders, rubbing his brow. A moment later he waves his hand:

"Ah, I remember!"

In the headquarters of the southern front, in a quiet house

surrounded by guards at Tuzla, General Oskar Potiorek sits down at a table covered with maps. They are Austrian maps— "specials," scale 1:75,000, and "general," scale 1:200,000—encompassing the southern districts of Hungary, parts of Croatia and Bosnia, and the northern regions of the kingdom of Serbia. The red rectangles and squares depicting his own units are concentrated in the region Neusatz-Peterwardein and are moving in the general direction of Ruma-Mitrovica-Jarak. A sizable unit of cavalry is forming north of Belgrade in the region of Zemun and Pancevo. Troop trains bringing the Eighth Prague Corps are on the way; some have already passed Budapest. The whole Croatian Thirteenth Corps was directed yesterday evening toward the Drina. The latest messages state that Serbian patrols are penetrating across the Drina into Bosnia and Hercegovina. General Frank, commander of the Fifth Army, is expected shortly at Tuzla. Artillery General Oscar Potiorek wipes sweat from his forehead with a handkerchief. He wants to speak to headquarters, then he revokes the order. He is pacing nervously in the large hut covered with soft Bosnian carpets.

Between Klenak and Sabac, Fifth Army pioneers are collecting material for building a pontoon bridge. Here and there, single shots are fired across the river. Sometimes from the Serbian shore a machine gun rattles and goes silent almost at once. An empty black canoe is rocking midstream in the Sava.

Just as General Potiorek gets his connection with the Seventh Corps headquarters at Peterwardein and learns that their unit left the city less than an hour before, to proceed by car to Mitrovica, Second Lieutenant Zdenek Kocourek says as he lights a cigarette:

"You must have heard about the White Lady?"

"Of course," says Kottfuss. "She appears, as far as I know, in Slovakia, in the castle of Krasna Horka or somewhere around there. Have you met her?" He laughs.

"Not her but another—the one who wanders about on the night express trains between Szolnok and Bekescsaba, and who lies in wait at stations. This is a different White Lady, modern and apparently quite real. No specter, nothing from a fairy tale, you know. A traveler who predicts death . . ."

"Have you met her? Have you?" laughs Baron Kottfuss.

Emil R. stands next to him, in silence. Gendarme Vilajcich has disappeared.

"Yes and no. You see, she only shows herself to those who are to die. She is death's messenger. Or a modern Fate. Take your choice."

"Where have you read about it? Tell us, Zdenek."

"I can't remember. Maybe I've read it, maybe somebody told me. I don't know now. Anyway, while traveling here by night across the Hungarian plains—you probably know all sorts of strange things happen there—I woke up in a station that we were passing without stopping and I looked out the window. I was alone in the compartment. The train had slowed down and was passing some brightly lit, empty platforms and in this light, very white and spectral, I noticed a woman walking beside the coaches, as if looking for somebody. When our coach passed her, she noticed me and waved a white glove that she had removed from her hand. Our eyes met briefly. I saw clearly how her lips moved behind a white, transparent veil and then curled in a kiss. I leaned out the window. She was still walking along the empty platform, waving her glove, then our train accelerated, and I lost sight of her."

"So what? Obviously, the lady thought the train might stop and then . . . I myself had a similar adventure a few months ago in Moravia. Listen—"

"No," interrupted Kocourek, who was pensive. "I looked at my watch. It was five minutes past two in the morning. At such an hour adventures, as you say, don't occur. Afterward I again dozed off and dreamed about a bewhiskered old Hungarian who told me that the White Lady regularly appears in those regions and that his young son, returning from Pest, had met her, and soon afterward died. My Hungarian of the dream, having said this, covered his face with his hands and began to shake with sobs. I woke up at dawn and the train was nearing Bekescsaba. I thought to myself—"

"So you see, my friend, you must have dreamed it all. I don't believe in predictions or premonitions. A gypsy woman told me two years ago . . ." And Willy Kottfuss begins to tell them, laughing, about a night of drinking with friends after a great shooting party on the estates of Count Andrassy some two years

before, and about an old gypsy who insisted on reading everybody's palm when all the Count's guests were assembled in the
tavern. But Zdenek Kocourek had stopped listening.

The proscenium emits a strange aura (this is after the second
act, and the Burgtheater is saturated with a mixture of smells,
ranging from perfume to the cigar smoke that clings to the
gentlemen's clothes), a ritual aura very different from the spectacle that the actors perform on stage. Emil R., sitting behind
his mother, can see only the right side of the stage. If he leaned
forward, he might also see the left side, but he does not care to
do so now. He is happy with things as they are. Against the
lighted scenery he can see Mrs. Jacobi's head. The councillor's
wife is sitting next to his mother in the front row of the box.
From time to time she puts her hand up to her head, to adjust
her hair. Afterward, her thin fingers in a white glove that
reaches to her elbow slide down her cheek, as if stroking it,
and disappear in the shadow of the box, disclosing another part
of the stage. From where he sits, Emil can see the space in
either of two ways, depending on the focus: in the foreground,
the head and part of Mrs. Jacobi's left shoulder distinctly visible, and the rest as a nebulous, hazy background; or the outlines of the boxes opposite, now vague and remote in the
darkness, then clearer, as the stage materializes sharply in its
glare, while Mrs. J. together with her left ear, the halo of her
coiffure, and her neck dissolve into a shapeless, almost spectral
apparition. In that uncertain light the stars of her earrings
glisten, disclosed by the successive movement of Mrs. J.'s hand
reaching toward her hair; then immediately they vanish.

That year was the time of the old apartment in the Stubenring,
on the mezzanine. The front stairs were covered with a crimson
carpet meticulously cleaned every day, the brass rods shining
on each step. There were mirrors in gold frames and potted
palms on each landing, and for the comfort of aged, obese, or
simply tired tenants, little semicircular sofas covered with
cherry-colored plush, in a shade of red that adorns the collars
and cuffs of the parade dress jackets of the First and Third
Imperial and Royal Dragoons. There, in the Stubenring, a young
man named Emil had been engrossed long ago in the pages of a
Zarathustra stolen from his mother's bookcase, trembling with

the emotion of discovery, then drifting into a state of exaltation. "So this is what it's like. Now I know. Somebody has said
about me everything that is to be said. Finis. Here begins the
requiem. Requies aeterna." Emil had just returned from the
Jesuit convent at Kalksburg, having been dangerously ill with
pneumonia.

Late at night, stealthily, hiding a candle behind a small
Chinese screen, and lying in the circle of shimmering light, young
Emil absorbs greedily the thoughts jotted down on paper by
Nietzsche, a thinker and poet previously unknown to him.

Nearby, behind the double door with the brass Art Nouveau
handle, there sleeps—or perhaps she still lies awake—Emil's
elder sister Elizabeth. In her room the lights are off. The large
crystal chandelier reflects faintly and icily the lights from behind
the windows—those late cabs that pass the house, or perhaps lanterns carried by pedestrians. Bernadette shares L.'s room, but she
doesn't count. Emil pays no attention to her. She is like a small
curled-up animal, only physically present in the neighboring
room. But Lieschen . . .

"What is man?" reads young Emil, propped on his elbow
while lying on his side so the flickering candlelight can fall on
the pages of his book bound in green morocco with gold edges.
"What is man? A collection of diseases that crawl out from his
soul to find fodder here. Who is man? A tangle of serpents that
rarely rest, one next to another. They crawl out, each looking
for prey. Look at this poor body! Everything from which it had
suffered and that it had coveted, the soul explains by the wish
to kill and by nostalgia for the knife . . ."

"Yes!" thinks young Emil, who shivers. "What a revelation!
This is the great truth—how terrible when discovered! The sudden clarity! Somebody is talking to me, speaking to me from the
pages of this bewitching book (the clock on the bedside table
says precisely nine minutes past midnight and it is Tuesday,
one day after the new moon, and behind the windows the night
is black because a thaw is coming), somebody has disclosed a
truth I didn't know but subconsciously anticipated, afraid to
descend into the tunnels and dark spaces without any hope of
redemption, as Father Cornelius Blatt would certainly say. Yes,
yes, yes! *Je suis condamné, maudit!* What a relief to realize this
at last! My feeble body emanates what so far I have dared not

name even in my most secret thoughts. And here I find a man, an undoubted genius, who has disclosed that truth to me openly, fearlessly, aloud . . ."

Fifteen years old. In the Stubenring, on the first floor. One night in November 1908. Or is it already the first week of December? Nietzsche. A volume bound in green morocco with gold edges. Most of the books in Mrs. R.'s bookcase are similarly bound. Only a few volumes—by mistake or perhaps on a whim—are bound in pale pink linen with decorated spines in the fashion of the 1890s. On the shelves there are also a few books in a larger format, bound in black. On their cover is an engraved Ariadne unwinding her thread, with silver gladioli in the background. This composition is a kind of *ex libris* of Attorney R., the master of the house. The black books are the classics: Goethe, Schiller, Grillparzer.

Lieschen is in the next room. While Emil reads and meditates, she is probably dreaming. Her brother assumes that she is dreaming about a winged cat that is stretching and sharpening its claws, or perhaps sniffing at the burrow of a mole. The cat will bury its claws in the soft fur of the mole as soon as it emerges. The eyes and ears of a cat. A cat's paws. A cat's tail.

In that room—formerly a small sitting room, but now that both girls are older, their bedroom, dressing room, as well as reception room—stand two painted white beds. Young girls' beds full of sleep and warmth, covered with blue bedspreads with borders of white rabbit fur. By the beds lie animal-skin rugs, each different. When their mother brought them from town, Lieschen without a moment's hesitation selected the one that looks like a tiger skin, leaving for Detta a uniformly grayish skin. Upon rising, Lieschen runs her feet over the long, dry hairs of the pseudo-tiger (or is it an authentic young specimen of this predatory species?) and does not quickly interrupt her game: sitting in a nightgown on the edge of the bed, she half closes her eyes with enjoyment and, wrinkling her nose, caresses the fur with her bare feet. Detta, if she could, would take a long stride to avoid stepping on her grizzly polecat's skin (or maybe it is that of an ordinary cat?). Before putting her foot on it, she thinks about it, hesitates, sits curled up and uneasy and then, as it happens occasionally, Lieschen jumps across the two beds, bumps into her sister, and sends her sprawling onto the rug. Detta falls, gets up clumsily in total silence, and without looking at her sister, begins to put on her winter underwear.

On the wall over Lieschen's bed hangs a small Oriental tapestry, silver on an azure blue background. Mr. R. brought it back from his journey to Bosnia in 1894. Next to it, above Detta's head, hangs a picture of the Virgin Mary of Maria-Trost.

Next to the bed on which Lieschen now is or is not asleep lie her slippers, the color of periwinkle in bloom. On the hills above Kreuzbach, the two of them, Lieschen and Emil, in the early spring two years ago . . . He picked a small bunch of periwinkles and fearfully, almost in a panic at doing something outrageous, offered it to his sister. Lieschen accepted the gift without a word, got to her feet, and ran with the flowers along the path down the slope. There, in front of a beer garden, several elderly gentlemen had taken off their coats and were playing ninepins. The knocking of the balls and the falling ninepins could be heard by the children while they were playing in the woods. Lieschen, passing her father, made a curtsy in front of one of the beer drinkers, a stout bald man, and handed him the little bouquet. Emil observed her from behind a big spruce.

During the picnic at Kreuzbach, Lieschen got her shoes wet and her knees dirty from the sticky clay. Emil remembers every detail: his sister's wet soiled socks and the brown shoes with a half-torn pompom. Hopping on one leg, holding onto a branch, she shook a small clod of earth from the shoe. On the tree trunks, beads of resin glistened in the sun.

"This looks like thick honey," said Lieschen, who licked a glob of resin, screwed up her face, and gave the resin to her brother. "Eat it at once!" she said in a tone of voice that forbore any protest. Obediently, Emil ate some; it glued his teeth together so that he almost choked. "Another little piece!" urged Lieschen. He swallowed it. Then Lieschen, cleaning her hands on the grass, said, "That's enough. I allow you to throw the rest away." Then she stroked his head.

Emil stops reading Nietzsche and listens carefully. He bites his lips. He frequently lifts his head and stares at the crack under his sisters' bedroom door. But there is silence in the next room and the crack remains dark. Even so he thinks that

Lieschen has got up stealthily from bed, come to the door, and is now peering through the keyhole. He imagines her standing there in her nightgown, her hair in curlers, and thinks he hears her breathing, as if she had put her pale, thin lips against the brass fitting of the door.

Behind the windows, crows have settled in the trees along the Ring and are cawing now. If one looked out, one might see them clearly against the snow. Black hieroglyphics or maybe musical signs among the bare branches. One of the birds opens its beak, as if yawning, then closes one thin eyelid over the protruding eye. It pushes its large head into the bristling collar of its feathers. It must be dreaming because it shakes itself again and again. If one had the time and the patience, one could watch the bird until it stops its nightmare-plagued dozing and, spreading its wings, flies away noiselessly over the Danube like a large bat.

The round pompom on Lieschen's left shoe has finally fallen off and is lost. The shoes lie one against the other, their toes touching, forming an obtuse angle. What does this mean? Can one ascribe to this fact any significance at all? Nietzsche might have found an answer.

Detta's shoes, on the contrary, are extremely well-bred and correct. They still have their pompoms. They look like clean toy kittens side by side next to a fireplace or straight from the box in which they came from the shop in the Kärtnerstrasse.

The windows of the room overlook the solid buildings of the Imperial and Royal Ministry of War. Through the partially drawn curtains, streetlamps glow in their halo of mist. This, however, is only an illusion. The night is frosty and clear, and the air glassy. The material of the curtains and the moisture on the windowpanes combine to give the impression of a fluffy fog.

Some windows of the ministry are still lit even at this late hour, and their curtains are drawn. One can count the lit windows: two on the first floor on the right, three on the second floor to the left. There is silence, and coming from afar—from Aspernbrücke and the Danube Canal—a cab is approaching. As one can tell from the rhythm of the hooves on the frozen street, it is one of the one-horse cabs so common in Vienna. If one rushed to the window and pulled aside the curtain, one could see it clearly. Now it is passing the family house in the Stubenring. The clatter of hooves increases, then dies away. For a moment one hears it faintly in the distance, then total silence returns.

No one will go to the window that night.

Yet somebody does come to the window and moves the curtain on the opposite side, on the second floor of the Imperial and Royal Ministry of War. It is a high-ranking officer who just left the table where he had been reading until this late hour when, from over the Danube, the first gusts of wind come announcing an imminent thaw. The officer has been reading a strategic study written by Lieutenant Colonel Csicserics von Bacsany, a former observer for the Imperial and Royal Army attached to General Kuropatkin's staff. Tomorrow or the next day he will give a shattering assessment of the new military tactics derived from the Russo-Japanese War. Infantry hiding in trenches? And what about the serried ranks marching beautifully to the accompaniment of the thudding drums? What about the cavalry? Bah! Csicserics must have succumbed to the poisons of Manchuria, must have been saturated by the yellow nights of panic, have listened to the screams from the thick bushes, seen the withdrawals in gale and snowstorm, the Russkis' bearskins covering the field of Mukden like the smallpox! But that was an exceptional terrain, quite different, contaminated by plague, while for us in Europe, even if it did come to war . . .! The staff officer approaches the window, moves the curtain, and looks down on the empty Stubenring. On the other side of the road, behind the curtains of the house opposite, a light is shining with a reddish glow. So somebody is still awake at this late hour. Away to the left, the tops of the trees in the Schwarzenberg Park are visible. Against a whitish background one can see the motionless crows. One of them lifts himself up, adjusts his position on the branch while slightly spreading his wings, then drops his head and becomes motionless again. The officer leaves the window and returns to his urgent work.

"When did this temptation beset me for the first time? Was it during the summer trip through the Grossglockner and by Heiligenblut up to Dölsach, and from there in several carriages to Tolbach? Myself with father in one cab, Mama with Lieschen in a second, Mr. and Mrs. Jacobi in the third. Detta, who had mumps, remained in Vienna under the care of Miss Traut. I could think of only one way to liberate myself once and for all, although I didn't yet realize, as I did a year later, what was at stake.

"That time at Tolbach I wandered one evening to the local cemetery, overgrown with tall mountain grasses and herbs smelling like a child's bathwater. There were bumblebees everywhere. I thought that some of the gravestones had rotted away to such an extent that they had reverted to childlike dimensions. The coffins of old people have changed with the passage of years into white or light blue boxes, containing the brittle, thin bones of infants. And at night, when a full moon rises from over the Dolomites, these childish graves begin to babble, slowly, one word an hour, with deliberation, like infants. Phrases taken from the store of memory, shreds of something that has or has not happened, that has never been said, but grows now like a soft white fungus. I even imagined broken sentences, perhaps declarations of love, gossip . . .

"In the evening of that day, in the inn at Tolbach, I tried to write on this subject the first poem in my life. I even thought that I had created something but afterward, when I reread it, I saw that I had failed. So I tore it up.

"Yes, it was in the Alps, and not at Grado a year later. Only not at Tolbach, but some two days later when we spent the night in a hotel high up on a mountain peak at Pustertal: our horses had difficulty getting our carriages up there.

"It was when L. propped her shoulder against the stone wall of a balcony overlooking a rushing stream. Some hundred meters below, a waterfall roared over pewter-colored rocks. The cascade fell in sections, from one level to another, thundering down the slippery walls. It was a magnificent romantic sight, or so I must have thought at the time, following L. to the balcony below the enclosed veranda of the hotel where our parents and the Jacobis were sitting. And only when I stood next to L., or rather closely behind her, as if fearing that . . . It was then. I still feel some of the enchantment: an authentic Gothic scene! And afterward . . .

"Mama decided that it was time to go back. Suddenly it got cold, a strong wind blew from the glaciers, born somewhere high in the clouds, and woolly balls of mist rolled soundlessly toward the west. If Mama had not appeared next to us unexpectedly—I thought she was still on the veranda—had she not come to sit next to me . . . I don't know . . .

"It turned cold suddenly when the clouds crept over the sun and the mountains around us deadened and turned gray. The waterfall turned a steely gray and became menacing. It had lost some of its fairylike colors but at the same time acquired hues that I might liken to an organ requiem. Perhaps this simile entered my head just now, years later, I'm not sure. A Gothic kind of Alpine death.

"Mama was visibly shivering under her fur coat. Father, I remember, had already gone with the Jacobis to a restaurant further down, because here near the top they didn't serve hot dishes, since the winter season had not yet begun. I remember the high-pitched, almost black roof of that inn in the valley below us. It stood over a swiftly running stream, probably flowing from the foot of the waterfall, some hundred meters below the rocky balcony where we had stood a short while before. When the three of us had made our way down over the stony ledges turned slippery by the wet mist that within seconds had obscured that whole magnificent view, my father, already settled in the other inn, was talking to the head waiter, who was excitedly explaining to him that the gentlemen who had just arrived by car were none other than Archduke Leopold Salvator himself, his aide-de-camp, and His Excellency Julius Latcher von Lauendorf, the Minister of Defense. Mrs. Martha Jacobi raised her gold-rimmed lorgnette and from the steps of the veranda observed the three officers entering the hotel, their spurs clinking.

"And more: fragments of landscape, absurdly remembered with clarity. A branch of a fir tree brushing against the window of the glass-fronted veranda. A segment of the meadow brightly lit up as the clouds moved away to uncover the sun. At one edge of that view seen through the small metal-framed windowpanes that looked like tiny stained-glass windows, a sheepdog lying on the grassy slope opposite. And close by, across the table covered with a checkered cloth, Lieschen, her pointed nose red from the cold and chapped at the sides, her narrow, half-closed eyes, set wide apart and truly catlike. And the return of that earlier temptation experienced for the first time up there, over the waterfall in the mountains. And around the two of us all the rest of the company, very excited by the arrival of the archduke and his companions. Whispered exchanges of information and suppositions about them. And the respectful bows of the waiters on approaching the table of the dignitaries. Even a detail of no importance: the archduke had ordered soured milk and hot potatoes, whereupon Mrs. Jacobi, adjudging that to be proof of exceptional distinction, at once ordered the same. Yet all the time I was thinking about one thing only. That if my mother had not joined us . . . When Lieschen, wishing to see the waterfall better, had leaned out over the slippery wall . . . A thought that lasted only half a second. And the beginning or only the intention of a move. That like Abelard and Heloise we two together . . . Or like Romeo and Juliet . . .

"And then the evening at the hotel. After the excitement caused by the departure of the archduke with his retinue, after a series of bows by the manager of the hotel and all the servants, after the assumed indifference to the event of my parents and the Jacobis (their assertions that they had hardly noticed it and would have preferred to be left in peace on the veranda), Lieschen, I remember, declared that one of the military gentlemen had bow legs and a paunch, for which she was at once rebuked by Mama. Behind the windows the evening mists, creeping up tier by tier, layer after chalk-white layer from the mountains, filled the valleys, and finally covered the meadow opposite the hotel. Then it began to grow dark quickly, the mists became first blue, then steely gray. And far away, on the range of mountains opposite, probably in a hut that I had not noticed in daylight, a small twinkling light appeared. Lieschen yawned then, declaring that she was sleepy.

"I was wakened in the night by a downpour beating on the steep roof of our hotel, and by thunder like the roar of an avalanche. There were flashes of light from behind the wooden shutters, which weren't tightly closed. The thunder resounded from the side of the Grossglockner, glum and fierce: a bell ringing the alarm, a bearded giant with a snowy hood pulled over his head. I sat on the bed and listened to that mountain symphony until the downpour ceased abruptly and through the gap in the shutters I saw the stars, cleansed by the rain, very bright and distant. I fell asleep and dreamed of the poem that at dawn I managed to write down in my exercise book.

I cut off my hand, sister mine,
Lest it push you into the abyss.
I gouged out my eyes so they would not sin in looking at you.
I severed both your arms
Lest you should embrace me and be damned for ever.

Something like that. Perhaps the poem was slightly different; repeating it from memory, I may have mixed it up. Later I mislaid this childish piece and never tried to find it again.

"Visiting my family at Graz a few days later, I went to listen to Beethoven's *Missa Solemnis* in the Leechkirche. I listened in growing excitement to the *Agnus Dei,* and the especially impressive *Miserere.* Not far from me sat a priest with an old, wrinkled, medieval face. I watched him from the pew where I was kneeling next to L., watched each movement of his narrow lips and folded hands. I tried to transpose myself, Lieschen, and that priest into the seventeenth century or even the *quattrocento,* and with us the tones of Beethoven's *Miserere* sung by the choir.

"And again, soon after, at Hilmteich: a pond full of swans; children and pensioners sitting on garden seats. And a silly tune, "Anne-Marie," played on mandolins by a group of students, and following it, "When the Hussars . . ." And a friend of my parents, an old colonel, who got up from his bench at our approach and attempted to engage us in conversation. I remember his name: Ferency von Franola. He had a dachshund that Mama stroked but that was kicked quite brutally by Lieschen, who was bored and made faces behind the old man's back. That summer was the first one that was authentic and knowingly sinful. It was then, in the mountain hotel at Pustertal, that I tried to describe my feelings, tried to write them down in a quasi-musical rhythmic verbal study or symphony. Later the same year at Grado I wrote some poems, attempts at a musical image, if it can be so described. The contrast of background: grim Alpine peaks swathed in cloud, an icy night, a star-studded sky after a storm, then a flat sandy Adriatic beach in two colors, dun and blue, soothed by the double murmur of approaching waves thinly bordered with foam; and receding waves that left small bubbles on sand as lifeless as an empty desert.

"My attempts at poetry, I know, were worthless, but at the time I wrote them they filled me with undescribable bliss. I went into a trance. I tried to transform musical impressions into words, into chords reflecting both sounds and colors. At times it seemed to me that at any given moment, with the next one or the one after that, I would reach the peak. Then, discouraged and in despair, I had to admit that it still was not what I wanted.

"The first time, at Pustertal, in the hotel at night, I sat by candlelight (the electricity had been cut off because of the storm) behind the window, from which an almost icy cold already penetrated the room. (In spite of my mother's orders, I had opened the window wide and was thoroughly frozen, with bronchitis again as a result.) Flocks of silvery, black-lined clouds raced across the now clear sky. Flashes of lightning appeared from time to time. I thought: wide-open, astonished eyes of clouds. And I tried to write a poem about it. It seemed to me that the clouds, chased away by the screams of a wild Alpine sorcerer, emitted a long-drawn-out moan, or that they were singing in chorus. I stood in the window and inhaled the air that smelled of snow and ice, until my lungs ached. I enjoyed the physical pain that was growing in me.

"I deluded myself that L. was also awake. That, like myself, she was constantly thinking of that moment when we both stood on the steep rocky platform over the waterfall.

"I felt giddy from these thoughts and had to hold fast to the window frame. The high attic room floated with me in the clouds, over the valley, rising and falling like the gondola of a balloon. I remembered that one of our friends had told us how from curiosity he let himself be persuaded into going up in the basket of a balloon: he was amazed to observe that high up in the sky there is total stillness and immobility. He could hear every word spoken by people peacefully working in the fields far below him, even the exclamation of a boy guarding a cow in a pasture: 'What's that funny thing up there?' And he could hear the mooing of the cow and the barking of a dog that began to chase the balloon's passing shadow.

"The next day I learned—not without bitterness—that L. had slept so soundly all night long that it was difficult to raise her for breakfast. She had slept through the storm, the thunder, the downpour, and the lightning, missing the whole uncanny spectacle, while I had passed a sleepless night. She came down to breakfast heavy with sleep, yawning and, worse still, had an excellent appetite. She ate not only her own two soft-boiled eggs but also my portion of ham, which I was unable to touch. I looked at her, gravely disappointed. She was as childish and heedless, as capricious and impossible as ever. I knew her well, so I should have known what to expect. And yet I felt aggrieved. I had imagined during the night that she was more adult, more grown-up, and more aware of my feelings. Perhaps that other time, over the waterfall, she didn't suspect anything, while I thought that she was impatiently awaiting my decision, prodding me in a desire of fulfillment—'Don't hesitate, make up your mind!'—while I was too weak, perhaps not mature enough, to do it.

"After the stormy night the day was fine. Drops of water sparkled on the branches of firs and on the white stars of Alpine thistles. Through the wide-open windows of the veranda where we had breakfast before our departure, I saw a child on the next grassy slope, a half-wit (there are many in those Alpine regions). He was rocking on his bandy legs, holding a cow on a tether and chanting monotonously. It was a semianimal hymn of joy in praise of the sun after the stormy night, a wordless gabble, but fascinating, full of resonant surprises. Sometimes squatting or half-turning, he performed a kind of ritual, in a desire to express something unattainable.

"This idolatrous hymn of the half-wit in the meadow, in the full glare of the sun, next to the quietly grazing roan cow, ended with a kind of grunt. That whole scene seemed to me a symbol of those moments when we feel a rising tide of creative inspiration. Already the previous night I had experienced the illusory bliss of such a mood. A few years were to pass before I realized the delusion of those sterile, uncritical moments.

"It was at Grado that I began to cover scores of pages with poetry in which I tried—ineffectually, as soon became apparent —to achieve a unity of words, colors, and music. I attempted to create a hybrid, a synthesis of the arts—which up till then had existed independently and parallel to one another—by trying to create an indivisible unity, a monolith, a new branch of creativity.

"That entire exercise book filled with notes in pencil—mostly written on the beach in the shade of a large parasol (I was forbidden sea bathing and even sitting in the sun)—I tore up and burned after looking at it a second time while in the sanatorium at Merano the following year. There at Merano I was given a notebook beautifully bound in green leather, in which I began to write everything that has survived until now. (I tore out some pages—very personal—lest they fall into indiscreet hands.) It was the story of several years of my life, or rather its most important fringes; the result, I now know, was a rubbish dump, a sorry testimonial to nonfulfillment, illusions, and the growing realization of complete defeat.

"Thus the date: Merano, Doctor S.K.'s sanatorium, April. I am lying on the veranda covered with blankets, a thermometer under my tongue and, in spite of the doctor's prohibition, I am scribbling away. Now, after a long period, I can properly analyze my pleasure when listening to the half-wit's pseudo-concert in the sunlit meadow at Pustertal two years ago. An unconscious impression, I see it now, of happiness in degradation, in passive acceptance. That babbling child, dancing in the meadow next to his cow, was unconsciously trying to break away from a condition into which he had been forced by nature, while I, in full consciousness, am willfully penetrating into an underground labyrinth in search of a hiding place from my own self, a passive witness of my sister's experiments, an only apparently objective observer. For L., I know it, arranged her 'performances' with me in mind, while Detta was a necessary but unimportant extra. Detta was the object of these experiments, but not their purpose. It was I, each time, who became the true object on which the experiments were performed. I shall never find out whether Detta also experienced pleasure from submission, or whether she agreed to everything only because she was afraid of her sister. And did she know that it was I who, by proxy, took the whole burden upon myself?

"What of it? The melody was born, the first primeval scream sprouted, just as with that half-wit who cavorted in the sun on a mountain slope amid clumps of gentians and juniper that emitted an alchemical scent. A condition of violent tension was followed by a release too shameful to mention. So perhaps each product of authentic art is born in a condition of semiconsciousness, at a point where plus and minus signs converge; a current that mounts, rises to a peak—a scream unchecked by reason or the consciousness of shame!—then falls when tension snaps. A pond full of warm muddy water, to the bottom of which one sinks passively, with a sigh of relief worthy of contempt. This occurs independently of the creator, who only transmits these forces which exist independently of him in the dusk of nature and gush out like a geyser, like an underground river that has at last cut through layers of rock to reveal to people (and to the creator himself) the true face of the abyss. The form is not quite clear to the creator, because he has extracted it from his subconscious, which is unknown to him and therefore unknown to the recipient. In those days I read Rilke's *Malte*. Did he realize what he was writing? I doubt it. He had descended into hell and brought back only a scrap of knowledge of the real depths, yet through his intermediary we learned enough to experience the taste of the Inexpressible. There is also *Le Jardin de Bérénice* by Maurice Barrès.

"I hear music from a distance. It seems like ice breaking under the hooves of a horse and the feet of a man, walking in step side by side in silence. The walking man leads the horse over the ice, under which fish sleep facing stiffly upward with glassy eyes. Fish with half-open mouths. Toothless mouths veiled with slime oozing out of bloodless lips. And still this innate fear! On the white surface of a frozen, empty river, its banks lost in a stifling mist, a lonely man is walking, leading a white horse by a white bridle covered with frost. (Similarly, in Mrs. Martha Jacobi's box a year ago, while listening to Bach I imagined perpetually changing forms—Gothic towers and galleries, and other visual elements that I tried hard to shake off, in order to achieve a pure, undisturbed musical vision.)

"Again and again these secondary images. Mirror reflections primarily, always incomplete, stunted in their definite form from their moment of birth and transformed into other equally stunted shapes. The scream of a madman whose impulses will always remain obscure to others. The gibberish of a half-wit dancing for himself and the sun on the grassy slope of an Alpine mountain covered with patches of yellow and violet crocuses that have opened up in the night after a storm. And close to the singing man, a cow quietly grazing on the greensward striped by fleeting shadows of the branches of a tree moving in a gentle breeze."

The same place: Merano, April 1909:

"A dream noted after awakening; an overcast morning, rain in the air:

"The interior of an antique shop. Perhaps not exactly that— I'm not sure. Rather a kind of a junk store serving as a studio. Where? Most probably in Paris. This might be a reflection, a repetition in dream of authentic thoughts remembered from a stay in Paris with Father, when we were walking through a dark, dirty covered passage near the Boulevard Montmartre. A junk-filled tunnel full of small shops with display windows squeezed into the corners and angles at the turns of a winding passage, a ghostly tunnel full of hellish stalls, shops selling curios for collectors, or toys for adults who still have the perverse curiosity and whims of small children.

"There I got lost in the dream, or rather I returned there quickly, eluding my father, who had stopped for a moment to buy some cigars. Behind a windowpane I saw the face of an antique dealer or a magician. His eyes looked at me through glasses, his gaze summoned me to enter, promising unknown delights for the eye, or for the sense of smell or touch. The whole shameless battery of temptations of a shameful Babylon. This eccentric character straight out of *The Tales of Hoffmann* wore a nightcap that hung like a limp triangle on his forehead, and a dressing gown or snuff-colored coat fastened with buttons and loops. He sold spectacles, perhaps, but for seeing what? Toothless jaws under a hooked nose, and small bony hands hardly protruding from the long sleeves of his garment. One of his fingers, the index, deathly pale and with a yellow nail, was upright, separated from the other fingers and clearly signaling to me, inviting me to enter the shop.

"While he was still behind the glass pane and I myself still outside in the passage, my father had passed from sight smoking his cigar. I only smelled the smoke, also somehow indecent, too adult for me and promising me something. The merchant showed me jars of various sizes, and in them, floating in alcohol, anatomical exhibits that smacked of some freak show: a miniature two-headed calf, and the aborted foetus of a cat or a dog, no bigger than a dry prune soaking in sugared water. Also frogs and reptiles such as I had never seen before, creatures reduced to the size of amulets and trinkets, lizards' eggs, and other curios. Then he whispered in my ear, in spite of the pane that separated us: 'I also have other goods for the young gentleman. Would you like to look at them?' He winked at me from behind spectacles pushed down on his nose, showing protuberant, red-veined eyes. Then I remembered that a few years ago L. declared that if you gouged out somebody's eye, you could boil it and eat it with mayonnaise instead of a hard-boiled egg; at the same time she directed her gaze at Grandmother Sophia, who had in fact protuberant eyes. I froze in terror and was afraid even to look at Grandmother. Meanwhile L. quietly went on eating plum dumplings and at every opportunity, nudging me with her knee under the table, she made faces, while at the same time removing the plums from the pastry and moving them to the edge of the plate. 'Just like eggs. The only difference is that they're dark red,' she said. 'Or like somebody's eye,' she added, to the horror of Mama and the rest of the company.

"That antique dealer from the dream gestured with his hand, and I at once realized that it was not an ordinary gesture such as children use in play, but something obscene. Then I woke up bathed in sweat, having raced along the stone tiles of that passage in Montmartre to escape into the arms of my father, who was placidly smoking his cigar while looking at posters at the entrance to a wax museum.

"I took my temperature after breakfast and it was 37.9 C., three points more than the previous day. So I had to stay in bed all that day: I wasn't even allowed out on the veranda, because a cool, damp wind was blowing from the mountains."

"Merano, May 1909, 6:00 p.m. For a week we have had marvelous weather. The mountains are visible through a veil of light mist and this means fine weather. Not a cloud in the sky. Have been sitting since early morning on a bench in the sanatorium park.

"A thought came to me in the morning: I believe that there is a real possibility of getting rid once and for all (or at least for a long time, which would be a good thing) of temptations of every kind (I prefer not to name them here or to be more precise) by putting them down on paper in the form of poetry, drama, or a musical composition. I name such a method expulsion. .

"The day before yesterday, having wandered, God knows why, to the railway station and sat there idly an hour and a half on a bench, I looked at the locomotive—an old veteran with a low body and a high stack covered with something like an icecream cone—that was shunting cars about for two different trains. It shunted them singly, or coupled together in twos or threes and, having gained speed, braked suddenly with a hiss of steam and a furious whistling, so that the cars rolled on under their own momentum to their destinations, their buffers hitting those of the other cars. There ensued a whole gamut of sounds: the clash of one car against another, then a whistle when somebody waved a red flag, followed by a minute of silence. Then the locomotive would resume its work from the beginning, snorting and emitting clouds of black smoke into the clear, limpid air, as if climbing the steep incline of an Alpine railway somewhere near Semmering or Mürzzuschlag.

"Sitting thus warming myself on the empty platform, a thought struck me: I must push that thing away from me, I must unhinge it, rid myself of it by putting it down on paper or translating it into music. That way I could unburden myself and become free. The thing would go away like the cars shunted by the old locomotive, and I would remain calmly on the empty platform. In the form of such a composition, it would begin to live its own life. Once fulfilled, clothed in the illusory shape of a work of art, it would cease to tempt me and worry me. If for instance I wanted to strangle Desdemona, I would write *Othello* first, and having acted vicariously perhaps I would be satisfied. The intended deed would have been committed in some other way, but still committed. But albeit in that artificial form, as if in effigy. One could also liken it to the part played by wax figures in the rituals of black magic. I just recently read about it. The difference however would be that, instead of a person represented by a figure, the figure itself would perish. This might be sufficient, if only for a time. It would be like tearing up or burning the photograph of someone you either hate or else lust for so hopelessly that you can't bear to look on their likeness.

"The destruction of a wax figure. That same day I tried to imagine L. in the form of such a figure. I tried to choose a shape most suitable for the part she was to play, and here the difficulties began. Now, two days later, I'm laughing at myself, realiz-

ing my own naiveté or stupidity, but back then, lying by the
open window in darkness, I took it all very seriously. The wax
figure should be immobile and remind one most accurately of
the chosen person, and my imagination was not equal to this.
The wax figure L. moved, making various gestures and adopting
various poses, as if conscious of her fate. She would not stay
still. There was L. in a 'tutu'—this, if I recall correctly, is the
name of the skirt worn by ballerinas—and in ballet slippers,
performing various dance steps to the piano accompaniment of
the dancing master and under his watchful eye. I saw our old
drawing room at the Stubenring, and even a fragment of the
view beyond the window and balcony. Quickly withdrawing,
erasing that scene from memory, I at once saw L. at a young
people's ball at Mrs. B.'s, in another drawing room, bigger than
ours and with windows in different places. A crowd of girls and
boys, and among them L. in a pale pink muslin dress almost
reaching down to her ankles, in white silk slippers and a hair
style specially made for the party: her short plaits undone, tied
with a ribbon and hanging loosely down her back in a pony-
tail. When I recalled her image and wanted to place it correctly,
she stopped but, looking at me out of the corner of her eye,
began greedily to eat wild strawberries in cream from a dish.
I saw her lips smeared with cream; when I walked up to her,
she squirted all the cream in my face. While I was cleaning my
face and my suit, she disappeared.

"I tried also to imagine her on the beach at Grado, but this
happened so long ago that apart from a multicolored ball
bouncing over the waves, I couldn't recall anything. As I began
to fall asleep, tired by the work of imagining, it seemed to me
that I was up to my knees in water, trying to retrieve the ball
that floated on the sea, and that as I waded in, the ball began
to change into L., but the image quickly dissolved itself into
something lukewarm and watery, and finally disappeared."

Grado, summer 1910.
"Somewhere in the distance one can see a small boat approaching. It's the *vaporetto* from Trieste. There is a faint smudge of
smoke in the windless late-afternoon sky. Above the boat two
gulls, one flying above the other by the side of the boat. The
second one dives and a moment later is high up, flapping its

wings and carrying its quarry away in its beak. Now I see quite clearly a lady on deck in a straw hat with a blue veil wrapped around it. She's throwing bread to the birds. Both gulls fly by low over the waves, screeching, then soar high up. I'm looking directly at the sun—a black orb and around it, bright circles that blind the eyes. They are turning like the Ferris wheel in the Prater. Looking up at it a few years ago Lieschen said to me, her head adorned with a straw bonnet tied under the chin with a sapphire ribbon: 'You'd be afraid. I know. Don't deny it. You'd be scared, you *would*, you *would*, you *would*!' And she stamped her foot. I stood next to her, hanging my head, and wanted to rebel. 'Not at all,' I began in an uncertain voice, because I felt I really lacked the courage to make a decision. But Lieschen wouldn't listen. She ran over to the Ferris wheel, which was stopped at the moment, and curtsied in front of a strange gentleman about to get in a little car with his lady friend. The man—I saw it clearly—laughed and put his arm around L. helping her into the gondola. And to my horror, the Ferris wheel began to turn. I could see L. leaning from the window and waving not to me but to Mother, who walked up quickly, clearly anxious, carrying some cakes she had bought for us. So I called at the top of my voice: 'Mama, Mama, she's riding on the Ferris wheel, she's up there and I've been left behind!' 'You'll ride next time,' Mama said, but I was still in a state of agitation, almost despair. I stamped my feet, refused the cake, and behaved so hysterically that Father had to take me away by the hand. 'You should be ashamed of yourself. Such a big boy . . .!' He shook me gently, irritated because people near us were watching with amusement.

"Above my head, the Ferris wheel was turning with its hanging cars. In the cars sat couples happily embracing, soldiers and ladies' maids, milliners and clerks, waitresses and salesmen from the stores. Close to us an elderly man wearing a bowler hat was looking up, accompanied by two boys slightly younger than I who had probably overheard our conversation and were now making uncomplimentary remarks about me while nudging each other. Even Detta, who never left Mother's side, was looking at me not without malice, asking over and over again: 'Mama, what's the matter with him, why is he making such faces?'

"When was this, I wonder. Probably in 1906—or perhaps 1907? I must have been thirteen or fourteen at the time, and Lieschen fifteen or sixteen.

"Now the sea is flat, immobile like a mirror, silvery white, and the beach is empty. The beach chairs are throwing elongated shadows. The hotel boy is collecting the colored beach umbrellas left along the shore. He is brushing the sand off, folding them, putting them to one side.

"The *vaporetto* is approaching the small wooden pier, where a few people are standing. A sailor in a white coat with a navy blue collar, and with a black, curly beard called *en collier* in French novels, is waiting for a line to be thrown from the steamer, so he can slip it over a post green with slime. The boat emits a piercing whistle, one blast, then another shorter one. The second one sounds merry, like a greeting. The steamer's bow sprays a swath of white foam, as she turns to come alongside the pier. A few short, gentle waves break against the supports of the pier. Arcs are imprinted on the wet sand. And there are voices. That of the woman who a short while before was feeding the gulls, and of her child. A little boy in a sailor's hat with a ribbon down the back and an inscription around the crown. He tears himself away and runs onto the gangplank, just set in place by the bearded sailor. The latter, laughing, grabs the child in his arms and carries him ashore. A fat man carefully steps on the gangway, holding on to the guard rope. From where I am standing I can see clearly his white silk suit and his piqué vest, over which he wears a dangling watch chain with several medallions. Wiping his forehead, he stops next to the booth where tickets for the *vaporetto* are sold. He asks something. Then he walks away and vanishes from my sight in the narrow street behind the Archduchess Valerie Hotel. The boat is emptying and there are few candidates for the return to Trieste. The sea becomes darker: cold azure, with white flashes on the crests of the gentle shallow waves.

"Some ideas for poems haunt my thoughts. Then music flows in, but I know that it's an imitation—not very accurate—of a Mozart étude. Next a poem floats in, not yet precise in form. An image of a poem, rather than its real shape. I get up from the garden bench and slowly, with my hands in the pockets of my light blue flannel jacket, walk toward the café close behind the Archduchess Valerie Hotel. I'm so deep in thought that I don't notice an acquaintance from Vienna, Mrs. Hansen, who is staying in the hotel and has gone out for a walk before dinner toward the pier."

At that time, in the summer of 1910, Emil R. decides to devote himself to art. He gives up the thought of studying law after his graduation the following year. Why study law? He will become a musician or perhaps a painter. He will write poetry. He makes this decision while staying in the boarding house of Mrs. Hilde Schautzi, née Ganzoni, in the Silver Gull villa. "One must," he thinks, "create a work that is a synthesis of music, words, and images. I don't yet know how to do it, but I've made my decision. A unity of impressions, connected with music chords. But I'm afraid that I won't be equal to the task, that I can't achieve anything of the sort."

Emil R. spent the whole of 1912 at Eger as a one-year volunteer in the army. He was admitted to the officers' school at the age of eighteen—an exception, because someone had pulled strings high up that reached almost to the Imperial and Royal Minister of War. At Eger he meets Zdenek Kocourek, and they quickly become friends. In the green exercise book one might find only scanty notes from that period—"Today, as usual, caraway seed soup for breakfast," or "The coffee in the officers' mess reminds me of burning rubber." Two pages later: "I fell off my horse in the morning and am now limping slightly."

The times were turbulent, there was war in the Balkans and the possibility of partial mobilization. Emil R. noted the slogans and pronouncements in the military and patriotic vein, adding malicious comments or even cartoons. We read, for example, "When Emperor Franz Josef mounts his horse, all his peoples follow," and in the margin: "I don't adore horses, I don't count myself a member of any of the loyally devoted nations, I'm exclusively myself." On the next page: "Every soldier, from the least foot soldier to the highest general, is fired by the desire to meet the enemy," and the following comment: "What next? I'm not stupid, you can play without me!"

Emil R. spent the Christmas of 1912 in Vienna on furlough, and in February 1913 finally discarded his uniform, with its newly sewn-on insignia of a second lieutenant of the reserves, and returned to civilian life. He had decided to comply with his father's advice and enroll at the Faculty of Law.

A date in the exercise book: May 25, 1913, Abbazia.

"Meeting with Liesbeth in the garden of the villa Wind Rose, belonging to our acquaintances, the Baron von Reisach und Gleiss and his wife. L. and I were able to exchange only a few words, because almost at once Mrs. Emma von Reisach came up to us. L. wanted to inform me herself, it seems, about her engagement. Her fiancé is also here. He arrived straight from Pula, where his ship is in port, for a twenty-four hour furlough obtained, apparently, with the exalted support of the admiral commanding the squadron. L. told me about it not without a grain of malice. She probably wanted to see my reaction. I did not speak to her, but instead began to ask Mrs. Reisach the names of the roses along the path to the veranda. I learned that they were: Marshal Niel, Empress Augusta Victoria, and Princess Annunziata von Hohenlohe. I felt deeply enriched by this information. L. stood beside us, digging the end of her umbrella into the soil and looking intently at me from the corner of her eye. She probably imagined that, upon hearing the news, I would make a dramatic and tragic scene, that I would exclaim something like 'Oh my God!' and take my head in my hands and rock from side to side, and also indulge in a kind of pantomime wringing of my hands, falling on my knees, etc. I deprived her of that pleasure. Perhaps if I had been taken unawares . . . But luckily my kind mother could not keep the secret, overjoyed about an engagement at last and the fact that L.'s future husband and my brother-in-law, Edmund von S., a naval officer assigned (that's the phrase they use) to the light cruiser *Admiral Spaun,* is such an excellent young man of good family with a 'von' in front of his name. So L. will also sign herself 'von.' Furthermore, 'they are very much in love.' Were it not for Mama's letter, I might perhaps have been taken aback, and couldn't have kept my composure throughout that difficult day, not to say my sense of humor. For I sparkled with wit, amusing all the assembled company, not excluding Edmund von S., who sat next to his happy fiancée in his becoming naval uniform, with a small dagger at his side with which he played all the time. I astonished only my mother, unaccustomed to seeing me so animated, and slightly shocked her with my stories, brought straight from the regiment at Eger. But I succeeded in vastly amusing Baron von Reisach, who laughed until he cried and asked me to repeat two or three of my jokes."

At the same time that the company was assembling for breakfast on the veranda of Mrs. Schautzi's villa, an elegant gentleman appeared in one of the post offices in Vienna and collected a letter sent to him care of general delivery, to be claimed with the password "Ball at the Opera." Alerted by a bell rung by a postal employee, the two secret police agents, Ebinger and Steidl, followed him out of the building. But the elegant gentleman had taken a taxi, so the two agents stopped on the corner of Kolovratring, deliberating what to do next. We who know the sequel can disclose that the mysterious gentleman pursued by the agents was Alfred Redl, a colonel on the general staff.

Through the wide-open windows of the von Reisach's veranda come fresh breezes from the sea. Mimosas flourish on the hilly slopes. Mrs. von Reisach lifts a cup of tea to her lips. A ray of sun is fleetingly reflected in the embroidered Dalmatian tablecloth. Now the faces of all those sitting round the table are turned toward the sea. A large passenger steamer can be seen in the Bay of Quarnero. Lieutenant Edmund S. explains: "That's the *Martha Washington* sailing from Fiume to Piraeus and Alexandria." Baron von Reisach lights a cigar.

At exactly the same moment the two police agents begin a pursuit that almost resembles a great film chase. Similarly clothed in black suits and bowler hats, the two men look like a double reincarnation of Max Linder. At precisely the same moment, Emil R. mentions the film (with the same actor in the title role) that he saw the day before yesterday in one of the theaters in Trieste. Meanwhile the police agents enter the hall of the Klomser Hotel. It was here, in room 1 on the first floor, that on a certain August night twenty years earlier—on the birthday of His Gracious Majesty—Mrs. Ethel R. conceived the son who was to be christened Emil. The same room was now allocated to Colonel Redl, who had arrived that morning from Prague. Having just returned from the post office, the colonel is now changing. His civilian suit has already been placed over the arm of a chair, probably the same one on which years ago the hastily discarded garters of Mrs. R. were hanging. Now the colonel is putting on the dark green uniform of a staff officer. In a moment he will go downstairs to the hall, where both agents are talking to the porter while scanning the list of hotel guests.

Colonel Redl's civilian suit, discarded a moment before, exudes the scent of "Violettes Impériales," recently less fashionable than of late, but still used by a certain category of officers of the Imperial and Royal Army, and by the habitués of a number of exclusive cafés in Vienna. That somewhat eccentric category of men is subject to private fashions and tastes shielded from human indiscretion. The silk handkerchief that Colonel Redl uses to wipe his glasses, holding them up to the light, also smells of "Violettes Impériales." So does the navy blue cloth of naval lieutenant Edmund S.'s uniform. It is quite probable that his silk underwear, usually bought in the most elegant London shops, is also tinged with that scent.

We are still in the era of the dying Art Nouveau, so we can afford a certain exaggeration in feelings and definitions, a rather sentimental immodesty imbued with this somber, now unfashionable violet. Maybe even a touch of melancholy would not be amiss. It is thus that one must view the musings of young Emil R. noted in his green book, soon after his return from the Reisach's villa to the Miramare Hotel, where he has been staying since his arrival from Trieste.

"I realize that I am being unfair at the moment. It isn't true that Edmund S., whom I met briefly last year at Marienbad, disliked me at first sight, as if he suspected something. On the contrary, he's been trying very hard to win me over. It is I—as if suspecting how things might end, and that something was in the air—I who, since Marienbad, have been prickly, unfriendly, and cold. Yet I ought to have foreseen that somebody like him would one day appear on the horizon. But at that time I didn't think about it. This might have been a simple lack of imagination on my part. Or perhaps unconsciously I've been trying to convince myself that everything would remain as it was forever. I treated lightly Mama's hints that it was time to look around. On the other hand, L. herself did not seem to think about the future. She shrugged her shoulders whenever Mama said anything. Even when Detta got engaged and then married, L. laughed and said: 'I have plenty of time! What does it matter that she's younger and that it didn't happen according to the rules of seniority? Even if I became an old maid, what of it? I don't care.'

"Reverting to Edmund, I only now realize that all his supposed dislike of me—even the disdain that I noticed whenever he addressed me—I myself had invented as a pretext. I felt a growing physical repulsion from that healthy, handsome young man literally bursting with male strength. I felt it again this morning when Edmund was rowing and the rest of us—the Reisachs, Mama, myself, and L.—were sitting calmly in the boat. I even tried at first to assist him, but he laughingly assured me that he could manage. Only then did I detect in his voice a somewhat contemptuous tone, referring probably to my physical condition, admittedly much weaker than his, as well as my lack of skill. Certain animals feel a similar mutual aversion, a distaste or even hatred at first sight. They avoid any approach, looking askance and ignoring each other's presence on the same feeding grounds.

"Luckily he left by the evening train, because his furlough was ending. The navy is now in a state of alert in connection with events in the Balkans. Edmund told us, probably disclosing a military secret, that the whole squadron of *Novara*-type light cruisers, to which the *Admiral Spaun* belongs, is lying in the roads of Pula under steam, ready to depart. I don't deny that the news did not upset me very much. I noted with relief that L., too, did not look disturbed by the news. If the Balkan countries decide to misbehave to the extent that we must restrain them, I won't much care. In spite of my quite unjustified, completely platonic feelings for Nikita of Montenegro. Let him occupy Skutari. Why shouldn't he?

"That night when, still fully dressed and feeling that I wouldn't sleep, I was standing in the open window, an absurd but revealing thought crossed my mind. There had existed once upon a time a *ius primae noctis*. Long forgotten, it is no longer exercised, but what of it? What if I addressed myself to Edmund man to man and told him straight, concealing nothing: 'You have my word of honor that when you come here tomorrow at dawn, I will be gone from this world. And apart from the three of us, nobody will ever know. Do you understand me, my future brother-in-law, Naval Lieutenant Sindbad the Sailor of the Imperial and Royal Navy, the future nourishment of sharks?' And I'm not exaggerating when I maintain that after the first indignant shocked reaction—perhaps the summons to an affair of honor, and an instinctive reaching for his naval dagger—he would hesitate. If apart from the promise of my death, I were to promise him, and even legally will to him, all my possessions, everything I'd ever inherit in the future . . . A man as worldly as himself—so modern and intelligent (if a career officer of the Imperial and Royal Navy can be all these things) —can't possibly attach an exaggerated importance to what one might define flippantly but quite discreetly as *la fleur de la virginité.* Whereas I . . .! Still standing at the open window of my room at the Miramar Hotel, I burst out laughing."

At exactly the same time that Emil R. was standing in the open window, leaning out over the thick tangle of branches growing in the seaside boulevard of Abbazia, we might have witnessed the last act of an unpleasant affair, had we been able to creep unseen into room 1 of the Klomser Hotel in Vienna. A shot resounded in the room and some time later, to verify what had happened, two secret agents looked into the room. Having ascertained what had occurred, they went downstairs on tiptoe, passing the porter who, not having heard anything, was quietly dozing, then went out into the empty street to impart the good news to the three senior officers impatiently waiting there. The officers made a note of the time and sighed with relief.

The scanty information about the events of May 24 at the Klomser Hotel in Vienna reached Emil R. through the press two days later, when he was already back in Trieste. It did not make a great impression on him. He glanced at the paragraph, then read on the opposite page about a concert that a famous lady violinist was to give in Trieste. He might have gone, had he wanted to. But Emil felt too lazy to make even this small effort, so he forgot about it.

At the same time, at the private apartment in Prague of Alfred Redl, former chief of staff of the Eighth Army Corps (whose body had been carried out down the back stairs of the Klomser Hotel), a search was taking place. The general in command,

Redl's superior, Baron Giesl, was inconsolable. His brother, the ambassador of Austria-Hungary in Belgrade, was reading at the very same moment the coded message sent him from the War Ministry in the Ballhausplatz. He looked worried. His secretary was knocking at his door.

Over the Adriatic the gulls circled, perching singly or in pairs on the roofs of the seaside villas. Dusk was falling.

Perhaps it is worth quoting a few additional facts, parallel in time, from private and public affairs. We will confine our attention for a moment to events of a highly personal nature such as Emil R.'s increasing feeling of doom.

The gypsy girl Marika was walking at dusk through the already deserted market square in the small township of Fehertemplom. She was swinging her hips and singing softly, while diagonally crossing the market full of rubbish, squashed vegetables, melon skins, bits of watermelon, horse manure, and straw. Somebody invisible in the dark, hidden behind the fence dividing the market square from the village slaughterhouse, gave a whistle. One whistle, then another. The girl stopped in the center of the empty square, listening. The whistle was repeated. Then the darkness became so dense that it was impossible to see her any longer.

Baron Giesl, the plenipotentiary, has just finished decoding the message and has pressed the bell on his desk. He stands looking toward the window covered with a heavy velvet curtain.

One must hurry to accumulate the details, because time is of the essence. If one wanted to, one might count the minutes remaining before the end. Only one, perhaps two minutes to go, and what is left in our hand will be an empty bottle of Puntigam beer with a label representing a white Styrian lion on a green background, and the memory of the name of the Archduke's confessor while the Archduke lies in agony at Sarajevo. And hands moving on the clock.

"Do you know . . ." says one of the lieutenants. It is now so dark in the narrow and winding Kerestesh Street, that only from his voice can we tell that the words are spoken by Sandor Viranyi, a lieutenant of the fourth squadron. Somebody else lights a cigarette; the flicker of the match falls for a moment on the officer's fingers, his lips, and his moustache. Then the darkness is deeper than before.

"Have you heard," he continues, "that not far from here the body of a murdered gypsy girl has been found?" He gestures with his hand, but no one can see his gesture; the darkness is so complete that one can only guess at the direction. A dense, opaque darkness. Above the acacias, the sky is full of distant stars.

"It apparently happened," Viranyi adds, as the officers continue toward Franz Josef Square while skirting the sleeping gardens, "while we were at Mother Bezsi's, no more than an hour ago."

They walk on down the middle of the road full of holes, or on the narrow pavement of rough stones with tufts of grass growing between them, stumbling, laughing when they collide with one another, their spurs and saber scabbards clinking. Only the light of their cigarettes betrays where they are at a given moment. But when they pass the junction of Kerestesh and Kiralyi Streets, where the gas lamps shine between the trees and a few windows are lit in the low village houses, one of them begins to sing an aria from the *Grand Duchess of Gerölstein*.

There is a stifling smell of dust and fading acacia flowers. Distant stars shine in the firmament. One of them detaches itself and falls in an arc somewhere in the direction of the Danube. The officers stop and look up. One of them hurries to make a wish for himself and the others. They wait for another star to fall. The silence is total. Then from one of the houses in the narrow lane, a woman's voice resounds, singing: "Nahorny, Nahorny, why have you left me? . . ." The officers listen for a moment, then turn toward the barracks.

In a field outside the station, somewhere near Slavonski Brod, stands a long train composed of boxcars for "forty men and six horses." The fields are bare after the harvest, the sun-drenched wheat stubble emits a strong smell. Soldiers leap from the cars, some clumsily sliding down from the wide-open doors, pulling heavy packs, knapsacks, and bound stacks of rifles. One can hear Czech, because this is the first train of the Landwehr from Prague, the Twenty-first Division, commanded by Major General Prziborski. In a moment the infantrymen in their field-gray uniforms will march toward the Sava, where they will embark on large rafts. The divisional pioneers and a few officers are there already. On the black waters of the river one can see red, white, and yellow flashes—the lanterns on the bows and sterns of the broad flat-bottomed barges. The water gurgles beside the bank. A young officer runs up the gangplank of the nearest raft.

At the same time, in the office of the Imperial and Royal Gendarmerie at Fehertemplom, three men are occupied with the case of one dead girl. Her body was brought there less than an hour before. Behind the window, the short July night is drawing to its close. A bird has awakened and emits cheerful noises in the dense bushes nearby. But the three men are too busy to notice the bird's early dawn hymn.

The local medical man, Barber-Surgeon Imre Ludasz, has authoritatively stated, after a preliminary examination of the victim's body and before the official post mortem, that the first assumption sustained erroneously by Gendarmerie Sergeant Vilajcich—namely, that somebody had cut the girl's throat— was false. It is a fact that the victim has a bloody mark on her neck, but it is not from a cut with a knife or a sickle; it was made without any doubt by the tightening on her neck of a thin but very strong wire with some cheap beads of colored glass threaded on it, the beads having been undoubtedly stolen by the victim from a stall in the market. Here the assistant commissioner of the gendarmerie, Bogatovich, interrupts the medical man. He reminds him—having opened a folder in a light blue but rather dirty cover, tied with a tape and with a reference number on it—that the deceased had a record of seven thefts committed over the last two years especially, but not exclusively, in the market. There is a complaint and deposition made in the commissioner's office by Ruth Wilnerova, a merchant, owner of a stall selling ladies' clothing. Date of deposition: February of the current year. Subject of complaint: a kerchief and a reel of cotton. In the current year alone, the deceased had spent as much as twenty-five days in the town jail. After her release no more than two weeks ago, she was caught attempting to steal a melon and some bread from the stall of a woman named Filas. And so on. Assistant Commissioner Bogatovich snaps his fingers and closes the folder, tying the black tape in a bow, then lights a cigar.

Surgeon Ludasz proceeds:

"Moreover, it seems to me that this was not an act of sexual violence. I have examined the deceased superficially. There would be traces, if there had been rape. The post mortem will confirm my opinion. So what if Marika's blouse had the fourth button undone, so what if it was missing? This might have happened independently, much earlier, or during a struggle with her assailant. There are no scratches or bruises on her body. Only that red mark. How might it have been done? Perhaps like this: when she was not expecting it, somebody grabbed her from behind by her necklace and tightened it so that the girl fell backward, strangled. Her murderer then dragged her about ten meters to the bottom of the clay pit—to be precise, a distance of nine meters and thirty-three centimeters." (Ludasz checks a sketch he has made on a greasy, crumpled piece of paper.) "After that, it seems, he left her there and escaped. But the wire, although exceptionally strong, did give way in the end, as some of the beads were scattered on the grass. Here are some of them, you can see for yourselves!" Here Ludasz produces from a piece of paper several small red glass beads. "This is material proof, and I will therefore deposit them here for the file."

Assistant Commissioner Bogatovich and the clerk of the court, the thin and slightly balding Mircsa, examine the beads, then turn their attention again to Ludasz, who is still talking.

"The body of the deceased was discovered. The first to notice the body was a gypsy youth, a certain Yano. I forget his surname." Assistant Commissioner Bogatovich nods assent, knocks the ash off his cigar against the edge of the table, and says: "He has already been detained."

"So this fellow Yano found the body of the deceased lying on her back with her head twisted to one side and her arms spread. This was confirmed also by the Gendarmerie Sergeant Istvan Vilajcich—who was on night duty at the police station. The fingers of both hands of the victim were bent, which proves that she had tried to cling to something as she was dragged on the ground. Under her nails I found bits of fresh clay, similar to that of the pit. Also quite a few blades of grass and some seeds of the plants that grow there. The victim must have literally torn the earth with her nails. Thus, I repeat, a classical case of death by strangulation. One of the veins in her neck was severed by the wire, hence the hemorrhage. That's all."

"And the motive?" asks the thin, balding clerk of the court, Janos Mircsa. He yawns, covering his mouth out of respect for the assistant commissioner. Behind his pince-nez, his eyes begin to water from his yawning. "Motive?" he repeats, tapping his nicotine-stained finger on the table top. The table is spotted with ink and has knife marks in many places. Some of the cuts, engrained with dirt, must be very ancient, others, rather pale, seem fresh. If one looks closely, one finds among them heart shapes and initials; one cut even attempts to represent the breasts of a woman without a head. The artist was obviously not capable of etching the features of a woman with his pocket knife. The people at the table are visibly bored.

"Hmm, motive . . . motive?" They both ponder: the assistant commissioner and the barber-surgeon.

"Not rape—there's no evidence of it. An attempted rape? Perhaps the attacker was interrupted at the last moment? Hmm . . . it's difficult to say. Considering however that Marika, while only fifteen, was a rather loose kind of woman . . ." Here Assistant Commissioner Bogatovich intervenes:

"She was twice apprehended and held in custody for prostitution in broad daylight, and also in the evening. Like all of them," he adds, and draws sleepily on his cigar.

"Exactly," continues Barber-Surgeon Ludasz. "That's what I had in mind when I eliminated sexual motives for the murder. Why should the attacker commit rape, when he could achieve his objective by simply paying her with a couple of cigarettes, or perhaps an unfinished cigar butt?"

"Exactly," confirms Assistant Commissioner Bogatovich. "It was not an expensive pleasure."

"We can also exclude robbery as a motive, for what did she have on her, that wretched girl? A dirty dress over her naked body? Beads not worth five cents? So what we're left with is revenge, in which case we must look for the murderer among her fellow gypsies. It could have been some youth, for instance a betrayed lover. Among the gypsies such matters are common."

"Otherwise?"

"Otherwise it's some kind of shady affair—who knows, these days? Political?" The barber-surgeon lowers his voice to a whisper and leans toward Assistant Commissioner Bogatovich who, still smoking his cigar, has now adopted a very official and knowing expression, important and threatening in its intent. "Perhaps some links with the Serbs . . . with the Black Hand. If not, only a pervert could have committed such a deed."

At this point Ludasz falls silent, as if frightened. He coughs softly and starts cleaning his pince-nez with a red-dotted handkerchief.

"In that case this is not within my competence, I am pleased to say." He smiles at the thought of shifting the responsibility to other shoulders, then rubs his hands.

"Now, gentlemen, the post mortem. Let's get to work! It's the devil's own making, in heat like this!" He walks to the window, which despite its bars is open to the song of night birds in the bushes. There is a heavy scent of wilting acacias. A noiseless cat sneaks past the window.

Assistant Commissioner Bogatovich remains alone in the police station. He drums his fingers on the table top, runs them over the initials cut in the shiny wood, and over the bosom of the headless woman that the unknown artist surrounded with a garland of sickle-shaped cuts. He grows thoughtful. He lights yet another cigar and takes from a drawer a pile of folders and loose papers. He rummages through them. When he is alone and the occasion is private and intimate, Assistant Commissioner Bogatovich thinks in Croatian. He does not resort in his thoughts to that language in matters of an official character.

Now, with a sharp pencil that has an eraser on its end and a metal clip for attaching it to the breast pocket of his uniform, he underlines certain items in a column of names. He puts brackets around others. It is a list of names of gypsies from the disreputable suburban district of the Gypsy Quarter.

Thus in turn: Andras Balos, Michael Silko, his younger brother Zaran Silko, their brother-in-law—that one will go to prison without a doubt!—Istvan Maruta (what a villain!)—and three or four other names at random. They will be locked up just in case, and pressed hard at interrogation. The assistant commissioner knows perfectly well—he would vouch for it—that the above-named had nothing to do with the murder, but one might get their statements on many other subjects. For instance, on the constant thefts in the so-called "German booths." And who stole a cow from Ilaticia Ferenczy? No doubt one or another of them will admit to it out of fear. Moreover, their being locked up will show the examining magistrate that something is being done in this affair. That the Royal Gendarmerie at Fehertemplom isn't asleep, that they're keeping an eye on the suspect and criminal elements, that Assistant Commissioner Bogatovich knows how to cope—you bet!

What is the life of one girl, when war against Serbia is in the offing, and another with Russia? Mobilization is imminent—so many military matters of supreme importance! Assistant Commissioner Bogatovich has a healthy dislike of his brothers across the Danube. This dislike turns at times into hatred. It is, one might say, a highly patriotic feeling, legal, correct, and completely understandable after the crime at Sarajevo. Assistant Commissioner Bogatovich repeats in his mind the slogan that has recently become fashionable: "All Serbs must die!" He adds another, the very latest: "A Russian with every bullet." That's how it should be. If he had his way, he'd show them, those Serbs from across the Morava! But for the moment, state matters and his feelings must be put aside; he must deal with the ugly case in the old clay pit. The devil take it! At a time like this!

At this point Assistant Commissioner Bogatovich opens a special folder. In it there is a register of names of another kind— seemingly untouchable names. The commissioner of the Royal Hungarian Gendarmerie smiles. He savors, while chewing on the end of his Virginia cigar, the sight of old family names preceded by "von" or "zu." The flower of the officer corps of the local garrison, a select cadre, far beyond his authority, contemptuous of him, not even noticing the existence of the Royal Gendarmerie of which he, the assistant Commissioner, is the head— are vastly supercilious men whom he hates.

Let's look now at this haughty company. Those grand Sicilian Lancers! They are certainly the worst! With the Honveds one can sometimes come to terms, especially after a few glasses of brandy, but with the Lancers—never! On this unofficial list— compiled for his own semiprivate use, whenever the opportunity should arise and the circumstances be favorable—the assistant commissioner has made various observations in the margin, the result of confidential information from trustworthy persons, a miscellany of tidbits. He ponders these personal notes. Leaning over the table on spread elbows, inhaling the aromatic Virginia

cigar, he probes the secrets of that list of hated names, that
untouchable and thus impervious elite. Just wait, gentlemen,
just wait, patience, patience . . .! And with his sharp pencil he
begins to go through the roll of Magyar, Croat, and German
names with or without titles, delicately putting question marks,
exclamation marks, and little circles here and there in the
margin.

Gently, step by step so as not to disturb the past, one might
withdraw from the stuffy room of the police station to the areas
encompassed by a number of obscure allusions in the green exercise book of Reserve Lieutenant Emil R.

"Club of the Fashionable—Paradise" is from 1912, when he
served for one year as a volunteer in the dragoon regiment in
the Bohemian town of Cheb, otherwise known as Eger.

And in the same year the desperate—for outsiders, incompre-
hensible—cry of agony of the young officer candidate: "End of
illusions! Let's abandon further attempts! What remains is deep
disgust and shame. The eyes of that woman whose name I don't
even know, in which, under the guise of sympathy—no, rather
a dismissal of my failure despite her attempts, though this is
nothing, it could happen to anybody, so I mustn't make a lot
out of it—I discerned a hint of mockery. I averted my eyes from
that contempt coupled with a sympathy born in hell." And a
date: Eger, November 7, 1912.

A few pages further on, notes of a general character, included
for reasons unknown in this book of intimate although allusive
confessions and attempts at creation of various kinds: "On October 7, 1911, Admiral Borea Ricci d'Olmo left for Tripoli. The
Caid of Tripoli, Hassan Pasha, participated in the transfer of
that city to the Italian authorities."

Next to it, several original pencil sketches of military subjects,
probably under the direct impression of war communiqués from
Libya and Cyrenaica. And farther down, in the margin of a draft
of a poem about Proserpine:

"Interesting attempt to land a Curtiss biplane on the deck of
the American battleship *Pennsylvania*. The pilot's name is Elly.
I saw his picture in the *Wiener Illustrierte*. There is plague in
Manchuria." Here, a photograph cut from some magazine is
pasted in the book: several figures in white coats, their faces

masked with cloths, erect or leaning over stretchers on which lie the victims of the plague. In the background, a column of smoke above a pyre on which, one must surmise, the bodies of the plague victims are being burned.

And again a note: "At the airdrome of Issy, near Paris, an accident of a military airplane. It crashed into a group of civilian dignitaries and high-ranking officers observing the pilot's acrobatics. The prime minister was injured and the war minister, Berteaux, killed. His head was smashed by the propeller of the falling airplane." The date: May 1911.

The next page is entirely occupied by a reproduction of Edward Munch's painting, "By the Deathbed" and—slightly smaller—a sculpture by Vigeland: "Marvelous! And how horrifying—especially the Vigeland . . ." (June 1911)

Under the date of October 12, 1911: "Vivaldi, Concerto in D Major for Oboe and Orchestra. Magnificent. Especially the largo. I'm in bed, repeating various passages to myself."

And the next day, October 13, 1911: "The two poles of life: creation and destruction (I think this is from Goethe's *Faust*). Must check who said it."

1913, Vienna: "I went to a film by Louis Feuillade entitled *Fantomas*: only two installments so far. Now I have a headache. Will films ever play a part in culture, or will they remain fairground entertainments?"

And two quotations, unattributed: "The devil's daughters with the Madonna's lips," and "Satan's messengers: witches." Remark in the margin: Bah!

And lower still, similar quotation: "Woman: halfway between devil and beast." Next to it a pencil drawing, later erased and unrecognizable. Only the date remains: "Horrible night of November 7–8, 1913."

An earlier date, April 1910:

"Although spring is well advanced here at Tolbach, winter is not yet over. Snow lies in heavy layers, especially in the shade behind our hotel, and also under the spruce trees across the road. The frost lasts until noon. Expedition to the chapel; at the turn, L. feels that her fingers are frozen. She pulls off her crocheted wool ski gloves, pushes them into the pocket of her fur coat, and blows on her red fingers. A sudden impulse made me take her right hand and cover it with kisses like a madman. With her other hand, with all five fingers of it she scratched my cheek and left red nail marks on it. Then, pushing me aside, she ran into the forest and stopped under a tall fir tree. She called to me while I stood still in the middle of the empty road: 'Come quick! Look at this lovely black squirrel!' After we returned to the boarding house and Mother noticed the marks on my cheek, Little Devil explained calmly, dunking a biscuit in her tea: 'He wanted to catch a squirrel and while it was struggling to get away, it scratched him. Serves him right! Don't worry, Mama.' Then, still eating her biscuit, she shrugged her shoulders. But Mama, very anxious, went to get some witch hazel.

"Vienna, March 19. (Written before going to sleep: Mama is at the theater with Mrs. Jacobi; Lieschen has a cold and has stayed in bed; Detta is playing on the floor with a doll, talking to it.) Poets often die young, especially in turbulent times (example: Byron). They are of no use, and even dangerous in foreseeing or explaining events in their vision. Unfathomable. Some acquire honors and positions that are a polite expression of society's derision and contempt. Future readers of encyclopedias will not know of their existence. Some will die along the way. But there are others who try to produce a golden egg during their progress toward the cemetery gates."

Then the draft of a poem (Vienna, early morning, after awakening, May 2, 19—) :

BURNING AND FLICKERING LIGHT

A whole realm of shadows is moving toward you and me
The nonfulfillment and nonrealization that you evoked.
We are sailing on a white plain,
Myself and the skeletons of riders on dead horses,
Into the void of wilting gardens and fallen leaves.
Oh rider on a black horse in a black cape
You wear a feathered hat. The hem of your crinoline hangs
On the silver caparison of your side saddle.
Your left foot in a white bony stirrup calls for my mouth.
Soft like satin, arched.
Alive. You lift your white-gloved hand. In it a hammer
On a long staff. You strike the knell of night.
Requiem aeternam. Mortuus enim. Requiescat.

This whole poem is crossed out and there is a comment in pencil: "A failed attempt. Nothing has come of it. At the time I made these hasty notes of words that came to me in the night I thought I had achieved something—grasped the shadow of God! But all I did was transpose—and awkwardly, at that—some painting of a danse macabre."

And without a date, in almost illegible writing:

"I was sitting on the edge of my bed, bent over a book, when both leaves of the door were pushed open soundlessly and I saw L. standing there. She was wearing close-fitting white silk pantaloons reaching to her knees—a novelty that Mrs. Jacobi brought her from her last journey to Paris, and that until now served only for charades—and on her shoulders something lacy, full of flounces that formed a kind of broad ruff round her neck. She was barefoot and looked at me in silence. I lifted my head, also in silence, then she stuck out her tongue at me and, slowly withdrawing, half closed each leaf of the door leading to the bedroom. And something else besides: throughout this short, silent scene, between the opening and the closing of this 'gate to hell,' I heard music: somebody in the neighborhood was playing the barcarolle from *Tales of Hoffmann*. Against that background, L.'s eyes, narrowed into two lengthy cat-like slits that reached almost to her temples, a birdlike but at the same time catlike look that expressed, perhaps (although I couldn't see her pupils) amusement or maybe (as I thought, petrified) a challenge and an encouragement? She stood in the half-open door; her head against the light of the bedroom was almost black, but with a halo of locks lit by the light of the chandelier."

And then:

"Grand Prix de France: Le Mans, July 23, 1911. Héméry in a Fiat, first; Friedrich in a Bugatti, second. Prix de l'Auto-Dieppe: Bablot in a Delage. The first *Rallye hivernal de Monaco* was won by Henri Reugier in a Turcat-Méry. Bravo! A man I know, Willy Kottfuss, was supposed to take part, but his Puch broke down at the last moment and the poor man only reached the Brenner Pass. I got a tragicomic postcard from him with his report on the unfortunate race."

Let us note it all carefully, because nothing will ever be repeated! Everything is unique and irreversible, first and last in its shape and expression.

• • •

And so one must hurry to keep up with the passing events.

Approaching stealthily in order not to frighten, not to offend by an unsuitable remark, by a louder breath or an accidental cough, we go back toward the sources. One might walk up to a ground-floor window of the villa in 3 Seebacherstrasse in Graz and look out of it. As we know, there is a small garden there surrounded by a wall overgrown with vines, and with honeysuckle that has just flowered and almost reaches the lawn with its festooning branches. There is also a chestnut tree in bloom. The year is such and such. A long time ago.

Sun and calm in the garden. We can guess that Mr. and Mrs. R. have gone visiting friends on this Sunday afternoon, and that the servants have a day off. That is why it is so quiet and peaceful.

In the middle of the lawn Detta is on all fours. Her hair the color of new carrots is undone and falls down her right cheek, her right elbow touches the grass. Over Detta stands her elder sister Lieschen. Their brother Emil is off to one side. In the full sun, insects are swarming and buzzing in the honeysuckle. A few bees also hum higher up in the chestnut tree. Its white and pink candlesticks jut upward and will remain in Emil R.'s memory as the background of the picture, preserved in the scene on the lawn.

Lieschen is standing over her younger sister with her legs wide apart. She is wearing a Scottish tartan dress with side pockets into which her little fists are pushed deep. She looks down on her sister from above, possessively and in silence. In her pose she is somewhat boyish and angular, serious and attentive.

Emil R. in the uniform of the Jesuit school stands immobile and silent. He looks at most ten or eleven years old, tall for his age, but anemic: a handsome boy with blond hair and light gray eyes with long, girlish lashes. He is standing in the shadow of the chestnut tree and will remain there throughout the experiment, looking on passively, apparently unseen by either sister. On the path nearby stands a green watering can.

"Why don't you bloom! Well? Hurry up, what are you waiting for?" Lieschen repeats stubbornly, towering over Detta and looking down at her. Detta does not look up at her sister.

Lieschen stamps one foot, then the other. Neither looks at Emil who with his arms hanging down, tense and alert, looks slightly frightened. But this might be an illusion. For the first time the scene is being played outside in the garden. Until now all these games were performed in the large drawing room at the front of the house.

"And now we shall make a flower bed," decides Lieschen, who runs toward a bed of irises. She stops, considering something.

"Here!" she decides. Detta obediently crawls on all fours in that direction, trailing her loose hair behind her. She takes up a position prescribed by the ritual invented by Lieschen.

Sometimes Detta's hands are tied behind her back, not to prevent any protest, which would never happen, but to make the ritual, according to Lieschen, "more grown-up and serious." This is an idea she got from an illustration in a magazine for grown-ups. Then follow some words of ritual warning: "If you dare to do anything . . ."—here Lieschen's voice and expression become threatening—"remember that there's something hanging in the pantry cupboard."

What she means is a carpet beater, used for both carpets and upholstered furniture. At the mention of this, Detta draws in her shoulders and hangs her head even lower. Now she is almost touching the grass with her nose. A carpet beater is of course similar in shape to a treble clef in sheet music, and in a more tangible form, to an ornament in braid on the red trousers of the Royal Honveds. It is elastic and flexible. It can clasp the body tightly when used in a particular way. Lieschen knows this, and so does her sister. This is why she shrinks so now and begins to tremble. Emil stands still, his arms hanging at his sides, and says nothing.

If one crawled under the drawing-room table covered with a fringed cloth resembling the sides of a tent, one might follow with the index finger the pattern of the treble clef ornament plaited with black and gold threads on the upper thigh of a hussar sitting at the table, a thigh that is taut and hard as wood. Each move of his hand reaching for a Tarot card, or for a cigar resting for a moment on an ashtray, causes an additional tension on the muscles in the hussar's leg, which is noticed by the seven-year-old Elizabeth, who is touching the leg with her fingers. Neither Emil nor Detta would dare to do such a thing. From a corner of the drawing room, they are observing in silence and horror the actions of their elder sister. Detta has opened wide her blue eyes, large and round, childish and trusting. Emil has put his palms together, as if praying for the salvation of Little Devil's soul, now irrevocably damned. Emil is having scripture lessons with Father Cornelius Blatt, who in a few years' time will be his confessor, so he knows the price of such misbehavior. Under the tablecloth hanging down almost to the floor, one can see only Lieschen's legs. One, then the other disappears under the table. The hussar major is so absorbed by the Tarot game, however, that he does not notice the light touches on his right, then left thigh. In any event, the children will soon be sent to bed.

This happened quite a few years before. In the garden now Lieschen is thirteen and has lost the habit of crawling under tables at which her parents' guests are sitting. This is another era with another range of interests, and there are other games.

The treble clef will remind Lieschen of a musical note between upper C and a sudden fall to perhaps A minor. She whistles at the revealing thought. The whistle resembles the voice of a solitary oriole at dawn, when the dew is still shimmering like silver upon the leaves, and eyes are rubbed to chase away sleep. It makes Emil, still apparently unseen by either sister, tremble, and he has to control the trembling as best he can. He may have to walk away, to leave the sight of the two young girls and hide in the jasmine bush under the wall where the honeysuckle falls in cascades amid the hum of insects. He emerges after a while from his hiding place, with the sense of having committed a mortal sin that he will have to confess to Father Cornelius Blatt of the Society of Jesus.

He will kneel at the confessional, through the grille of which he will see the priest's dry fingers making the sign of the cross. While confessing he will become confused, afraid to conceal a recent sin, constantly repeated, threatening him with blindness and perhaps madness. He will not admit to it clearly or precisely, but in a muffled whisper, yet Father Cornelius will understand. "You've been playing naughty games again!" And Father Blatt will sigh behind the grille of the confessional, and mumble the words of some Latin prayer. He will stay thoughtful for a moment before bringing his mouth close to the grille, behind which Emil will be waiting for his verdict, standing on tiptoe to put his ear close to his confessor's mouth so as not to miss anything that the priest is saying. Perhaps the medieval Latin prayer is meant to chase away the devil, who has crept into the church and even now is hovering between the rows of somber, empty oak benches?

A kind of exorcism over the head of the lost boy, now kneeling in humility and shame, aware of having committed a sin possibly of greater consequence than the one he has confessed to, for he did not reveal its cause. Not a word about the source of his fall, about his two sisters—especially about Lieschen. So he will walk away from the confessional into the unlit nave of St. Leonard's Church like a creature damned beyond reprieve.

The treble clef. Also a maple leaf if suitably dried, not flimsy, but sufficiently stiff while still supple. The ends of the leaf might be used for various purposes. Just like cat's claws. Lieschen has already thought of this—such ideas come to her before she falls asleep. When, having said her prayers under the eye of Miss Traut, she slips under her blanket, curls up, and draws her knees up to her neck, she begins to think, and quite often she invents something new. A new variant, an interesting detail never before used, for the next day's games. Detta, quietly falling asleep in the next bed, hears her sister's soft giggles from under the blanket that covers her head. Devils must giggle like that. Detta begins to shake. She does not possess enough creative imagination to foresee what lies in store for her the next day, but knows that something will inevitably happen. She thinks about her sister with fear and respect, mixed also with a fervent doglike love and fascination. Falling asleep, she repeats the prayer, said previously in too much of a hurry, for the salvation of Lieschen's soul. She prays softly, piously, and sincerely.

A maple leaf in Lieschen's hands transforms itself into an experiment with the sense of touch. If one lays it carefully against Detta's bare arm, having pulled up the sleeve of her blouse, it causes an electric shock on the nape of Detta's neck and between her shoulders—the result of expected pain rather than of real pain: a shiver will pass across her cheek and the bulging veins of her neck, and disappear somewhere lower down in her back. While Detta is crouching on the grass, Lieschen, still in her tartan dress, moves the leaf along Detta's palm to her elbow and above. The area of the elbow and its inner side (Lieschen knows this because she has tried it out on herself) are the most sensitive places on the skin. It would be a waste of time to experiment anywhere else.

"Well, how is it?" inquires Lieschen, holding the leaf by its dry stem between two fingers. Detta mumbles under her breath. Lieschen gets angry and impatient: "Do you feel anything or not? I'll go look for something else—guess what." Lieschen smiles—as she imagines, ominously and cruelly. Her wideset eyes narrow into slits. "Well . . .?"

But now she has seen something so interesting that she turns away from her sister and smiles even more wickedly. On a flower growing on a long, pliable stem only a few inches from Detta, who is kneeling in the grass, a brown-black, furry bumblebee has just settled.

Buzzing angrily, it struggles among the petals that stubbornly refuse to open. It has put its head inside and, still humming, pushes the petals aside with its feet. Mr. Bumblebee (Lieschen bows to him deeply) has feet that are thick and knotty, covered with rough black down. Maybe also with some tiny hooks, although this is difficult to verify, since the welcome visitor might fly away.

"Welcome, dear sir!" Lieschen greets him. "How nice that you have decided to visit us. You are quite well, I hope?"

Detta has also noticed the bumblebee. She looks at it out of the corner of her eye, holding her breath. From so close up, the insect seems enormous.

Mr. Bumblebee, if he wanted to, could easily transfer himself from the bluebell straight to her ear or cheek. At the thought of this, Detta is shaken by stifled sobs. Tears fall from her eyes. Lieschen touches Detta's forehead with the tip of her shoe. She puts a finger to her lips: "Shhh!"

The bumblebee has finally squeezed itself inside the flower. Only a pair of rear legs and the end of the hairy abdomen stick out. Its abdomen is pulsating. Apparently it has found nectar and its mouth is working, which is why its abdomen is swelling. It moves all the time, splaying its feet. There are, in fact, tiny hooks on them; one can now observe them from nearby. Lieschen leans over the flower. The three children are waiting until the bumblebee, filled with food, extricates itself from the petals and perhaps decides to land on Detta's ear or her bare neck or at least her shoulder, in order to rest before buzzing off into the sun.

It is a known fact that Detta fears bumblebees most of all. Even the hairy caterpillars that Lieschen calls "furries" and that she intended to breed with her sister in mind, do not cause Detta such agonies, do not fill her with such intense fear.

Emil anticipates what will happen next. He sees goosepimples on his younger sister's skin. Above her elbow, her skin has suddenly become dull and rough. Emil, inwardly trembling, awaits the insect's moment of decision. But without hurrying, the bumblebee is now cleaning its forelegs and mouth, sitting on the stem of the flower. Emil knows how it will end: by the dizzying completion of a painful ecstasy followed by torment. He prays that the insect will fly away, that the experience he will have to confess with shame to Father Cornelius should this time pass him by.

Mr. Bumblebee, if he wanted to—Lieschen repeats her girlish curtsy, holding in two hands the hem of her dress and gracefully putting her left foot behind while leaning down—might decide to sink his sting into Detta's flesh. Best of all would be the tip of her pink ear, visible under her long hair, quite a tasty morsel, soft and plump, or perhaps her upper lip, now limply protruding in expectation of the insect's sting.

But do bumblebees have a sting? We read a short while ago in the Schmeil's *Zoology Manual* that, alas, they probably do not. Lieschen crouches again and, looking intently at the bumblebee, puts her palms together as if in prayer. The insect has stopped cleaning its mouth and now sits immobile, exhausted. "Maybe it's eaten too much?" says Lieschen. And if it has no sting, might it not simply bite? But with what? Does it have tiny teeth or a kind of sucker or a snout like a fly? Otto Schmeil maintains that it has not. But is this not an exaggeration, a lie spread by grown-ups in order not to frighten the children and to end every fairy tale on a cheerful note? At any rate there remains the fact of the bumblebee's extreme hairiness, its spiky legs and body, and especially the elastic mobility of its abdomen—less hairy, but capable of funny movements. It can blow up and raise itself stiffly, then suddenly become limp and slowly subside.

"Well get a move on, you lazy creature!" Lieschen urges, still squatting next to the bluebell on which the insect is perched. Discouraged, she gets up and starts fidgeting. Detta is watching the bumblebee in growing panic. At the same time, not realizing it entirely, she feels a secret desire for martyrdom and sacrifice.

Lieschen wrinkles her freckled nose. She sniffs, not being able to use her fingers to wipe it, as she often does, lest a misjudged gesture frighten away the insect which, as if to irritate her, can't decide what to do next.

"Get on with it, get on with it," Lieschen whispers, more in her thoughts than in words, although she is moving her lips and frowning.

Detta, her eyes closed now in silent prayer, feels her throat contract and her tongue stiffen. It fills her mouth, as if suddenly swollen. It seems to reach the roof of her mouth like a hard foreign body that is trying to penetrate her gullet and, not able to turn and curl up because of its size, decides to leap forward between her lips and her teeth so as to find its way out. Its red tip is now jutting out; from it a thick glob of saliva trickles down the girl's chin onto the grass like honey.

Trembling, Emil turns away, covers his face with both hands, and withdraws into the lilac bushes. Lieschen, standing on one leg, the other bent at the knee and raised, slowly turns her head and watches her brother escape. Only Detta, absorbed in what is happening to her, sees nothing. She is shaken by short, spasmodic convulsions. Her eyelids remain tightly shut, while tears begin to flow. Lieschen, impatient and irritated, stamps her foot and calls to her sister: "Shhh! Be quiet!" She even uses an expression heard on the streets: "Keep your trap shut!" Serious and collected she continues to observe her brother. Behind the clump of lilac one can see the back of a young boy wearing the dark blue uniform of a Kalksburg student, with the silver braid sewn on the azure tabs of his collar. One can also see the movements of his back and shoulders. His sister might even hear a soft, stifled moan.

("Lieschen, Lieschen, look, look at me!")

Attracted by the expected sound, Liesbeth will run toward the lilacs and there, on tiptoe, observe her brother through the dense branches covered with purplish brown clumps of flowers. She will intently follow all that occurs, still standing on tiptoe, with her hand to her mouth. She will step back cautiously and softly and then, putting her finger to her lips, she will once more admonish her sister: "Be quiet, you!"

The bumblebee has flown away. The bluebell is still swaying on its long, frail stem, but it is empty now. It is still oscillating when Emil R. emerges from behind the lilac bush and, not looking at either of his sisters, rushes up the steps into the villa and, reaching his own room, throws himself on his bed, hides his face in the pillow, and bursts into tears.

Father Cornelius receives the penitent as usual on Saturday afternoon. He hears his confession. He may realize that some details have not been admitted, may have an inkling that there is more to it than meets the eye. So he will ask a few additional questions that he would prefer to avoid. Not having obtained an explanation, he will decide that the young man is at an age when various temptations arise in the imagination. There are sins of eye and sins of ear. "If your eye offends you, pluck it out!" he might think, but will not say it aloud. He will impose a penance, three Hail Marys and, extending his hand, wrapped in a stole, to be kissed, he will dismiss him with a knock on the grille of the confessional. Young Emil will walk into the darkened church and kneel by one of the benches. Here and there at the side altars, red oil lamps are burning. An old woman is sitting immobile a few benches behind him. Emil's inner disquiet grows.

The stalls are silent in horror and condemnation, as are the empty confessionals. A blackened Christ looms on the large, black cross. The ample baroque clothes of a bearded saint look as if ruffled by a wind from hell.

Young Emil gets up and wanders on tiptoe about the silent church. His steps on the stone floor awake echoes on the flagstones. "Sacrilege!" whisper the black chapels, the secret nooks, the extinguished candles in their candlesticks. He passes a painting that he has looked at repeatedly: the Last Judgement, Hell. Father Blatt spoke about it at the Easter retreat. He described the vision of the fiery stake crawling with worms, seething with boiling pitch. And the eternal stings of remorse! The drying of the flesh, muscles, and eyes, the withering away of all the organs during the infinity of torture. Infinity! A year, two, even ten years—one can imagine this, but what is infinity? The sticking of fingers to red-hot metal? Blindness? Emptiness filled with the cries of the damned? An unending sleepless night when the past is remembered? Will the memory of life persist, will it shrink to the size of a hazelnut? He recalls Doré's illustrations in a luxury edition of *The Divine Comedy* that lies on the table in his parents' drawing room, together with other albums. Will he encounter Lieschen in the corridors of hell? As a she-devil? As an angel fallen into the abyss? As an eyeless specter in a black veil? As a bird or a cat, a black insect?

The picture in the aisle of St. Leonard's is very old. It dates from the Counterreformation, the reign of Ferdinand II. In it there are rocks from which devils with forks push the entangled naked bodies of the damned into the flame-filled abyss. Behind the highest rock, a hand raised in condemnation can be seen. A lone, disproportionately large hand of the Supreme Judge, God. In the chasm of hell dogs are visible—emaciated, resembling jackals or hyenas. There is a cat with glowing eyes and several rats, and at the top, bats and owls in flight. A witch flies into the abyss riding on a black buck. The whole fauna of hell is crowded together here in a rush to the bottom of the pit. But the bottom cannot be seen. Perhaps the artist's imagination failed him, or perhaps he did not wish to offend the eyes of the faithful with such infamies.

Dressed in his school uniform, Emil R. gazes at the painting. Somewhere down below, there must exist a bottom. Or perhaps hell has no bottom and this is what makes damnation eternal—without hope? The constant falling, tumbling from one level to another, and the constant lack of any bottom or end, the impossibility of any respite.

Years later, standing in the Sistine Chapel and looking up at the ceiling, viewing a masterpiece of another era and another dimension, Emil will think: "Hell is beautiful!" But here in the dusk of St. Leonard's, Emil is in anguish.

Back home, he cannot fall asleep. He turns from side to side, shivering in spite of the warm May night. He relives the visions of hell. The next morning, at Sunday breakfast, Miss Traut notices that Emil has rings under his eyes and, worried about her favorite child, tries to question him. But Emil remains silent, swallowing his cocoa with difficulty. He feels sick.

At early morning mass, he had taken the sacrament. He fought with himself to the last because he knew that he was about to commit the worst, the unpardonable sin, the one against the Holy Ghost—He who, of the Holy Trinity, seems the fiercest, because inhuman in his birdlike guise, deprived of human eyes and their glimmer of forgiveness. Receiving the Host, Emil feels that he is committing sacrilege.

But it is difficult to withdraw. Father Cornelius Blatt used to celebrate morning mass for the schoolboys in a side chapel. He knows his students. He knows to whom, the previous day, he granted the grace of forgiveness, absolution for sins confessed in contrition; he knows from whom he got a promise of improvement, on whom he imposed a penance, and what the penance was. Emil looked at Father Cornelius when he turned his face toward the faithful; the priest certainly saw the kneeling pupil. And when Father Cornelius walked to the rail sticky from the touch of hands and covered with a narrow strip of linen bordered with lace, among those waiting composedly for the acceptance of God's flesh in the form of a wafer, he sought Emil with his eyes. He could not have forgotten that he gave absolution to Emil yesterday, so why did he do it?

Yes, but the absolution was obtained by a ruse, thought Emil, because he did not confess everything. In his meek admissions to his confessor the thing that was most essential, because most horrendous, had been omitted: the source of sin, growing in him and filling him. In his confession the hell of bliss that, having achieved its peak, crumbles again and again into the mire of humiliation and shame, had been omitted. The eyes of his sister, awaiting that moment with trepidation, were not mentioned. But the feeling of her participation has not yet been completely realized. These are still early stirrings, the Ur-Strata.

And so, still unclear about the feelings growing in him, Emil attributed that threatening but still half-realized condition to his own weakness, and having returned to his seat, secretly spat out the Host into a clean handkerchief neatly folded into a square. A minute before, in accordance with the rules, he had held the handkerchief under his chin while kneeling in a row with the other boys, so that when the priest handed him the Host, it could not be dropped on the floor. With a feeling of growing horror he carried it home, tightly wrapped. He felt its presence in his breast pocket while he was drinking his cocoa. His sisters were quarreling over some trifle, Lieschen impossible as usual, and Detta as usual feeling wronged and near to tears. They did not pay much attention to the somber mood of their brother, tired from lack of sleep. Emil did not look at them. Miss Traut had to separate the sisters, who had come to blows.

Emil intends to bury the defiled Host at night in the garden. Has the worst happened or, since he did not swallow it, has it only happened indirectly, not finally or without appeal? And in view of this, will there still be any hope for him? Perhaps a hundred years of purgatory? Let it be a thousand years, provided that it not involve, as in the painting and in Father Blatt's words, an eternal descent into a bottomless pit. Emil R. dares not pray for fear of committing another sin in the absence of any fervency of feeling: the sin of defiling words. He sits over his mug of cocoa, hanging his head. He pretends to his mother and Miss Traut that he has a headache. So in spite of the lovely weather he has to stay indoors, while the two girls go out to the garden with their ball. Not daring even to look at them through the window, he is lying turned toward the wall, with a thermometer under his arm and a compress on his forehead applied by the anxious Miss Traut.

The eagerly awaited evening comes at last. When everybody at home is asleep and the big clock in the dining room strikes midnight, Emil sneaks out, a coat thrown over his nightshirt, into the garden full of creeping specters. Each step costs him a year of his life—each step along a path well-known in daylight, but now transformed into a dark winding passage. Where is he to bury the sacred object? Under the Turkish lilac? Bright purple in daytime, it seems now, against the background of a slightly lighter sky, to be hung with black clusters resembling vultures' nests. Perhaps vultures are indeed nestling there, ghostly and asleep, their beaks plunged into the feathers on their throats, with film over their eyes, and bare, wrinkled necks like those of old witches. The stifling scent of flowers and an intense heat rise from the earth. Over the center of the city the sky is brownish red. From the direction of Hilmteich one can hear distant echoes of a waltz. It is Sunday and people are still having fun.

Creeping on tiptoe, overcoming his growing fright, Emil

walks step by step into the black garden. In daytime quite small, it now seems as vast as a primeval forest.

Emil kneels down, wraps the Host in a red currant leaf, covers it with a handful of loose, dewy earth, then kneads it with his hands. He gets up, stands still for a moment, listening. The silence is complete; even the music from Hilmteich has stopped. Emil runs quickly toward the house, stops on the porch, and hears the violent beating of his heart. Something is moving in the grass, in the black threatening bushes. A mouse or perhaps a lizard? The bushes seem to rise up from the soil to surround him. With bare feet, in his nightshirt, he returns on tiptoe to his room and sits on the edge of the bed, shivering with the cold until his teeth begin to chatter.

After a few minutes he decides to return to the place where he has buried the defiled holy object, the living body of Christ, to make sure that ants have not found it and are even now desecrating the relic. Or perhaps a mouse, enticed by the unfamiliar smell. It might now be sitting on its hind legs, digging away with its forelegs to uncover the little casket.

And so, combatting his fear, Emil returns, digs up the Host, blows on it, wipes it with the flaps of his nightshirt, and takes it back indoors. He sneaks into the bathroom, rinses the earth-spattered treasure in the basin, tries to dry it on the towel. He carries it to his room and hides it in an empty match box lined with tissue paper. On the cover he draws a cross with a crayon. For a long time he is unable to settle down to sleep. He checks if the box is in its place, under his pillow. Is this a suitable place? Perhaps he is committing another sin, becoming familiar with something whose proper place is inside a monstrance, in the middle of the golden sunflower, at the center of shining rays. Emil in turn sleeps and wakes up briefly, filled with feverish visions.

In the morning he decides to burn the Host. That would be best. But at once he is horror-stricken: to burn Christ's living body? What has got into me?

The next day is Monday and a warm wind that augurs rain rattles the windows. Then the worst thing imaginable happens: Lieschen guesses her brother's secret and volunteers as a partner in what she considers a fine lark. Having come back from school and thrown her satchel aside, she catches her brother before lunch when their parents are not home yet and, trembling with a curiosity that makes her eyes sparkle, she whispers, holding him by the sleeve of his uniform:

"Admit it! You went out into the garden last night, didn't you? Tell me! . . . You're lying! You'd be scared. What? Show me at once, or I won't believe you."

And when Emil, completely despondent, defenseless after a sleepless night, shows his sister the small box with a cross drawn on it, she tears it out of his hand and, jumping with joy, escapes with it to her room. Her brother follows her and tries to retrieve the wooden coffin, the small tabernacle, the sanctuary of his misfortune, but he cannot because Lieschen, quicker than he, jumps on her bed and, holding the box in her raised hand, dances about, laughing and mimicking her brother's entreaties. He falls on his knees before her, but she jumps down from the bed and races toward the kitchen. Out of breath, she stops in the dark passage, clasping the box to her breast. There, completely overwhelmed, Emil finds her. Lieschen says:

"We'll divide it, all right? The thing . . . the thing inside. Half and half. All right?"

Emil tries again to persuade his sister. He fights to tear the box from her clenched fist, but Lieschen is stronger: she puts her hands behind her back, and pushes him away with her elbow and knee. After some moments of struggle, Emil gives in. Then Lieschen, in spite of her brother's protestations, opens the little wooden coffin, takes out the Host wrapped in tissue paper, and tries to eat it. But at the last moment she changes her mind. She puts it on her tongue and orders her brother to bite off a piece; in a moment of distraction, he does so.

Just then somebody rings the front door bell and the maid, calls out, "I'm coming!" and appears at the kitchen door, wiping her wet hands on her apron. The two children cling to one another, trying to hide in a dark corner of the hall under the coatrack, next to the Chinese vase with a full complement of their father's walking sticks. Among these is the famous stick with his initials and the silver head of a greyhound—a historic prop from their childhood, and two rolled parasols that belong to their mother. The coats among which they are hiding emit familiar domestic aromas of their mother's perfumes and father's cigars. Lieschen whispers into her brother's ear, while she holds him by the neck so he cannot escape: "You see, it's over: we're even now, just as I wanted. So be careful, because if you ever get in my way, I'll tell all. To Mama, Papa, and the priest—that bald one. I know you fear him the most. You'll go to hell anyway, but that is unimportant. Me, I don't fear hell at all. Besides, what you did isn't *my* fault—you're the one who took it. Anyway, if they ask, I'll deny everything. And don't you tell them it was me who broke Mama's scent bottle."

After a while, hissing straight into his ear, she says: "If you behave and do everything I tell you to, perhaps—who knows—perhaps I'll marry you. I'll think about it. Now get away from here—Mama's back!"

Emil says nothing. He stands completely still, hiding under his father's summer coat, then slowly goes to his room. He cannot collect his thoughts; his hands are sweaty and cold.

When all this happened many years ago, Emil was just eleven and his sister thirteen. It was in May 1904, an exceptionally sunny, warm month. In the public park at Hilmteich the jasmine and lilac bloomed in unusual abundance. The Third Japanese Army, commanded by General Noga, was besieging Port Arthur. There was fierce fighting for the fortress of Vodoprovodniye. In the inner roads the masts and funnels of the scuttled battleship *Ryetvisan* and the cruiser *Bayan* were jutting from the water. In the mountains behind the Yalu River General Kuroki's guards were pursuing the retreating armies of General Zasulich. Blériot would fly over the English Channel only four years and six months later. It was the fifty-sixth year of the reign of Emperor Franz Josef and the third of Edward VII, King of England and Emperor of India. Emile Loubet was President of France. The Austro-Hungarian minister of war was his Excellency Artillery General Heinrich von Pitreich, and the chief of staff was Baron Friedrich von Beck. We cannot tell whether Swann was still alive, but the Princesse Oriane de Guermantes still spread around her the aura of her beauty and charm, and Guillaume Apollinaire, Madame Kostrowicka's son, had become editor of the magazine *Guide des Rentiers*. In that same year he made his second journey to England and proposed to Annie and was rejected by her. Afterward he wrote a poem entitled *La Chanson du mal-aimé* that young Emil R. read seven years later and was so enchanted by it that he did not get to sleep until sunrise lit the windows of his room in the boarding house of Mrs. Hilde Schautzi at Grado, and the Adriatic shone with the colors of mother-of-pearl.

We are approaching the end.

Soon we shall leave sun-dried, dust-covered Fehertemplom, full of rich Banat Germans and little naked gypsies, its market square strewn with melon skins and other garbage, and its acacia trees with their pods bursting in the heat and scattering little seeds like dwarf lentils.

Soon the hour of departure will come. The last horses led by their bridles by the Sicilian Lancers will walk up wooden platforms into the cars. The semaphore behind the station, behind the warehouses and the crossing guard's booth, will lift up its green arm. And somebody in one of the cars will shout: "Cheers!" in Hungarian and Croatian and the troop train will pass over the switches outside Fehertemplom's railway station. Good-by, Fehertemplom—good luck!

Tomorrow there will be the clash of wheels on the rails, the rhythm of an accelerating train increasing to a thunderous roar as it passes the small stations of the Banat and the plain of Vojvodina, and the booths with crossing guards standing to attention in front of them, holding signals in their right hands. Bearded and bewhiskered old Hungarian and Croatian peasants, gypsies and Jews, and Banat Germans mobilized a few days before and detailed for the defense of the railway lines will salute the train that rushes past at great speed.

Troop trains will pass through this area one after another, by day and by night, by night and by day at short intervals, and the local people gathered in groups beside the railway will cheer in a multitude of languages: "Long live the Emperor!" The Sicilian Lancers, sitting in the open doors of the boxcars ("forty men and six horses") with their legs in red trousers and high boots with spurs dangling over the side, will reply to the Hungarian and Croatian peasants and especially to the buxom girls who, giggling and nudging one another in assumed embarrassment, will acknowledge with concealed laughter the good wishes and propositions hurled as the train flashes by. After the train has passed only a memory will remain, a faint image that might return after many years, perhaps even in old age: the black upturned moustache of a hero going off to war, and under it the red lips open in an exclamation or a burst of laughter. And the obscene gesture of his fingers.

Already the train is far away, but remembered by the people standing beside the track: the sound of singing; the green branches and the bunches of wild flowers decorating the cars; forecasts of triumphs to come written in chalk; the letters M.A.V., the insignia of the Royal Hungarian Railways, and K.u.K.St.B. on the Austrian cars; cars, cars, and more cars, and on the last one of each train a flag and a lantern swaying from side to side.

Click by click, the train will proceed toward its destination, while the old men and children slowly move away from the railway track, sighing and gossiping about the rumors that have multiplied over the last few days, since the mobilization of the nearest army corps—the Seventh, the Thirteenth, or the Fourth—when the troops were directed to the assembly centers commanded by Infantry General Oscar Potiorek, governor of Bosnia and Hercegovina, somewhere on the Danube, the Sava, or the Drina.

Our train will most probably pass under a stone bridge arching high above the track, and on it a cart might be seen from one side by the passengers, foreshortened because seen from below. This short glimpse might remain in the memory of those on the train: a cart full of cut corn pulled by two white Hungarian long-horn oxen, and the silhouette of a peasant in a pointed hat and dark blue apron seen against the sun, completely black, like a shadow on the light background of the summer sky.

Now there is a thunderous roar as the cars speed across a bridge over a river lit by the low, blinding sun: the Danube, seen through steel girders, its yellow, foaming water carrying great branches of trees from recent floods. Among the reeds on the banks, a girl stands up to her knees in muddy water washing clothes, now staring for a moment at the train speeding overhead, and waving to the lancers (to her, a row of red trousers and boots)—a sunburnt face glistening with perspiration, and a mouth open in greeting. But the girl will hear nothing because of the noise of the train crossing the bridge high above the water. Now the bridge has been left behind a bend in the track, while the train continues across cornfields covered with stubble, clouded by dust and the heat haze. Beyond, a plain stretches as far as the eye can see. In the vast fields, outlines of people walking, difficult to recognize from this great distance. A silvery golden horizon of summer on the Banat plain. A few lone wheat sheaves far away on the horizon; nearby, a high embankment.

The troop train has passed and disappeared. Each station has in a steel safe three envelopes to be opened after the receipt of a coded telegram. The first, white, to be opened on receipt of the code word "Poplar." The second, blue, to be opened upon receipt of the telegraphed code word "Istvan Szent." The third, red, to be opened on receipt of the code word "Arpad." The telegraphs click in the small stations as the train passes. "Palonta Nagy speaking, Palonta Nagy speaking: train number — just passed. Train number — has now passed." "Thank you, message received. Traffic duty officer, stationmaster at — Fähnrich Imre Kalay speaking. Imre Kalay here. Message received." "Palonta Nagy speaking. Palonta Nagy here."

Somewhere far away, *S.M.S. Tegetthoff* puts to sea at this moment from the port of Pula, her steel prow cutting through the green waters of the Adriatic. She is followed by *S.M.S. Kaiser Karl der Sechste*. Behind them a few torpedo boats and one submarine sail toward the island of Pelagosa.

Russia has ordered total mobilization. The German ambassador in St. Petersburg, Pourtalès, a courteous man of some distinction, has delivered an ultimatum. The day darkens. Somewhere in the region of the Bay of Kotor lightning flashes in the sky, then a thunder clap resounds that echoes in the rocky clefts of Mount Lovcen. A Montenegrin officer observes through his binoculars the steel-green waters of the bay. Then he descends a steep path. In a moment he will disappear into a thicket of silvery black bushes that will rustle for some time before closing again behind him.

Egon Erwin Kisch, the future chronicler of the first months of the Serbian campaign, is still in the town of Pisek. He will not reach the Sava and Drina, along with the complete Nineteenth Division, for two or three days. He is an acquaintance, almost a friend, of Reserve Second Lieutenant Zdenek Kocourek, and their paths during those August days will cross and then diverge.

While Kisch will approach the place where the Drina flows into the Sava, Zdenek Kocourek together with the whole Twelfth Regiment of Lancers, forming part of the Eighth Cavalry Brigade of Colonel von Woyciechowski, will go north, to arrive on August 24 by train at the station of Lubaczow in Galicia. On the night of August 27–28 near Posadowo, a white lady will cross Zdenek's path. She will emerge at night from a pine grove swathed in mist, and will put her white hands over his eyes. But this will not happen for some twenty days or so.

For the moment the train is still moving through the fertile plain of the Danube. Traveling in a second-class coach, Regimental Surgeon Oplustil will in a moment take off his gray-blue field officer's cap, with its round, dull insignia bearing the Emperor's monogram. He will probably wipe his perspiring brow because the heat on that day is unbearable, especially in the airless train compartment. When he finally opens the window (its strong green sash embroidered with silver thread now slightly tarnished and covered with soot), he will find that the heat outside the train is also unbearable. So Oplustil will close the window again.

Just then Lieutenants X and Y will decide to kill time by playing cards or perhaps—having found partners—tarot. Their faces too, like that of the luckless Dr. Oplustil who can hardly breathe, are red and puffy from the heat and shiny with perspiration. They will unbutton their collars and unbuckle their belts. In the closed compartment there is a smell of male sweat mixed with eau de Cologne and the Russian leather of the field belts and the slings for the officers' sabers, supplied by the mobilization depots in Temesvar. In addition, the air is heavy with the smoke of cigars, cigarettes, and Pursiczan tobacco. The sabers in their broad scabbards of camouflage have already been laid on the luggage rack. Now they will clink at every bend in the track, making a steady and monotonous accompaniment to the long journey. The black leather in which the seats in the second-class compartment are upholstered will also play its small independent part in that travel symphony, exuding a more discreet yet distinctive smell, easily recognizable in the gamut of all the other smells: the specific smell of the Austro-Hungarian trains whose network spreads from the frontier stations of Eger and Passau in the west to Temesvar, Arad, and Nagy Varad in the east—just as a trained ear can discern the sound of a violin chosen at random from among a whole symphony orchestra, even if more than one violin plays in it.

So much for the journey today, tomorrow, the day after, or even in three days' time.

At the moment, the cars brought to the ramp in the railway siding at Fehertemplom are being filled with squadrons, platoons, and auxiliary units. The loading of military personnel proceeds accompanied by the shouts of corporals and sergeants, giving orders and cursing in Hungarian, German, and Croatian. The horses step on the platforms cautiously, putting their freshly shod hooves on the thin diagonal slats. Some are afraid to proceed, draw back their ears, and resist in panic; the eyes of the most nervous ones must then be covered by a band. The soldiers try to comfort them, patting their necks while holding them on a short rein. The horses step from one kind of heat into another, into the airless cars overheated after a long wait in the sun. On some roofs the tar has melted and seeps down in black rivulets. Brightly shining puddles, patterns, and stains are formed. And one can smell soot, as well as the disinfectant with which the interiors of coaches have been sprinkled. Their doors and barred windows have been decorated by the lancers with branches of linden and rowan trees, also with sprigs of acacia and large unwilted sunflowers. In the morning some cars will look like green arbors. But the sun is so strong that the leaves will wilt and hang limply from the branches within an hour. Maybe a few sunflowers will survive until morning.

The troops loading are the first squadron under Captain Mala-terna, the second under Captain Istvan Koronyi, and the third commanded by Captain Count Kray von Kraiova. By nightfall probably the First Division will have been loaded. But when will the order for departure come? During the night or the next morning? No one knows. In the station master's office the tele-graph clatters, the white tape continuously emerging.

Activity at the railway siding has not ceased since dawn, when there was still dew on the axles and buffers of the cars and on the roofs and bars of the windows, and when one could breathe the fresh morning air blowing from the great plains that reach as far as the Danube. It will continue through the white hours of the afternoon and probably into the night, when lofty constellations will appear in the velvety black sky. And then, when total darkness falls and only the green and red eyes of the semaphore are alight, and here and there the smooth rails shine at the switches, and above them on the signals, the vertical or horizontal white rectangles below, pointed summits that look like hooded monks standing singly or in twos and communicating by an obscure, secret blinking of the eyes—then only will a moment of respite come. From time to time, far away beyond the supply depots, over the tops of the black trees the arm of a semaphore will rise. Second Lieutenants Zdenek Kocourek and Emil R., while observing the loading of the third squadron and walking up and down the platforms and the tracks, will be struck by the strangeness of the signals that loom in the darkness. It is Kocourek who would liken them to hooded monks. Both young men will stop under the acacia tree near the now closed depot. Between the rails a greasy, iridescent puddle of spilled oil will shine. And a drunken man will go staggering along the fence dividing the railway area from the gardens in Temesvar Street and disappear in the darkness. Far away in the town, a dog will bark.

Emil R. will now say something that he had thought about frequently before: that both of them at that particular moment, two second lieutenants of the reserve brought to that station by a strange fate, torn away from normal life, are participating in a rather important event. Despite appearances, it is not the outbreak of war against Serbia, not even the seemingly inevitable war with Russia or even a general war (since France, probably England, and perhaps Italy might join in)—no, this is not what matters most. There is a much more important problem: standing here in the station of this small Banat town, we are witnessing the end of the nineteenth century. "Do you feel the breeze of its departure?" asks Emil R., and his friend Zdenek denies it at once. According to Zdenek, the nineteenth century died of old age at the moment when the poet Lautréamont wrote his immortal work—a milestone of human thought, more than that: of imagination exceeding thought—in a word, when *Les Chants de Maldoror* was created. Or maybe even when Baudelaire's *Les Fleurs du Mal* began to bloom? At any rate, back then. We (Kocourek goes on) were both born in the twentieth century. The previous one—the century of steam, electricity, and Karl

Marx—was born when the Bastille was stormed and it died when a new era began in the arts, when new creative ideas appeared in music and in visual art, when the paintings of David and Delacroix became museum rubbish and, after the visions of Van Gogh, when the first Cubist paintings appeared in the studios on the Seine. You must have read Musil's stories, *Vereinigungen*? You must have seen the catalogue attached to the latest issue of *Die Fackel*? And those paintings by Braque? And Picasso? From Prague, I sent to your Vienna address several reproductions that I brought back from Paris.

But Emil R. remains unconvinced. The thing that will occur after the moment now being experienced, of which we are passive witnesses, is a great unknown quantity. A tunnel that our old-fashioned train is just entering. Will the train emerge at the other end of the tunnel? And is there anything beyond it? We're playing a rather pathetic role on this platform—the role of participants at a funeral. *Nous sommes des croque-morts, tous les deux.* We hold invisible candles. After which he adds: "Solferino." Zdenek Kocourek is silent. Somewhere far away a red light appears on a semaphore.

In a long row of cars, standing on the tracks, among the snorting of the horses, the stamping of hooves, and the clinking of chains, flickers of cigarettes appear here and there, and the black oily patches on the gravel faintly reflect the lanterns that the lancers have lit in the cars. In one of the more distant cars, somebody starts singing a nostalgic Magyar song.

When Lieutenant Kocourek returns to the barracks with a group of officers, from inside a room behind a second-floor balcony of one of the houses in Kerestecz Street, the words of a song are heard: "Nahorny, Nahorny, why have you left me?" One of the officers walking in the darkness stops and asks another who has been singing, and the other, obviously more familiar with the town, explains that the house from which the song comes is the town's prison. Prostitutes apprehended for some misdemeanor are held there. "The one who's singing now is a Croat. I know her, her name is Desha." And the informant so well versed in the affairs of Fehertemplom laughs loudly. He calls something in Croatian to the singing girl. The officers stop near the balcony and raise their heads, listening. The song stops, but heads appear in one of the windows and laughter resounds.

The officers continue on their way. One of them suggests they spend the evening—if they feel like it, the whole night—in Mother Rozsa's tavern. There are four young ladies on duty there, and now a fifth has arrived, imported by Mother Rozsa from as far away as Arad, in preparation for the expected flow of guests.

But when they reach Mother Rozsa's tavern, talking about one thing and another, it appears that since that morning it has been under martial law. On the ground floor Sanitation Sergeant Augustin Prchlicka is on duty, wearing a white apron and a Red Cross arm band on the sleeve of his jacket. At the sight of the officers, he gets up from a table and salutes them smartly. The tavern is now under the jurisdiction of the city commandant. Naturally, for the gentlemen here . . . But he, Sergeant Prchlicka, must warn them that in the hall there are also the noncommissioned officers of the local honved artillery regiment, and so . . .

On the table where the sanitation sergeant is on duty, stands a large glass jar with a muddy purple-red solution of potassium permanganate with a large wad of cotton beside it. A notice has been tacked on the wall setting forth the regulations, in the event of war, concerning the sanitary rules and the conditions for the use of premises of a given type, applying to members of the Austro-Hungarian forces. Sergeant Prchlicka has a sizable upturned moustache and a jovial, kindly face. The officers stand around, undecided. Since the honveds have already been admitted under some regulation or other . . .

At the same moment, Mother Rozsa comes down the stairs. She carries a candle in a silver candlestick and wears a flowery housecoat and slippers trimmed with white rabbit fur. Her high heels clatter on the stairs. Mother Rozsa becomes lyrical at the sight of regular and valued customers. She makes something that resembles a girlish curtsy, after which she spreads her arms wide as if she wanted to embrace and press to her heart the whole hesitating bunch of lancers. For old friends, of course! For them she has reserved her own small sitting room on the second floor, having admitted the others—she means the honveds—to the ground-floor hall with the buffet. Fat Marishka and two other girls are there with them, but awaiting the gentlemen officers— here her voice falls to a whisper, while she half shuts her

made-up eyes and half closes her lips—are Ilonka, Clara, and
Erzika, yes, yes, little Erzika, the same one that some of the
gentlemen might remember from last year when they had
seemed so satisfied: Erzika is back, she arrived yesterday straight
from Arad where—I will tell the gentlemen a secret—she performed at the Orpheum as a Spanish dancer, yes, yes, and a
young count fell in love with her! Mother Rozsa and her candlestick move nearer the wall to make room on the stairs for the
gentlemen officers: "Please come up, I hope you won't refuse."

So they go up, one behind the other because the stairs are
narrow. Sergeant Prchlicka looks up and smiles kindly. "Good
luck!" he says to himself and perhaps to Mother Rozsa, who
slowly climbs the stairs behind her guests. She is extremely fat
and her shape, especially seen from the back during the difficult
ascent of the stairs, makes some impression on the sergeant. How
much there is of her! He smiles and twirls his moustache. He
knows that in a few moments Mother Rozsa will remember him
as well. She will send him little Bezsi, a sixteen-year-old servant
girl who has been working there for some time, with a jug of
new white wine. He will gladly have a glass, as his throat is
quite dry. He will pour it into the beer mug beside the jar with
the gray sticky ointment. It is also in the cards that in a burst
of good humor the jovial sanitation sergeant will embrace little
Bezsi in a corner and pinch her you know where. He smiles at
the thought and lights a cigarette. At that moment three honved
artillery officers, somewhat drunk, enter the tavern, talking
loudly in Hungarian, so that Prchlicka adopts a sternly official
and yet, because of the officers' superior rank, subservient and
respectful look; straightening up, he stands at attention and
salutes. The officers are still talking noisily in Hungarian. Augustin Prchlicka, the true-born son of a Prague suburb, does not
understand a word of that language, which he despises with all
his heart, so he continues to stand at attention in his white coat,
seeing out of the corner of his eye his cigarette that rests on
the edge of the table, slowly burning and about to burn the
table's already singed and blackened wooden surface. In the
presence of officers, however—even the despised honveds—he
cannot remove his hand from the visor of his field cap nor make
a gesture contrary to regulations. Yet in spite of this, Augustin
Prchlicka has an advantage over the three noisy honveds: being

a health officer in charge of that establishment to ensure that
all eight paragraphs of the regulations displayed on the wall be
obeyed, he can make some difficulties of a sanitary and admin-
istrative nature that might cause displeasure and bitterness
among the noisy representatives of the country's armed forces—
in other words the Landwehr—on the territory of St. Stephen's
crown, as distinct from the imperial and royal units. In case of
necessity, he will point to the relevant paragraphs. The regulations are printed in three languages: German, Hungarian, and
Croat, because they apply in the area encompassing the monarchy's three southern corps: the Seventh with its base at Temesvar, the Thirteenth at Zagreb, and the Fifteenth at Sarajevo.
Had Sergeant Prchlicka been on duty in his white apron and
with the syringe, the permanganate, and the jar of gray ointment
somewhere in the kingdom of Bohemia and Moravia, the regulations of which he is guardian and executor, instead of being
in Hungarian and Croat, would have been in Czech.

While in the entrance hall Prchlicka, still saluting, denies the
paradise of bodily pleasures to the three officers of honved artillery, up in the attic, in a small room with a tiny window in the
sloping roof now darkened by a curtain with red roses and green
foliage, three young girls reserved by Mother Rozsa for her
regular and best clients—the officers of the Sicilian Lancers—are
busy making up. They are the jolly Ilonka with black eyebrows;
Clara, who is slightly too fat and lazy; and Erzika, the star of
the Orpheum at Arad, who has arrived for a guest performance
at Fehertemplom, summoned by Mother Rozsa who, two years
before, sponsored her entry into the wide world, giving the simple country girl advice and instructions, and transforming this
daughter of ordinary peasants into the prima donna of the
establishment. At that moment all three, in conformity with the
assurance given the officers by Mother Rozsa, are making preparations to receive the visitors, like any young ladies of the best
bourgeois families who spend the last minutes before their first
ball in front of a mirror, with excitement and a certain
trepidation.

Struggling with her corset, fat Clara begs her two colleagues
to help her. Next to her, resting her leg against the frame of
an armchair with torn and shabby upholstery, little Erzika tries
to fasten the garters that she bought at Arad. They are red, and

adorned with a kind of bow or rose made of scarlet elastic. Proudly she has just shown the garters to her two colleagues and been rewarded with what she had hoped for: cries of admiration and envy. Now the lazy Clara and the fiery Ilonka, excitedly leaning over Erzika's leg, are examining the marvel from Arad, bought in the shop of a certain Dumitrescu, the best ladies' fashion shop in that city. Squealing with excitement, they stroke the scarlet elastic tapes with their silvery metal clasps, they even test the elasticity of the bands. Erzika explains with pride that they have come straight from Budapest.

Ilonka is curling her black hair that falls on her shoulders. In a few minutes she will tie it with a scarlet ribbon that she has ironed; the iron is still on the window sill. Clara at last, helped by her two friends, has won the struggle with her corset and is now so constricted at the waist that she can hardly breathe; she is powdering her pink décolleté in front of the mirror. She is holding in two fingers an enormous swansdown powder puff dipped in pink powder. The giggling of the three girls will bring to the room for a moment the bald and sarcastic Joshka, the waiter and, in peacetime, the porter of the establishment. Putting his head in the door, he will say a few words in Hungarian that all three girls will greet with even noisier bursts of laughter. One of them will even quote a Hungarian proverb that will shock the old waiter, who wags his finger at them and then, having spat in disgust and muttered something under his breath, he withdraws. Erzika sticks her tongue out at him.

Ilonka, having dealt with her fringe, puts down her curling irons with a sigh of relief and blows out the bluish flame of the alcohol lamp. Both Erzika and Clara, as the final touch to their preparations, put on white starched pantaloons adorned with flounces. Fat Clara inserts a medallion of the Holy Virgin between her large breasts. All three cross themselves piously and sigh—the night promises to be busy—and then descend one by one the squeaking, narrow stairs to the little drawing room reserved for the best guests.

In the room stands a long table covered with a white cloth, a battered sofa upholstered in red velvet, a few chairs, a piano with its lid open, and an artificial palm in a square wooden pot painted green. And at the table, the officers are seated. One of them, a young second lieutenant of the reserve, is writing a letter

to his mother or perhaps his fiancée. Another—this must be
Captain Karapanca—twirls his long pomaded moustache and un-
buttons the three-starred collar of his uniform. The room is
stifling. A large hairy moth is fluttering round the lamp on the
ceiling. One of the officers talks about an operetta by Lehar that
he had seen only a week before at Budapest. Another counters
with a report on the recent horse show at Temesvar, in which
he got a first prize riding the mare Rosina, and mentions the
gold cigarette case that the jury presented to him after his
triumph. He takes it from his breast pocket and passes it around.
When he opens it and displaces the row of elegant cigarettes held
in place by a gold ribbon embroidered with silver patterns, one
can read the engraved signatures of the donors. The first is that
of Count Apponyi, the honorary president of the horse show
society at Temesvar. As a bonus, he describes a certain dancer
in a night club there, and expands upon the superiority of
Trabuco to Temes cigars.

Then the girls file in. They are greeted by the officers, who
rise from their seats and raise their glasses. Captain Karapanca
grabs Erzika, whom he has not seen for a long time, and to the
joy of the assembled company lifts her up onto the table. The
star of the Orpheum at Arad, now restored to Mother Rozsa's
tavern, is greeted by the applause of the whole party. Thus
encouraged, she performs on the table, at the request of all
present, a few steps of the can-can now fashionable at Budapest.
Everybody has an opportunity to admire her open-work stockings and red garters. Her colleagues, who have never seen or even
heard about the can-can, stand wide-eyed in amazement. The
high heels of Erzika's patent leather shoes, as tall as champagne
glasses, stamp among the plates, dishes, and bottles. In Erzika's
interpretation the can-can, very provincial and deriving from
Arad rather than Paris or Pest, is soon transformed into her
native czardas.

In spite of the many attractions, the mood of most officers is
far from entirely carefree. In spite of the tokay, the apricot
brandy, and the trio of willing girls. In spite of the ice bucket
with bottles of champagne brought in by the old waiter Joshka,
who for years has been the informant and confidential advisor of
Assistant Commissioner Bogatovich. Mother Rozsa also maintains the closest cooperation with the commissioner, without

whose good will the running of the tavern would be impossible. The commissioner comes here sometimes to the second floor. The premises are empty and the girls asleep, compensating for their sleepless night. At such moments Joshka watches to see that no uninvited person should interrupt the commissioner's siesta or his tête-à-tête with Mother Rozsa. He keeps watch downstairs at the entrance. The commissioner usually sinks into a soft armchair and lights a Virginia cigar. He graciously accepts a glass of apricot brandy, or even two glasses. He asks a few unimportant questions. If in a good mood, he may plunge a hand in Mother Rozsa's cleavage, and with his fingertips investigate and stroke her warm and generous bosom, while Mother Rozsa accepts the gesture as homage to her charms. The commissioner's hand, which never strays in a caressing gesture toward any of Mother Rozsa's girls, provides her with a moment of singular bliss. She will close her eyes and wait until he slowly removes her brassière to attain his goal. This will last for a minute or two. For a long time no one has been allowed a similar privilege and no one, alas, has asked for it.

When the commissioner leaves; and his heavy steps have been heard descending the stairs and old Joshka with a bow has closed the street door behind him, Mother Rozsa, sighing, sinks in the armchair still warm from the commissioner's body and falls into a lyrical meditation. She may yet drink a glass of her favorite liqueur, or even two or three in a row. Lingering in the small empty drawing room upstairs, immobile, she suddenly looks much older, with flaccid cheeks, and heavy folds under her chin hanging over the cameo brooch in gold pinned to her lace collar. She even forgets to button up the small buttons of her silk blouse that have been undone by the commissioner. She sits inwardly relaxed as she used to, many years ago, when a novice at her trade. Then at last Joshka, entering, gives her a discreet signal with his eyes, and Mother Rozsa comes to her senses. She gets up, adjusts her blouse and brassière, and smooths her red-tinted hair. She transforms herself again into a busy manager, severe but fair. She looks at the time on her gold watch with a gold chain, states that it is late, and climbs to the little attic room to wake up her girls. "It's time!" she calls in the doorway, half serious, half joking: "Get up, girls!" She may walk over to one of the beds that stand in a row and remove the blanket, under which nestles the sleepy and yawning Ilonka or Clara, now rubbing her eyes with her fists. And she says something like, "When I was your age . . ."

Now the establishment has been placed under martial law and thus officially mobilized and, alas, demoted. Everybody has the right to come in now. Would not the gypsy women ambling in droves suffice for mere privates and corporals—all those who under normal circumstances would never dream of coming here? And what about the embarassing, disconcerting presence downstairs of the representative of military hygiene! And those tickets or entrance cards that he is issuing, torn from a little block after the payment of a fee fixed not by her, the boss and legal owner of the establishment, but by the rules and regulations of the Imperial and Royal Army in wartime! And the initial daily inspection, made by the already mentioned representative of the medical service of the Seventh Corps—not to mention everything else! No question about it: war is inhuman and contrary to nature! Only from a sense of duty does Mother Rozsa go down to the ground floor, now full of soldiers and noncoms. The large hall with the buffet is filled with smoke and smells of beer, brandy, and disinfectant. It is full of drinking honveds, and noisy with the shrill voices of girls and sounds of gypsy music. Madame Ilonka Rozsa prefers to stay on the second floor, which for the moment is not covered by martial law. But for how long will she be able to enjoy that peaceful haven, that luxury, that calm and certainty that nothing can happen there that might compromise the excellent reputation of her establishment? For how many years has it enjoyed that reputation? Fifteen, maybe sixteen?

In the small drawing room there is merrymaking, but the atmosphere is not of the best: more melancholy than Magyar fire. In spite of themselves, the three girls have to adapt to that mood. They sigh frequently and become sentimental. Fat Clara, perched on the arm of Captain Karapanca's chair, looks with interest—maybe her sentimental heart has really been moved and she is now near to tears—at photographs shown to her one by one as he takes them from his wallet. The first is a wedding photograph taken years before. Milan Karapanca explains that his wedding took place in the church at Vukovar, the birthplace of his wife. She can be seen in the wedding picture in a veil, with a wreath of small roses on her head; next to her stands Captain Karapanca, then several years younger and still a second lieutenant, somewhat stiff in his dress uniform. The next photograph represents a little girl, perhaps six years of age, in a winter bonnet, her hands inside a muff, and next to her, slightly older than on the wedding photograph but still young and radiant, her mother. Karapanca, forgetting that he is speaking to a fellow countrywoman, explains in German, as if to underline the importance both of the picture and the situation: "My daughter is named Clara, like you," forgetting that Clara does not speak German. But she is full of goodwill, deeply touched and close to tears. She strokes the captain's cheek and to console him, moves from the arm of his chair onto his lap. She hands him a glass of tokay. "Cheers!" she says, settling more comfortably and putting her arms round his neck.

Meanwhile Second Lieutenant Wilhelm Kottfuss Freiherr von Kottvizza—the habitué of cabarets in Pest and Paris, of Ronacher's in Vienna and Maxime's on the Seine, former tennis champion of Davos, participant in motorcar races, and a great favorite of ladies in at least three European capitals—observes the proceedings at Mother Rozsa's languorously. Once a few years before, when invited to join a shooting party on the estate of one of his titled cousins in Moravia, after an evening spent in select male company, he met in the corridor a young kitchen maid saturated with the smell of fat, cabbage, soap suds, and the kitchen hearth and persuaded her, after brief resistance, to visit him in his room. In her company—unable to talk to her, because the girl did not understand a word of German, nor he a word of Czech—he experienced a number of ecstatic hours and such heavenly pleasures that he remembers them still, although he did not learn even the name of that kitchen nymph whose chapped, red hands he had covered with kisses in a euphoria never felt when caressing the most famous stars of the Casino de Paris. So that now, without taking any active part in the fun, he gladdens his heart at the sight of provincial manners in all their glory. Having put on his monocle, he admires the oleographs in the small drawing room, the tapestry representing a pair of swans, and the patterns on the tablecloth. He is enjoying the brandy that is not of prime quality, and the tokay that he does not normally drink. He even reaches for a piece of cake that under different circumstances he would not touch. He is even moved by Captain Karapanca showing yet another of his family photographs to the girl sitting on his lap and embracing him—a girl who is too fat, wears too tight a corset, and whose chubby face is flushed under the powder. She has drunk quite a lot and now, with true motherly concern, is stroking Karapanca's neck and cheeks. She has tears of authentic emotion in her eyes as she comforts him in a plaintive voice, praising the beauty of his wife and children.

Willy Kottfuss is amused by the expressions on his colleagues' faces, as with assumed earnestness they all listen to Erzika's report on her triumphs during the spring season at the Orpheum in Arad. And by the elegance acquired in that same Arad, whereby she eats a cake while hardly moving her teeth. And by her gracefully raised little finger when she holds a glass. She sits between two officers on the plush sofa in the pose of a prima donna, and does not stop talking while they, hot and tired, have already unbuttoned not only their collars, but all the silver buttons of their blue uniforms.

Today is the first of August, a Saturday, so that ahead of us there are still twenty-six days of beauty of the August moon. Yet we must hurry! It is less than four weeks!

At Posadowo, on the edge of a forest, during the night of August 27 a bearded Kuban Cossack will lean over Willy, who lies on his back. He will go through the pockets of the dying officer and take from them a gold watch made by Patek, a cigarette case, and a wallet of light gray suede. He will look at these in the moonlight that penetrates the branches of the trees. On the leather wallet he will notice gold initials. The letters W.K. and over them a seven-peaked baron's crown. In a fold of the wallet he will find the photograph of an elderly lady in mourning, several visiting cards, and some Austro-Hungarian banknotes. From the side pocket he will shake out a few crumbs of tobacco and a handful of glass beads. He will look at these in astonishment. Perhaps he will take them for precious stones. From the shadows a Cossack officer in a torn gray bearskin with a scarlet top will emerge, cutting through the branches with his saber. The Cossack soldier has already hidden in his pockets the more precious booty. The bearded officer orders him to open his hands. He will find in them the pink beads. After a moment's hesitation he angrily knocks the soldier's hand, and the beads are scattered in the grass.

Before the officers of the Sicilian Lancers proceed to Mother Rozsa's establishment—even before the cars destined for the transport of the first squadron of this regiment have been shunted here—there will arise a certain commotion in the small open space near the warehouses where in peacetime the fattened cattle of the region were assembled, before being despatched to the central slaughterhouses of Vienna and Budapest.

Escorted by soldiers with blue tabs on the collars of their field jackets (which, as everybody knows, indicates that they belong to a unit of the supply column) almost the whole stud of Anglo-Arab horses requisitioned that very morning from the various estates of Count Festetics de Tolna, are herded past in the paltry shadow of acacias scorched by the heat. Horses of various colors, stallions, geldings, and mares with necks like swans and manes like Lorelei's hair, mares that move like ballerinas of the Vienna opera, are stamping impatiently in the heat, swishing their tails to keep off the flies.

In pursuit of the brutally confiscated horses, two farm stewards arrive in a yellow carriage and, jumping out, demand to see the officer in charge. All their attempts, however, to obtain at least the release of four breeding mares—medallists of the provincial exhibition at Debrechin: one completely black, two black and bay, and one chestnut, the dam of Agamemnon, the famous winner of several races at Pest—are in vain. They meet with the obstinate inflexibility of the commandant, Lieutenant Colonel Ilija Gavrilovich, a native Croat from somewhere beyond Varazdin. He feels extreme satisfaction at being able to exert his authority, supported by a paragraph of a new law in force as of that very day. He has every right to show these Magyars where they can get off. Summoned by the transport officer at the request of the two stewards, he arrives straight from the railway buffet now occupied by troops, where he has been peacefully drinking the local brandy. He now stands facing the two Hungarians who are clad in breeches, high boots, identical summer jackets, and straw hats. He spreads his legs, puts his hands on his hips, and begins to roar in German: "Watch out—I give you fair warning, gentlemen! Don't you know that for two days we've

been at war with those Serbian swine—those bandits? . . ." He
ends the tirade, somewhat quieter, in his native tongue: "You
motherfuckers! So there!" Then, imitating the words with which
the two representatives of the count had introduced themselves,
he adds with utter contempt: "The 'gentlemen stewards,' the
'gentlemen stewards'—goulash gobblers! For me there's no more
count, baron, or civilian—go to hell!" And he turns his back
on the stewards and walks away.

The desperate stewards try to telephone the head manager of
the count's estates, residing at Kecskemet, since there can be no
question of notifying the count himself and asking him to intervene at the imperial palace. No one knows where Count Festetics
de Tolna is at the moment. Both stewards only know that a
month before he was cruising on a private yacht in the Mediterranean, because the head manager showed them a postcard
from Taormina, asking about the results of the harvest. But now,
at this moment? He might be in Vienna with the Emperor, perhaps in Pest, God only knows. The stewards have never set eyes
on Count Festetics de Tolna, the owner of over 80,000 hectares
of land.

So they climb into their yellow carriage to ride to the post
office, unaware that from that very night, from Zero Hour, all
post offices in that area are reserved for the prior use of the
Imperial and Royal Army. The postmaster at Fehertemplom,
whom they know, gestures in frustration: he cannot help. In his
place behind the desk now sits a lieutenant, sent here by the
Fifth Army command. A private telephone call to Kecskemet?
You're joking!

So by order of Lieutenant Colonel Ilija Gavrilovich, commanding officer of the supply column, the horses will travel in
three boxcars attached to the next train as far as Mitrovica,
where they will be directed straight to the headquarters of the
Fifth Army of General Liborius Frank. The general loves beautiful horses and will certainly praise Lieutenant Colonel Gavrilovich. So the count's stewards can only return to the farm twelve
kilometers from Fehertemplom. They set out like two widowers
in heavy mourning. They will ride along a side road, raising
clouds of dust that will hang in the motionless air. In Hungarian
they will curse the war and its stupid laws, and especially the
damned transport officers with that fat Croatian at their head.

Then, passing an old inn, it will occur to them to have a drink
to cheer themselves up. Having started from home at dawn, they
had no time for breakfast. They will get out of the yellow carriage, tie the horses to a tree, and enter the inn. There they will
lament their own fate and that of the brutally requisitioned
horses. And also the fact that the almost imperial power of His
Excellency the Count will not absolve them from the inevitable
conscription. Under the general mobilization order their year
was called up this very morning; they just saw the posters in the
post office at Fehertemplom.

On the road along which they had ridden, they met young
men walking in groups toward Fehertemplom, still wearing
civilian clothes, but with wooden boxes scrawled with the names
of the future warriors. There they will put on the field uniforms
of the Home Defense Infantry, otherwise known as the honveds.
In supply depots they will be given caps, jackets, and trousers
protective silver gray in color. On the trousers they will have
treble-clef markings differentiating the units of the territories of
St. Stephen's Crown from the others beyond the Litava. The
trousers will be tight in the calf, Hungarian style, but the remainder of the equipment will not differ from that of the whole
great army of the realm lying on both banks of the Litava. The
same carbines, the same coats and knapsacks covered with hairy
calf leather, the same saddlebags and pouches. And the same
metal identity disks, in case they get killed.

The men walking toward the town and the barracks are
accompanied by weeping women. Groups of children also follow
them for several kilometers. The sound of farewells, the weeping
of peasant women, and the carefree, lusty shouts of the farmhands can be heard even here, in the roomy interior of the inn
where at a separate table of honor, under the portrait of His
Most Gracious Majesty, the two stewards of Count Festetics de
Tolna drink brandy and eat strips of salted bacon served with
new, pale green, almost white onions. A good thing that the
harvest is over, think the stewards, for who will be there to finish
it? How many hands are needed to reap so many thousands of
hectares of wheat? And corn? And tobacco? And sunflowers?
Not to mention the hundreds of harvesting and threshing
machines being used on the plain on the count's model farms.

A group of gypsies enters the inn—there are numbers of them

hereabouts—and ask for brandy at the counter. The mobilized
men are accompanied by a few older ones. A very old gypsy,
having downed in one gulp a full tumbler of brandy and dried
his long moustache with his sleeve, puts a shiny violin under his
chin and looks at it lovingly. When he tunes his instrument the
others at the counter stop talking, and their faces adopt a look
of concentration. The old man begins to play. And the room with
the beamed, smoke-stained ceiling, its door wide open because
of the intense heat, and the low fields now empty after the harvest, and the immense Danube plains will resound with the tones
of plaint and melancholia, regret and sorrow, but also of love of
the intense beauty of life, the unforgettable tones of a gypsy
violin. Even Count Tolna's now almost completely tipsy stewards
will grow silent, put away their glasses, and listen entranced. One
of them will throw to the gypsy across the width of the room a
silver coin bearing the portrait of His Most Gracious Majesty.
The coin will roll over the floor of blackened, knotty planks,
rebound from the side of the counter, spin like a top, then come
to rest at the feet of the musician. Still playing, he will bend
down and pick it up. His eyes gleaming in his dark, wrinkled
face, he will walk across to the stewards' table and play a gypsy
tune. The stewards burst into tears, in the presence of the whole
crowd. Resting their chins on their hands, bending toward each
other until their heads touch, they will rock in time to the wist-
ful music as tears flow down their young faces. Then they will
embrace each other. With tear-stained faces and gabbling drunk-
enly, they will recall the names of the horses that they have
known and looked after since they were young colts. The mares'
names—Duna, Tisha, Viorica, and Etelka—repeated over and
over again in a caressing tone, ever more lovingly, will mingle
with the music of the violin. The young gypsy recruits will
remain standing at the counter covered with tinplate and wet
from spilled drinks. They will observe the stewards and the
violin player from a distance, not daring to approach them. One
of them will wave a branch of mulberry, picked on the way, to
keep off the bothersome flies. And the fat innkeeper will remain
behind the counter, listening intently to the music, suddenly
serious, solemn in his dark blue overalls, conscious of the pathos
of the moment.

The well-known gypsy horse thief, Andras Balas, arrested on the orders of Assistant Commissioner Bogatovich, is snoozing as he sits on the stone floor of the town jail. His curly black head rolls in sleep and he wakes up with a start. He then props his head on his left forearm, sighs deeply, and falls asleep again. He dreams of fruit and water, of a large river filling a broad bed, and of an apple offered him by a hand with thin, sunburnt fingers. And then the apple changes shape and becomes a sliced melon dripping a thick orangy-golden juice. Andras Balas sighs again in his dream and lifts his hand to his face. In a landscape that is green and orange, limpid and yet opaque, across something that might be a green meadow shiny with dew, or perhaps his own extended hand, a young gypsy girl will appear, running. She will hold in her hand a sprig of blooming acacia. Andras Balas, now lying on his back on the stone floor, snores, in his sleep scratching his hairy chest glistening with sweat. He clenches and loosens his fingers in turn. In his dream the warm melon juice drips on his chin, neck, and breast down to his bare muscular stomach. Then the jaws of the sleeping man will move and Andras Balas will turn his face toward the brick wall.

In the office of the Royal Gendarmerie, Assistant Commissioner Bogatovich has been working since early morning. He had already questioned three male gypsies.

A regular customer of the town's detention center, and even of the district jail at Arad, the twenty-eight-year-old Andras Balas is questioned first. He stands in front of the assistant commissioner's table, and somewhere to the side sits the clerk, Clement Marina. The latter constantly wrinkles his pointed freckled nose, and scratches himself behind his ear with a penholder that is bright red, highly polished, and new. Each time the assistant commissioner looks away, Marina stealthily puts his red penholder inside his ear. He turns it this way and that, removes it, wipes it on his trousers and, awaiting the words of the deposition to be entered in the suspect's file, he dips the pen into the glass inkwell. Next to it is a blotter of light wood, with an inscription burnt into it: "Souvenir of Ragusa."

The gypsy shifts his weight from foot to foot. He is black-haired and unshaven; his shirt, tucked into his loose, slightly frayed linen trousers, has lost all its buttons. It is grease-stained,

and open over his chest. Andras Balas stands barefoot in front
of the table.

The bottoms of Balas's trousers are clearly smeared with clay.
These traces of clay might serve as evidence against him. After
so many weeks of drought, this kind of wet, bright yellow clay
can be found only at the very bottom of one of the two old clay
pits that are never entirely dry. The two gentlemen behind the
table raise themselves in their chairs and look at the trouser legs
of the suspect. The commissioner knows that his regular customer, Andras Balas, is not guilty of the death of Marika Huban,
but takes this opportunity to settle his other accounts with Gypsy
Balas. He wants to frighten him. Balas denies everything. On the
evening of the day in question he was at least two kilometers
from the scene of the crime. What was he doing there? Balas
good-naturedly admits that he was trying, under the cover of
darkness and the commotion caused by news of mobilization and
the war against Serbia, to steal a little corn from a sack. The
commissioner looks at him severely across the table and coughs
meaningfully. He knits his brows that are half an inch thick,
black, bushy, much thicker than usual in these regions abound-
ing in men with thick growths of hair. Bogatovich's pomaded
and upturned moustache rises sternly, showing a row of white
teeth. He smiles in his usual, ironically cruel way, but Balas,
knowing the commissioner quite well, suffers this terrifying sight
with resignation. He wipes his nose with his fingers. As before,
he shifts his weight from foot to foot.

"And what about the cow?" the commissioner insists. "What
about Widow Miller's cow, eh?"

"The cow?" Balas scratches his tousled black hair. "With the
cow, Mr. Commissioner, it was like this . . ." He begins, weigh-
ing every word, and Clerk Marina at last can dip his pen in the
glass inkwell and get to work.

At the same moment a troop train is crossing the bridge over
the river still muddy from the recent floods and carrying
branches of willow, splinters of timber, and streaks of yellowy
foam. In a half-ruined gypsy hut at the very end of Zsak Street
one of the gypsy women wakes up and having bared her brown
breast from under a shirt that is dirty, saturated with tallow to
keep insects away, and scorched by fire, gives it to her baby to
suck. The dark, curly-haired child climbs clumsily on top of the

half-reclining mother and greedily begins to suck her great, broad, almost completely black nipple. A few large flies circle about, coming from outside where chickens are pecking and a mongrel dog tied on a long chain is yawning.

The horizon against which looms the black silhouette of the tall chimney of the brickwork has become green. The sky is celadon-colored, saturated at the edges with red, and on the stubble fields, in spite of the early hour, the air trembles in the heat. Another scorching day. In the honved barracks reveille resounds and sleepy soldiers rush with their buckets to the well. In one of the smaller rooms in the Emperor Frederick Barracks, young Second Lieutenant Emil R. after a sleepless night takes an exercise book from his valise and writes the beginning of a lyrical diary or a prose poem: "Once upon a time there were two sisters, Elizabeth and Bernadette, who had one brother, Emil . . ."

The other occupant of the room, Second Lieutenant Zdenek Kocourek, is still asleep at this early hour, facing the wall. In his shiny, well-cleaned high boots with spurs that stand by the bed, the first pink rays of the dawn shining through the open window are reflected.

At the same time, in the outer roads of Spalato four light cruisers—the *Novara, Saida, Lika,* and *Admiral Spaun*—lie at anchor, ready to depart. From their funnels streaks of transparent smoke rise into the clear air against the background of a cloudless sky. The protective coverings have already been removed from the barrels of the guns. There is feverish activity on the decks. The officers are issuing orders. On the foremast of the light cruiser *Novara* flies the flag of the squadron commander, Vice Admiral Horthy. The old walls of Diocletian's palace shine in the morning sun.

On the deck of *Admiral Spaun* stands Naval Lieutenant Edmund von S. Leaning against the steel turret, from which two long light-gray gun barrels project, he is writing a postcard to Elizabeth R. in Vienna. He intends to send it by field post.

At Fehertemplom the whole mail consists of letters sent by persons in uniform, so it will be stamped "Field Post No. —" Place names are forbidden. The postal inspector and the military censor employed there will obliterate with black ink all details of date and place that might provide information to the enemy.

Just the previous night two gendarmes brought to the commissioner's office at Fehertemplom a young suspect caught in the neighborhood of the barracks of the honved artillery. Assistant Commissioner Bogatovich has ordered him locked up for the time being in the cellar of his office. He is now questioning yet another gypsy from the Gypsy Quarter. He does not realize that as of the previous night all cases of a civilian nature have entirely lost their importance, that the death of some gypsy girl is of no interest to anyone any longer. But Commissioner Bogatovich's thinking is still prewar and civilian, almost anachronistic and behind the times. He does not know that while the young gypsy Yano stands in front of his table—the same Yano who was the first to inform him about finding the body of Marika Huban —the auditor of the Fifth Imperial and Royal Army, Lieutenant Colonel Karel Lammasch, will arrive at the town of Fehertemplom. That he is indeed already alighting from the dust-covered motorcar in which he has traveled straight from Temesvar with his assistant, Second Lieutenant Alfred von Letnay of the Military Judicial Service.

Confident in his not-yet-threatened power, Commissioner Bogatovich is questioning Yano. Yano had boasted to the boys in the shanties at Zsak Street how, while searching for something in the bushes on the slopes of the old clay pit, he found somebody's corpse. And how, having lit a match, he saw in its faint light the face of Marika, whom he has known from childhood. He crouched next to the deceased and looked at her closely. He touched her almost cold arm and noticed that his fingers were sticky from her still moist blood. Then he got frightened. He got out of the pit and ran to report the fact to the police while Sergeant Vilajcich was on duty.

"But why did you go to the clay pit?" was the commissioner's first question.

Yano was somewhat hesitant in his answers. He couldn't remember what he had been looking for in the old clay pit. He just went there, he says, but for the Royal Gendarmerie such an explanation is not good enough. Nobody who is honest and sane "just goes" anywhere. So it would be better if Yano stopped quibbling and joking because this is no joke, and Commissioner Bogatovich can prove it to people who are more important than

Yano. And Yano, having been slapped for good measure, is led away to the cells.

Another gypsy youth, a certain Lupa, living in the same shanty as the deceased Marika Huban and quite probably her lover for some months, has declared that he clearly saw the silhouettes of two people walking at the critical time toward the clay pit, and that he recognized Marika's laughter and heard her whispering to someone who was walking behind her. Lupa stood for a moment at the crossing of the roads near the brickworks, considering whether to follow the two, but then he thought better of it and walked away toward Zsak Street. What did he do when he returned to the Gypsy Quarter? Nothing. He lay on the grass in front of Hut 5 where he lives, and lit a cigarette. The night was very beautiful, so . . .

"And is that all? I'm not interested in the beauty of nature," says the assistant commissioner.

No, that is not all. With regard to Marika's necklace, he knows everything about it and if Mr. Assistant Commissioner considered it important, he would . . .

"Everything is important that concerns a crime!" replies the commissioner, adopting a severe look. But Lupa smiles and is not at all taken aback. Well then, with regard to those beads, Marika had stolen them in the bazaar a few days ago. She grabbed a handful of them and escaped. Several beads fell to the ground, scattering, and he, Lupa, picked them up. He also helped Marika to thread them on a strong thin wire that he found in the market, such as is put round boxes of fruit destined for export. The place is full of them there beside the Fento Brothers warehouse in Franz Josef Square. Mr. Assistant Commissioner can see for himself. No, he won't deny that he and Marika were in love, and he had even promised her that they would go away together with Papa Gyula's band. Why then, when he assumed that he had recognized Marika's laughter that night near the clay pit, did he not follow her to find out with whom she was walking, if only out of jealousy? Lupa smiles. He is a handsome, dark, sixteen-year-old youth. He shrugs, wondering at the ignorance of local customs displayed by the commissioner, who should know that . . .

"That what?"

"That if it really was her, she was going to the clay pit not with a gypsy but a soldier. If it had been a gypsy, then . . ." Angry fires glint in Lupa's eyes. "Then," he concludes, looking into Bogatovich's eyes, "then I would have dealt with him and with her. But since it was some stranger, some soldier or officer, that doesn't count."

Both men behind the desk listen with moderate curiosity. Bogatovich lights a cigar, bites off its end, spits it out and, sprawling in his chair, emits the first cloud of bluish smoke. Clerk Marina is playing with the red penholder.

Marika often went with soldiers into the bushes behind the brickworks. Before the harvest, when the corn was high, she went there, and when the corn was cut she went to the clay pit. Lupa used to wait for her on the road leading in that direction, to take her home. They lived in the same shanty, in the same room.

"So you recognized the soldier, did you?" asks the commissioner. Clerk Marina now dips his pen in the inkwell and awaits the gypsy's answer.

"Yes, by his uniform and especially the hat. He had on a field cap."

"Careful now! Perhaps it was an officer, eh?" The two gentlemen behind the table become watchful and attentive; they even lean forward.

"It might have been an officer. I'm not quite sure. It was dark and then," he adds after a moment's thought, "having smoked the cigarette in front of the shanty, perhaps an hour later I went toward the brickworks. For it had been too long. Then I met Yano running and out of breath, and he told me what he had found at the bottom of the pit. He even showed me the beads he had in his clenched hand. He picked them up in the grass, at the bottom. He gave me a handful."

"What did you do then—go look for yourself?"

"No, I was afraid. I felt such fear that I ran back to the shanty and wakened old Papa Gyula—the leader of the band. I told him everything and he ordered me not to tell anybody, because somebody might think one of us had done it. But it was a stranger, I swear to you. A soldier. Perhaps one of those who pass through here. Or perhaps one of the local ones. I don't know. It was dark."

When Lupa has been led away to the cell where he will be kept, just in case, until the end of the investigation, a smile of triumph spreads on Bogatovich's face. "Didn't I tell you? I was certain from the very beginning! This must have been done by one of the officers! But which? And will we be able to question them all before the local garrison leaves Fehertemplom? Because afterward he'll vanish into thin air! We've got to get down to work while there's still time!"

And the assistant commissioner, for order's sake, looks through the papers relating to the deceased: born probably in 1900, while on the road with the tribe, somewhere in the region of Kecskemet, daughter of the late Miklos Huban and Ilonka Rajicich, address now unknown, because she left Fehertemplom with the tribe as long ago as 1909 and it is not known whether she is still alive. Her daughter Marika was raised together with other gypsy children in the Gypsy Quarter, where she lately lodged in Hut 5 in Zsak Street. She was repeatedly apprehended for theft, for tricking drunken soldiers into parting with their money, for vagrancy and begging. Examined prophylactically in the town's health offices on July 7, 1914, by the town physician, when brought there by a gendarme. No venereal disease was found. Seal and signature of the town physician. That's all. List of penalties. Fingerprints. No photograph. As a minor she did not have any personal documents. And that's it.

Bogatovich puts the papers away in a drawer of his table. He gets up and begins to walk up and down in his office. Every now and then he stops next to the barred window. In the street some officers are walking, their sabers rattling. Chewing the end of his cigar, Bogatovich observes them closely.

In the town, meanwhile, posters are being stuck up proclaiming the order for general mobilization throughout the entire dual monarchy. The posters are in the three local languages: German, Hungarian, and Croat. Under each text there is a slightly different signature of His Gracious Majesty: Franz Josef der Erste, Ferenc-Jozsef, Franjo Josip. The imperial manifesto begins: "To my Peoples." A few persons gather in front of the still wet posters stuck on the post office, the directorate of salt mines, the tax office, and a few other buildings. Somebody is reading aloud, moving his finger under the lines of print, patiently explaining to others who listen intently.

A young boy crosses Franz Josef Square. In the station a locomotive whistles, then slowly begins to move. Over the roofs of
the low station storerooms a cloud of black smoke rises, produced by the regular breathing of the locomotive. It hangs for
a time in the windless air, then disperses among the tall, shaggy,
sun-scorched crowns of the acacia trees.

Yano, the gypsy youth, is being interrogated again. He admits
that on the day in question he did not accidentally "just go"
down the slope to the old clay pit. He had been loitering around
the establishment of Mother Bezsi in Kiralyi Street, where the
military gentlemen were having fun. He stood in the shade of a
tree facing the tavern—he can pinpoint the very spot—leaning
against the shutters of Winter's bakery, closed at the time. What
was he doing there? Nothing in particular. He found a large
cigarette butt, so he lit it. What was he waiting for? Marika,
whom he had known since they were both children, had asked
him to watch over her. She had quarreled for some reason with
her lover Lupa, so she asked Yano to do this. He saw her walking
up and down under the chestnut trees behind Mother Bezsi's
tavern, waiting for an opportunity. But she was afraid. He
doesn't know why. She had a bad premonition. So she said:
"Wait for me, and follow us without being seen." She needed
two crowns urgently and was going to get them at any price.
She wanted to buy a shawl that she had dreamed about for a
long time—a green shawl with red roses. She had tried to steal
it, but couldn't because it was in the window of Turner's shop
in the market. He, Yano, knows all about it, because they both
had stood together several times in front of that shop window.
To steal something from a shop isn't like stealing from a stall.
If she had dared to enter the shop, Mr. Turner would have
noticed and immediately chased her off. He might even have
added, if he caught her, a few resounding slaps. He had done
this once before. He, Yano, had witnessed it. And that shawl
with flowers cost all of two crowns. A soldier, Mr. Commissioner,
will give at most fifty filers or a cigarette when he is drunk. But
an officer . . . Once already she had succeeded in squeezing a
crown from one of the gentlemen officers. She had shown it to
him. So on that evening, standing in front of the bakery, I saw
how she walked up and down in the middle of the road, how

she came out of the shadow of a chestnut tree, and how an officer stopped next to her. Did he have a moustache? Yano considered for a moment. Maybe, maybe not. In any case he was very slim and young. It was too dark and they were too far away to see exactly. They stood for a while together in the street, then she walked away first and he a few steps behind her. Yano then left his hiding place near Winter's bakery and began to follow them. The officer gave Marika a cigarette, or rather she herself took it out of his mouth and, laughing, even blew the smoke into his eyes. Then they both turned to the right, onto the path that circles the bricksheds, and went into the bushes. Yano stopped there and waited. How long? Perhaps ten minutes, perhaps a little more. It was completely dark. They probably went down below, to the bottom of the clay pit. He isn't sure, but he now realizes that he heard Marika's laughter from down below. Then silence—and a sudden scream. A short scream, and again silence. So after a moment's hesitation Yano ran down the slope to the bottom of the pit. In the darkness he began to call, "Marika! Marishka!" Then, after some little time, he stumbled upon her. "Mr. Commissioner knows the rest. She lay there, and strewn around her were the beads from the torn necklace. I stepped on them with my bare foot. I don't know why, but I picked up a whole handful of them."

Yano cannot explain now why he did it. Perhaps instinctively or perhaps to show them to somebody as proof? He crouched near the girl lying on her back and touched her delicately. He felt blood on his fingers. Marika was not alive, but she was still warm. Yano got up and stood there for a moment, not knowing what to do. Then he climbed up the slope and ran toward Kiralyi Street. There, smoking a cigarette, stood Lupa. Yano showed him the beads, unable to speak because of shock. But Lupa probably understood. "I ran to Mother Bezsi's tavern, for at first I thought I would tell her what had happened, or perhaps tell the old waiter Laszlo. But a group of officers was just leaving the tavern. So I changed my mind and ran toward the police station. I spilled the beads in front of the tavern. I remember that they shone in the light of the lamp hanging over the entrance, and one of the officers stooped down and, I think, picked up a few of the beads and looked at them as if astonished. And as for Lupa, I don't know whether he went down there to the pit or not. I can't remember. I left him standing in the path. Yes, Mr. Commissioner, it was an officer, I'm certain. As for the moustache, I don't think he had one. He was very young. Yes, a Lancer, I'm sure. I would have recognized one of ours by the cords on his uniform. It was an officer of the Lancers, I know for sure. No, when I got down to the clay pit, looking for Marika, he wasn't there. He had disappeared. I'd have heard his steps. There are dry stalks there that crackle when you walk on them."

Clerk Marina notes painstakingly, with careful penmanship, every word of Gypsy Yano's deposition. When the record is ready, Yano puts a cross under it. He cannot write. He remains in front of the table and looks at the two officials. Commissioner Bogatovich is enjoying moments of unclouded triumph. Now he has proof. He believes every word of the gypsy youth's story. So, just as he had expected, the murderer was one of those fancy boys who don't even deign to notice him! And since, as the gypsy maintains, the officer who went with the deceased to the old clay pit did not have a moustache, one must eliminate all the moustachioed ones—that is, the majority. Bogatovich reaches for his private list. He strikes off several names. Several officers have a clear alibi. At the given time, they were at Mother Rozsa's. He also has a list of those who that evening were in Mother Bezsi's tavern. She knows them all, of course. She has named each of them in turn, except two or three reserve officers, new arrivals, whom she did not know. Waiter Laszlo confirmed her deposition under oath. Here is the pile of documents. Bogatovich puts his hand on them as if it were a heavy seal. Now one must act cautiously but at the same time quickly, for there is not much time. One must make a final selection of names and strike the guilty man unawares, for he probably thinks that the Royal Gendarmerie does not reach so high. It will reach that high, and how! Assistant Commissioner Bogatovich gets up from behind his table and resumes his diagonal march across the little room with barred windows. He reaches for another cigar and lights it. He stops in front of the portrait of His Gracious Majesty hanging on the wall. It is a portrait of the Emperor in Hungarian coronation robes. Such portraits are seen only in the territories of St. Stephen's Crown or beyond the river Litava. With his calm, majestic gaze the Emperor looks confidently at his loyal liege,

Assistant Commissioner Bogatovich. Next to the portrait, lower down to the right, nearer the window, is displayed the mobilization decree. But the decree is now of less interest to Bogatovich. In this post of the Royal Gendarmerie it is the harbinger of a somewhat different, still unknown era, unfamiliar and only half real. The glue with which the poster was stuck to the brown wall is not yet dry. Bogatovich disregards two texts—the German and Croatian—and reads the Hungarian one, in spite of its being his adopted tongue. In his childhood—he remembers well—his mother, a peasant from one of the Banat villages, sang songs for him in Croatian. And he himself, before he went to a Magyar school . . . But later, when he put on his head that magnificent symbol of authority, the hat adorned with green cock feathers, and when he had buttoned up all the buttons of his gendarme's jacket . . . Since that time, only in moments of complete inner relaxation—after drinking wine or brandy, or when in bed with his wife—does he allow himself to think and speak in the language of his forebears. Here in the office he never allows himself to do so. So that now, thinking about something else, he reads mechanically sentence by sentence the text signed by the name Ferenc-Jozsef.

At the same time His Excellency the Minister of Finances of the Dual Monarchy, Governor of Bosnia and Hercegovina—lands belonging to both crowns, the imperial and the royal—finds on his desk a handwritten letter from the Monarch: "Dear Minister von Bilinski: I have seen fit to order the general mobilization. Franz Joseph."

His Excellency Minister Bilinski puts on his pince-nez and reads the text of the imperial handwritten letter aloud, standing up to show respect and moving his lips. His short gray beard moves, too. Up and down, up and down.

The letter written by Reserve Second Lieutenant Emil R. will never reach the Fifth Army censor in the imperial and royal post office at Fehertemplom. When writing it, Emil R. does not think of the war censorship. He is in a state of utter irritation, exaltation, and depression. Half reclining, half sitting on the camp bed in the little room on the first floor of the Emperor Ferdinand Barracks, he writes the letter that will never be sent. The windows of the room are wide open, admitting the growing heat of the morning. In one of the windowpanes the interior of the barrack courtyard is reflected, the tips of the half-dried acacias, the slanting roof of the lancers' stables. And now there moves on it the reflection of a black and bay horse led by the bridle by a soldier. The horse, trying to drive the flies away, shakes its head; then its thick, carefully groomed mane spreads out like a fan, for half a second hangs almost unmoving in the air, then falls to the side. The lancer and his horse disappear from Emil's field of vision; on the windowpane there remains only the reflection of the dusty orange courtyard.

And now another window, in another wing of the barracks, obviously pushed by somebody's hand from the inside, will throw a wavering reflection on the wall of the room in which, half reclining, half sitting on a bed covered by a reddish blanket Emil R. is writing a letter. The luminous reflection will create for a moment a kind of mirage, wavering and almost tangible: the view of a boat rolling in streaky waves. Emil lifts his head and, his pen poised over the paper, he shivers. But the image of the boat has vanished. The pane darkens.

Infantry General Liborius Frank, commander of the Fifth Army, leans over a staff map spread on a large table in his headquarters. Considering, he holds in two fingers a paper flag on a pin. While Emil R. bends down and starts writing the first words of the letter that he will never send, General Frank pushes the pin into the staff map lined with canvas. The pin is inserted into the slippery paper of the map with such strength that it squeaks. The general adjusts it with his index finger, pushing it even deeper in the place named Mitrovica. The flag is in two colors. It designates a unit of the Imperial and Royal Cavalry, to distinguish it from the one-colored flags for units of the Imperial and Royal Infantry. On the flag designating Mitrovica is the number 8. This means the Eighth Cavalry Brigade, consisting of the Twelfth Regiment of Lancers and the Ninth Hussars. Following it is the flag marked with the number 4, designating the Fourth Brigade composed of two hussars regiments: the Tenth and Thirteenth. Together they form at Mitrovica the Tenth Cavalry Division under the command of Lieutenant General Mayer. At that very time General Mayer is buckling on his saber in the divisional offices at Arad. His orderly is taking his luggage out into the courtyard. In the street a large dark green car, a Laurin & Klement, is waiting. The canvas roof is down, because the general cannot stand the heat. His aide-de-camp, a young second Lieutenant of the hussars, is standing by the automobile awaiting the moment when the Tenth Division Commander will descend. The general's spurs can be heard clinking on the steps. The scabbard of his saber, catching on the banisters of the staircase, is also clinking.

General Frank, leaning with both hands on the wide table top covered with the large sheets of staff maps, considers the next move to be made with the flags of many sizes and colors. The latter rest for the moment on the rim of the map, in a disordered heap, like a bundle of colored toothpicks.

Altogether, in the area of Mitrovica the general collects twenty-four cavalry squadrons and three batteries of horse artillery, each composed of eight M5 guns. A moment ago, with one swipe of his hand, General Frank moved that group of forces from the region Temesvar-Arad-Fehertemplom to the region of concentration Mitrovica-Nikinci-Klenak, facing the Serbian fortress of Sabac on the other bank of the Sava. Here, over two hundred years ago, the armies of Prince Eugene of Savoy were concentrated to storm the Serbian fortress. It is possible that now the commandant of the Serbian fortress, designated on the Austrian staff maps by a black circle surrounded with red points of a star, is observing through his field glasses the Austrian bank of the river, which is almost completely empty. Only infantry patrols operate there, hidden in clumps of osier. But the movement of the general's commanding hand, changing the position of the flags on the map, will make the other bank swarm, if not the next day then the day after that, with numerous units of the Imperial and Royal Army.

Over two hundred years before the Pasha of Sabac observed through a long telescope, in a similar manner and with similar anxiety, the yellowish plain on the opposite bank of the river. At a certain hour he probably also saw a cloud of dust raised by the galloping regiments of Prince Eugene's army approaching the river. And lances glistening in the air, and flags flapping in the wind. And then, having for a moment put down the long telescope mounted in ebony and brass, he lifted his eyes to the cloudless sky. Somewhere above him, on the minaret casting a sharp blue shadow on the sandy river banks and on the river itself—a shadow reaching to the other bank, where hosts of giaours were approaching at high speed—a muezzin raised his arms and made his call to Allah resound from the battlements. The muezzin, seen from below and in perspective, looked like a yellow bird perched on top of his tower. The sleeves of his long, loose robe fluttered in the air like wings. Shading their eyes from the sun, Prince Eugene's soldiers, reining their galloping horses at a ford of the Sava, saw him against the background of a cloudless blue sky like the background of a Venetian painting. The grenadiers in white collars and high bearskins advanced in serried ranks to the roll of drums, then stopped and pointed their muskets at the silhouette of the man praying on the high tower at Sabac. But in those days the weapons were not like the long-range rifles of 1914. The heavy lead bullets of Prince Carignan's musketeers fell like hail in the Sava, where bubbles rose as during summer storms, and a white smoke spread over the river meadows.

Infantry General Liborius Ritter von Frank, colonel of the Sixty-first Regiment of Hungarian Infantry, former commandant of the Seventh Corps at Temesvar and lately inspector of the army, is an old man. He is sixty-eight. With a perfect part in the middle of his head, he sports a long, pointed, upturned gray moustache and an equally gray short beard. Above his fleshy red nose there is a deep line between his bushy eyebrows that gives his face a fierce appearance. The general is considered fanciful, somewhat hard to live with, unpredictable when aroused, and rather obstinate. When he commanded the Seventh Corps at Temesvar, he was seen parading on horseback in the city streets, straight-backed and stiff, riding next to a carriage with high yellow wheels, pulled by a white Arabian mare and driven by his daughter, Christina. Miss Frank, who held the reins in her outstretched hands, was usually clad in a riding jacket and, like her father, loved horses—and also hats imported from Budapest that influenced feminine fashions in Temesvar. Most famous were the hats adorned with aigrettes in 1909.

Despite traits that might have been considered by some, especially by his immediate subordinates, as faults, General Liborius Ritter von Frank (ennobled by the imperial decree of February 1910, as proof of the highest esteem for his achievements) is considered one of the most eminent strategists of the Imperial and Royal Army. He has displayed his talents on imperial maneuvers. Now, when placing the little flags on pins in his maps, he is the nearest collaborator of the commander of the whole southern front, His Excellency Artillery General Oscar Potiorek.

Time flies and the goal approaches: on the birthday of His Most Gracious Majesty, August 18, one should be able to offer him the keys to Belgrade on a satin cushion. One must show these swineherds from over the Danube the worth of the Imperial and Royal Army, covered in glory by the victories on the Senta and at Aspern, Custoza, and Novara. And the superior minds of the two generals, their modern and advanced strategic thinking. King Peter has already left the capital that was captured years before by Prince Eugene, and whose sloping streets will soon resound with the steps of the Imperial and Royal Infantry. The Serbian king has escaped to Nis, and the two Serbian commanders—Bojovich of the First Army and Jurisich-Sturm of the Third, as well as the commander in chief, Vojvoda Putnik—are awaiting a pincer attack by the two Austrian armies, the Fifth from the north and the Sixth from the west. The Austrian guns are already firing over the Sava and the Drina. The light naval squadron that sailed at night from Spalato is heading for Antivari. Two Aviatic-type airplanes are circling over the Montenegro coast. A moored silver balloon floats over a yellow cornfield. The flags on pins, reminding one of counters in a children's game, are now moved in swift gestures by the commander in chief, denoting a change in the routes of troop trains. They mean hours of white, cruel heat in cattle cars and passenger coaches; stops at stations, in open fields, and at barred closed crossing points; and black nights full of the noise of crickets on the grassy slopes of the railway embankments of southern Hungary and Croatia. Meanwhile, the soldiers sit with their legs dangling from the cars stopped in empty fields, and listen to the nighttime noises coming from fields and vast meadows along the Danube and the Sava.

In the office of General Liborius Frank at Fifth Army headquarters, on his large map spread on two tables pushed together, all these troop movements are seen in one move of a hand emerging from a blue sleeve decorated with golden braid—one gesture of the elderly fingers that during a moment of reflection hold a colored flag in the air, before pushing it firmly into the name of a locality.

When the pin perforates the stiff, smooth surface of the staff map, telephones will start ringing and the white tape covered with Morse code will begin to festoon the floor, until somebody who until then was busy drinking tea, or reading the last number of the *Pester Lloyd*, or playing cards with an office colleague in some village station, gets up to read the message, after which he will walk to his safe and take out a sealed envelope with the inscription, "Secret—to be opened only when password *Arpad* is received." And the troop trains will start on their way.

But before the last train moves from the station at Fehertemplom—a train carrying the Sicilian Lancers, heirs of the defeats at Solferino, Magenta, and Montebello, marked forever by the double stigma of the death of a kingdom that, like a skeleton, rested its feet on the two stone sarcophagi of Scylla and Charybdis —before that train departs, in a small room in the left wing of the half empty, almost abandoned Emperor Ferdinand Barracks, young Reserve Second Lieutenant Emil R. (in civilian life, a law student) will write a letter that he will never send:

"My beloved! I tore up my last letter on the train coming here a few days ago from Trieste. And this one? I've been writing it, tearing it up, and writing it again, and I know that I'll tear it up this time too and burn the pieces as before, so that no trace is left of it. I've lived through a bad night, perhaps the worst night of all. I hope it was my last. What shall I write you that you don't already know? Perhaps only that I have constantly before me your narrow, half-closed eyes, always, always. Wherever I look I see them. When I strain my eyes to look at the sun until blinded, and at the stupid, uninteresting, alien world of other people around me whom I care nothing about. Neither their worries nor their joys, not even the war and its goals, nor death that awaits all of us who go to that war, interest me. I think about you by night and by day, sleeping and waking. I feel your hands on my eyes. Ah, to end one's existence imprinted with your image for the eternity of nonexistence! You will never read these words written in the consciousness of the growing emptiness and nonsense of existence, in a state of utter collapse that will accompany me to the last. Only you will understand why I have knowingly chosen such a way out. And only you will guard the key to our common secret. See, see, I call you for the last time by your most beautiful name, the only one in the world for me: Elizabeth! Lieschen! I call you to confess once more what you have known for a long time, while I was completely blind and not aware of anything. There was no one but you in my whole life. Nobody ever! And now? Tell me! Will this be an escape? A betrayal? Will this be one more, the most heinous mortal sin? And will you understand me and forgive? Poor Mama! Tell her that I was killed in the war, as were so many others. Or better still, don't tell her anything."

A large group of officers is leaving Mother Rozsa's establishment. The jackets of some are unbuttoned, others are fanning themselves with their forage caps. They are yawning. It was stuffy inside. The night is still dark, but dawn is approaching. Over toward the city brickworks and the Gypsy Quarter the sky is getting lighter. Between the branches of the trees a greenish streak is visible in the sky and a light green, and very bright star is shining in it. Over the entrance to Mother Rozsa's the lanterns have been put out and the street is almost uniformly black. On the opposite side of the street a running dog disappears round the corner.

Cavalry Captain Malaterna stops, strikes a match, and checks the time on his gold watch. It is five past four. On the scabbard of his saber the green streak in the eastern sky is reflected. When the saber changes its position, moved aside by the hand that puts the watch into a trouser pocket, the reflection disappears.

Other officers also look at their watches. Then they walk in a group down the narrow street toward the barracks. They are silent and sleepy. Their spurs clink, their steps resound on the pavement. They pass the low, one-story houses, the dark gardens, the smells of morning. The herbs and corn drying in bundles smell strongly, as does the dust on the road. In the area of Franz Josef Square it is much less dark. In front of the post office and the Müllermann Brothers store, lanterns are burning with a weak, flickering flame. Under one of them somebody is standing. Near the empty stalls, a lean dog is sniffing. At the sight of the coming men, it disappears in the dark corner of the square behind a black fence. The man standing under the lantern calls in a soft voice into the darkness of the courtyard beyond Hoffbauer's restaurant: "Yozska!" and falls silent, but for a few moments does not move away. Only at the officers' approach will the man disappear. In the windowpane of one of the corner houses the glare of dawn will be reflected for a moment.

Suddenly it becomes cold, or perhaps it only seems so to the tired officers. One of them stops, shrugs his shoulders, shivers. They begin to speak in German. None of them will get any sleep this day. They will doze off in the train coaches, one leaning against the thin wall of the compartment, his head hanging on his chest, another with his shoulder and cheek wedged into the corner under the window, still another with his head resting on his crossed arms. They will all sleep an uneasy sleep, and dream various dreams connected with the past and with the landscapes seen through the windows; they will be interrupted by short nervous awakenings, premonitions that seem like snatches of a loudly spoken sentence, words of prophecy spoken by some gypsy woman two years before and recalled to memory, fragments of reality and its deformations, returns to their childhood worlds.

In the drawing room on the second floor of Mother Rozsa's tavern, Captain Karapanca sleeps on the plush sofa lying on his back, his mouth open, snoring. His boots are standing under one of the armchairs removed from the table, which is covered with bits of food, its tablecloth stained with wine and brandy. The captain has stretched out his legs in his red trousers that become narrower below the knee, very tight at the ankles, and end in straps. When a fly settles on one of his feet, he moves his toes in his sleep while his moustache bristles.

Fat Clara is there, too. Yawning and rubbing her eyes with her fists, she sits in an armchair, legs outstretched. She has been able to unlace her tight corset. It is stuffy in the small room, although half a window is open. The window faces west and one cannot see the dawn from it. The other girls have been sleeping in the attic for a long time. Only one of those who had spent the night in the communal room is now taking leave of a soldier by the fence overhung by branches. Tightly enlaced, almost completely immobile, the couple stand on the other side of the street.

The room on the ground floor is empty. Here too the windows have been opened wide. Over the buffet an oil lamp is lit and a large hairy moth is circling around it. Little Bezsi comes in from the kitchen with a mop and a bucket of water. Having pulled up her skirt, she kneels down, barefoot and sleepy, to wash the floor. The water from the bucket flows toward the door in a wide stream spreading over the uneven boards. In the small porch, the table at which the sanitation sergeant had been sitting now has a chair on it upside down. On one of the legs Bezsi has hung a wet cloth. Through the open door the curly head of a gypsy youth appears. Ready to flee at any moment, he whistles softly; little Bezsi, her back to him, scrubbing the floor on her knees, turns her head. She gets up and collects butts of cigarettes and cigars on an old newspaper, then from behind the buffet produces a bottle of brandy and hands it to the boy, who disappears at once.

Mother Bezsi's tavern is also empty and shut at this hour. No one is walking along Kerti Street. The thick bushes on the path leading toward the old clay pits are dusky and impenetrable. It seems that there are no birds in them. It is the frontier of night and dawn, a poignant hour, neutral and equivocal, when demons and phantoms are easily conceived. But now there is no one awake to meet them.

In one of the windows of the police station, a light is burning. Assistant Commissioner Bogatovich is at work at this early hour.

He is making corrections to his private list of suspects. After some thought, and having eliminated all the Sicilian Lancer officers who have whiskers, he erases with some regret the names of two cleanshaven ones, Reserve Lieutenant Zdenek Kocourek and First Lieutenant Franz Svoboda, because their alibis are, alas unshakable. So there remain only three, whom the commissioner does not know because they arrived at Fehertemplom only after mobilization; therefore there are no details, no results of observation, and no reasons for a personal dislike at all. These are: Reserve Lieutenant Franilovich (still in civilian clothes, it seems—the commissioner is not absolutely sure; a solicitor's assistant from Zagreb) ; Reserve First Lieutenant Stavaruka, who arrived from Dalmatia, probably from Split; and young Emil R., domiciled in Vienna. "How did this one get into the Twelfth Regiment, whose recruitment is in principle from the territories of St. Stephen's Crown?" wonders Commissioner Bogatovich with suspicious distaste, as anger increasingly takes hold of him. He puts three thick red crosses against the three names, then pours himself a glass of brandy, takes a long sip, frowns, wipes his wet moustache with his fingers, and lights a cigar. He stretches his legs under the table, calms himself slowly, even smiles. But his smile is fierce, ominous. His sharp upturned moustache rises almost to his eyes; it looks like two black tusks.

All the others can go to the front as fast as they like, they can beat the hell out of those damn Serbians, but these three will stay here until one of them has been proven guilty of the crime committed on the young gypsy girl. The commissioner rubs his hands together and starts work again. He prepares official summonses that he will send by Sergeant Vilajcich to the barracks, to the hands of the suspects, with copies to the commander of the regiment. But the laws of war are cruel. A few short hours later the office of Assistant Commissioner Bogatovich will be invaded without so much as a knock by military justice, in the person of a man on short legs covered with new shiny leggings of yellow leather who, without so much as a perfunctory military salute, will give orders in German. The auditor lieutenant colonel of the Fifth Army, wavering before Bogatovich, the representative of civilian justice now standing at attention, a pile of those unfortunate summonses addressed to the three officers of the Twelfth Regiment, will declare that there can be no question of any investigation of that kind. He, the auditor lieutenant colonel of the Imperial and Royal Army now at war, is the only one empowered to conduct an investigation, to pass sentence, etc., on persons under arms—is this understood?

"All you here," shouts the auditor, red in the face with irritation, "instead of pursuing the enemies of the monarchy, the spies and subversive elements who poison wells and the flour destined for the Imperial and Royal Army—you amuse yourselves with trifles! You're surrounded by the Black Hand and what do you think about? Some rubbish! Some gypsy girl, some thief! Right?"

"Yes, sir! At your orders, sir!"

Standing close behind his superior, Lieutenant Alfred von Letnay, who also wears on his collar the black velvet tabs of the Legal Branch, looks with some satisfaction and even amusement at the frightened expression of the gendarme. Like most career officers, he dislikes gendarmes.

"I, sir, just this moment . . ." mumbles Bogatovich. Lieutenant Colonel Lammasch, angrily pulling himself up and then relaxing in turn, interrupts him: "Enough! Understood?"

"Yes, sir."

"All right." Somewhat appeased, the colonel, while adjusting his saber entangled between his legs, adds in a didactic tone:

"Generally speaking, I must now observe with all severity that to suspect officers of the Imperial and Royal Army in wartime of deeds contrary to their code of honor and rank is blameworthy and insolent. It smacks of hostile diversion! Right?" And the lieutenant colonel tears up the summonses with passion and throws them on the table. "At ease!" he roars as he turns to go. Their spurs clinking, Auditor Lammasch and his young assistant, Lieutenant von Letnay, leave the police office without a further word, without so much as raising the tips of their fingers to the visors of their field caps. Assistant Commissioner Bogatovich continues to stand stiffly at attention. The flies scattered lazily over the walls and the window begin to fly noisily round the office, buzzing and brushing against the windowpanes and the doors of the cupboard, against the ceiling and the glass of the lamp, and also against the portrait of His Most Gracious Majesty. A few minutes will pass before they calm down and hide again in their corners.

Many minutes will pass before Bogatovich sinks heavily into his chair. He takes in his trembling, sweaty hands his worried head, in which the threatening shouts of the colonel still resound. He will remain seated thus for several minutes. Then he returns to his senses and reaches into a cabinet next to the table. He takes out of it a thick tumbler and a bottle. After he has uncorked it, the office will fill with the pleasant smell of Banat brandy. "Guaranteed natural brandy." Commissioner Bogatovich holds the tumbler to the light, then drinks its contents in one gulp. He wipes his moustache with his hand and pours himself another. He is about to put both the bottle and the tumbler back in the cabinet, usually locked with a sizable padlock, but at the last minute he changes his mind and fills his glass once again with the golden liquid.

And after he has drunk five, six, or seven glasses, he suddenly decides to get up. He puts on his hat with the green cock feathers, checks the details of his uniform, his jacket buttons, and belt, and with unsteady steps, feeling his way along the wall and the banisters, proceeds to the cells. There, in complete darkness, he finds a padlock and with some difficulty opens the door to cell number one. Holding onto the door frame, he switches on his flashlight. In its white glare he sees a young man in a cassock, with an Orthodox cross on his breast. The man, blinking in the blinding light, has a black beard. Still standing on the threshold of the windowless cell, Bogatovich looks at the prisoner through eyes that are watering from drink. The prisoner moves and the irons in which his hands and feet have been shackled emit a metallic sound. Commissioner Bogatovich gestures to the man to come nearer, but the man will not budge. His eyes, already accommodated to the light, are glowing in his swarthy face. He observes the gendarme with utter contempt. The beam of light from the torch Bogatovich is holding in his shaky hand reflects on the cross of the Serbian priest, caught two days before by the gendarmerie in the gypsy suburb of Fehertemplom. The beam is split into a mass of sharp rays, like a starfish, or like petals of a just opening sunflower. The pupils of the prisoner's eyes shine.

The commissioner blinks in the glare, then in a sudden flash of insight he realizes that the prisoner standing in front of him is not only a dangerous spy, personally despatched for the ruin of the monarchy by King Peter Karadjordjevich, but he is also the perpetrator of the dastardly crime committed in the old clay pit, near which he had been caught the day before. Still holding the flashlight in his left hand, he approaches the young priest and slaps him hard.

With some difficulty, panting and staggering, he walks upstairs and, seated again at his table, on which the portrait of the Most Gracious Majesty looks down benevolently, he dictates to Secretary Marina the deposition of the Serbian priest. He signs it himself with a cross on behalf of the priest. He adds this document in a sealed envelope to the letter of transfer of the prisoner to the military authorities. Only then does he sigh with relief. He undoes the buckle of his belt, loosens his collar, wipes his forehead with a handkerchief, lights a cigar, and stretches his legs under the table.

Several hours later Secretary Marina observes through the barred window the act of transfer of the dangerous spy and murderer from the Royal Gendarmerie to the imperial and royal military authorities. Standing by the window and picking his teeth, he looks on while Gendarme Vilajcich takes the shackled Serbian priest away, prodding him with the butt of his rifle.

In the street in front of the police station, two soldiers in honved uniforms are already waiting for the prisoner. The honveds still have a moment, so they light their cigarettes while laughing and talking.

At the same time in the town of Fehertemplom/Bela Crkva some other events are taking place, seemingly unimportant, but to some extent essential. In a dark blue apron and striped trousers, innkeeper Willi Hofbauer opens his premises. He looks up at the cloudless sky and yawns. Two peasants in tall black hats enter the inn. Three women vendors get busy around their fruit and vegetable stalls, which have been closed for the night. They chase away a stray dog. Old Laszlo, the waiter in Mother Bezsi's tavern, comes out yawning from the kitchen, puts a mug of coffee on the tinplate-covered counter, eats a bit of white wheat bread with a slice of paprika lard, and becomes pensive. Little Bezsi empties the slop bucket into the gooseberry bushes by the fence. Their leaves begin to tremble, covered with drops in which the pink glare of the rising sun is reflected. Fat Clara gets up from the armchair and laboriously climbs the squeaking stairs to the attic where her colleagues, Ilonka and Erzika, have been asleep for hours. Captain Karapanca left an hour before. In spite of the open windows, in the empty room the air is still heavy with the sour smell of wine and brandy and the smoke of cigars. In the honved barracks reveille is sounded, and at the station a semaphore light over one of the tracks turns to green. In the transparent air of the early morning a high column of smoke rises from a locomotive, then from a second, then a third. And their large red wheels start turning.

And when troop train no. — has passed the last switch, just as might have been expected, the officers make themselves comfortable in the first and second-class compartments, unhook their sabers, and put them in the luggage nets; some begin to doze, others look thoughtfully out the windows, still others play cards.

They discuss how, when the train was about to depart and they were leaning out of the windows, they saw Mother Rozsa trotting along the platform in her long skirt, in a black lace blouse adorned at the neck with a brooch—a Maria Theresa thaler framed in gold—carrying as farewell presents for her friends (how many she had among the officers of the Sicilian Lancers!) an enormous bouquet of flowers and two bottles of wine. She was late and couldn't catch up with the accelerating train. Finally, she had to throw the gifts into the nearest window of the passing train; then, out of breath and perhaps even shedding tears, she gave up the pursuit and stood helpless on the empty platform, waving the handkerchief with which she had wiped her eyes a moment before, until she disappeared behind a clump of trees when the train rounded a bend—the last view, the last memory: "God save you, Sicilian Lancers! Farewell, my dear children!"

And that was all. They entered the compartments and sat down. Now Chaplain Dziedzina in a long service jacket places his suitcases and boxes on the rack. The folding field altar and the whole apparatus of the rites—a chalice, a chasuble, his stole —is in the charge of his orderly, who sits in the next coach. Chaplain Dziedzina pulls out from a side pocket of his jacket a small flat bottle of brandy. He unfastens the metal top that serves at the same time as a cup and invites his fellow officers to drink: "May God bless!" Captain Malaterna laughs, twirling his moustache. Baron Kottfuss is in an excellent mood. Just before departure he took a photograph: the heads of two comrades in the window of a coach on which somebody had written in chalk in capital letters: "Long live the Emperor! Death to the Serbs!" Both officers in the narrow window, their cheeks touching, made comical faces, and thus Baron Kottfuss's camera has eternalized them. In this amateur snapshot they will look like two clowns. Perhaps somebody will find this photo many years later, developed and printed at Mitrovica, or else lost in the turmoil of the war like so many other objects on this train.

In the mess of the empty cavalry barracks at Fehertemplom at that time the young kitchen porter goes up to the portrait of the former patron of the regiment, Ferdinand II, King of the Two

Sicilies, and with a bundle of feathers on a bamboo stick sweeps the face of the deceased ruler clean of cobwebs and dust. A lot of spiders have nestled in the vine growing on one wall of the barracks.

The name of the long dissolved Kingdom of the Two Sicilies has always been connected with the Twelfth Regiment of Lancers. It began in the days of Magenta and Solferino. A dual, dead kingdom. Like the mask of a tragic clown—a plaster mask, with dead, empty eyes.

On the train, Lieutenant Emil R. will talk about these things to his friend Zdenek Kocourek. He will speak chaotically, excitedly, as if in a trance. His condition will worry his friend. The twenty-one-year-old officer of the Sicilian Lancers, Emil R., will say a lot, much of it in words his friend will not be able to understand. About the premonition of an approaching end, defeat, destruction, ruin, the violent desire for death, about an etching seen years before, on which a lonely rider gallops into the night across the battlefield of Solferino strewn with the bodies of the fallen. And about a moon behind a balcony in the opening of a campanile that is black and threatening like a specter. And about many other matters. About a torn bead necklace and somebody's eyes. About a dream foretelling the end, and a painting on which a woman rider leaning from the saddle and rising in the stirrups strikes a bell with a hammer on a long wooden handle. And even about the tone of that bell: "*Requiem aeternam*! Solferino, Solferino!" He will repeat this several times. "It is for us, riding in this ghostly train across the scorching, sun-drenched plain. And for the beauty of despair, the hopelessness and fear of love, and for the sleepless nights dense with floating evanescent melodies, pictures, and colors. This is the end, the end." As he talks, Second Lieutenant Kocourek becomes more and more uneasy about his friend's state of mind. He listens to his words seriously and with a heavy heart. He feels he cannot comfort him; discouraged, he enters the compartment. Emil R. remains alone in the corridor of the train.

This might be the end of the story about several hot summer days, about the last years of a vanishing era, about the death of the nineteenth century, a century of great hopes and great disappointments. A kind of ballad about a dual kingdom and a time that is irrevocably past. But there is still the last act.

Emil R., alone in the empty corridor of the train, takes from his breast pocket the letter he has not sent and tears it into small pieces. He puts his clenched hand out of the window, then spreads his fingers. The scraps of the letter are carried away and scatter on the dew-covered meadows. A few of them will flutter in the wind like white cabbage butterflies, then they too will fall among the riverside rushes. Emil R. will next throw out his green-bound exercise book.

Just then the train begins to cross a long bridge over a large, broad river. It rushes between the iron girders with a roar and short, blinding flashes of light. Then a door of one of the coaches opens and a man falls on the track or even rolls off the bridge, smashing his head against the stone pillars. No one on the train has noticed it and there will be no witnesses who can testify to the truth, because no one has seen the accident—if indeed such an accident has happened at all and it is not an illusion born of the heat and travel fatigue, or just the inevitable end of a ballad. The train has already passed the bridge over the great river.

The image of the river and the empty bridge spanning it might be accepted as an end and a symbol. Looking back from the perspective of years, with cool reserve, caution, and calm born from experience and knowledge of the future, one can properly assess the importance as well as the relative unimportance of facts parallel in time and already accomplished, their illusory and not entirely accidental interdependence, and also the somewhat bitter taste of things irrevocably past. *Images d' Epinal* of that era; its lack of luster, its pallor, its antiquated air, as if not just half a century but whole centuries had passed. The relativity of what is important can be judged only from the perspective of history—in other words, of the time that is passing.

One might therefore begin everything anew, in one way or another. The end even so would be the same, because the past, down to its least details, is irrevocable and indivisible. In spite of the fact that since then so many matters have lost their importance and even become somewhat ridiculous, like the fashion for affectation in feelings, for despair, for hopelessness. And for exaggeration. Like the sentimental silent pictures of the early years of this century. Or like Vienna dress fashion *Wiener Mode* of 1900. Like the faint scent of perfume rising from the pages of the *Wiener Illustrierte* of 1914, or from a box found years later and containing, along with visiting cards of persons unknown to us and programs from dances, a few yellowed photographs.

On the evening of that last day, when the setting sun is reflected like fire in the river and the rifle shots from both its banks have ceased, two Serbian officers emerge from the thick rushes and observe through field glasses the Austrian side. One of them notices an object floating in the river which, after being fished out, proves to be an exercise book bound in green calf leather. Crouching in the rushes, the officers try to decipher the text smudged and washed away by the Danube. With difficulty they succeed in reading only the first sentence: "Once upon a time . . ."